The Scarred Highlander

Donna Fletcher

The Scarred Highlander

Cover art
The Killion Group

Visit Donna's Website
www.donnafletcher.com
http://www.facebook.com/donna.fletcher.author

Chapter One

Perched on his horse, Cavell stared at Dundren Abbey that emerged after he crested the rise. Without the favorable vantage point, he would have missed the sight of the abbey altogether, hidden amidst the ethereal mist and shielded by the imposing barrier of solid stone. His eyes remained locked on the structure, wondering what his wife was doing there.

A wife he never met and one he did not want.

"The marriage is beneficial to the clan, and it is past time you had a wife."

So his father, Lord Philip, and his older and only brother Harcus had claimed, but Cavell knew both men well. The decision had nothing to do with it being past time for him to wed and everything to do with what benefitted Clan McCabe.

He made his descent down the rise toward the abbey. His father had made it clear what he expected of the marriage. His wife Elsie was the only daughter of Chieftain Norris of Clan Murdock, who was ill and not expected to live long. Cavell would become chieftain upon the old man's death, securing more land for Clan McCabe. He was to collect his wife and settle in his new home with her, claiming the chieftain title upon the old man's passing.

Cavell had his own plans, and they did not include a wife or becoming Chieftain of Clan Murdock. But to

3

see his plans to fruition, he first had to rid himself of an unwanted wife.

There was something about the abbey that set him on edge. The place appeared more like a prison than a sanctuary with the high stone wall surrounding it. He did not fear entering it, though those beyond the wall might fear granting him entrance once they looked upon him. But this was where his wife was, and he was curious as to what she was doing here rather than at home with her clan.

Women were sent to an abbey for any number of reasons and some women even chose to retreat to one from time to time. Had his wife chosen to spend time here in prayer or hadn't the choice been hers because she was a difficult woman who required lessons in being an obedient wife? Either way, it did not matter to him. She would not be his wife for long and, if by chance, she felt as he did about the marriage, she would readily agree to dissolve it.

He dismounted in front of the thick wooden door and gave a yank on the bell rope to announce his arrival. He kept the hood of his cloak pulled down to cover a good portion of his face. He would not have anyone see it before he was granted entrance.

A small square in the center of the door suddenly opened and someone demanded, "Who bids entrance?"

Cavell's substantial height would have forced him to bow his head to see who was speaking, but he bowed to no man.

"I am here to fetch my wife, Elsie of the Clan Murdock," he called out, not giving any other indication as to his identity.

The door creaked open, and Cavell entered, one hand giving a tug on his horse's reins to follow behind him and his other hand near the hilt of his dagger at his waist. He had learned well not to trust and to always be prepared to defend.

The monk's head barely reached Cavell's shoulder and his considerable girth indicated that he surrendered often to the sin of gluttony, and while most would think him no threat, Cavell knew better. He had known many a man the monk's generous size to be a worthy opponent.

"I am Brother Emanual," the monk said and waved to a nearby monk. "Brother James will see to the care and feeding of your horse while we speak and partake of our delicious mead."

Cavell grew suspicious. What was there to speak of? He was there to collect his wife. He chose to say nothing and followed Brother Emanual into the abbey. He kept his head bent just enough so no one could glance upon his face, though that would not be for long.

They had barely made their way into the entrance of the abbey when a horrific scream echoed throughout the structure and sent Cavell's hand clutching the handle of his dagger.

"This way," Brother Emanual said, leading the way and paying no mind to the scream.

As a warrior, Cavell was well acquainted with paying heed to one's senses. It saved many a warrior's life. Right now, his senses were warning him that something was not right there.

Not sure where he was being taken or the monk's intention, he didn't wait. He shoved his hood back off his head.

The monk stopped at an open door and turned to Cavell to allow him to enter first and his gasp sounded more like a scream as his eyes rounded in shock when he looked upon his face.

"Good Lord," the monk said and crossed himself.

"I wear the scars with pride as do any Gallowglass warriors," Cavell said, knowing the name alone would instill fear in the monk while his many scars intimidated. Some scars were still healing, while others had taken permanent residence on his once handsome face. He kept his auburn-colored hair at shoulder length so when he bent his head the thick strands fell forward closing off the sides of his face like shutters upon a window concealing a view.

Brother Emanual paled and was unable to hide the tremble that took hold of him.

Cavell understood his fear. The Gallowglass were a notorious mercenary group of superior skilled aristocratic warriors. They were well known for their exceptional strength, their cruelty, and their lack of compassion. They would die before they would yield. His scarred face proved that there was nothing that could stop him. No matter what a Gallowglass warrior suffered, he continued to fight as Cavell had done the day he had gotten the scars.

Brother Emanual's hand shook as he filled a shallow, wood cup with mead and he had to grip it with two hands, he trembled so badly, to offer it to Cavell.

"I am not here to harm you or those here, Brother Emanual," Cavell said, taking the cup from the monk. "I am here to collect my wife."

"I was only recently notified of the arranged marriage and—" He took a fortifying swallow of mead before he continued. "I must say I was opposed to it."

An encouraging response for Cavell since if the monk opposed the marriage, it would make it easier for him to have it annulled.

That the monk opposed it had him asking, "Why would you oppose it, and did you share whatever concern you have with my father, Lord Philip?"

"As I said, I only recently learned of the arrangement or else I certainly would have alerted your father to my opposition," the monk assured him.

"And what is that opposition?" Cavell asked.

"It makes little difference now."

"Why is that?"

"Your wife has escaped the monastery. It has been three nights now since she has been gone," the monk said.

Had she opposed the marriage as well and fled to avoid it? If she did, it boded well for his plans. Still, he wondered how she had escaped a place that appeared more like a fortress than a place of worship and comfort.

"How did she manage to escape when it appears you have only one entrance and egress?"

"I have given that thought and have yet to discover a suitable answer. She was here one day and gone the next."

That his wife had escaped from this place made him think that she was far from a weak woman, and he admired her courage and ingenuity. Unless?

"Have you searched the woods?" Cavell asked, concerned she did not have the skill to survive on her own and had fallen prey to any number of possibilities.

"Aye. As soon as she was discovered missing," Brother Emanual said. "I sent a group of monks out to search the area, fearing what harm might befall her. Unfortunately, no signs were found of her. I do fear for her safety. She is skinny with little strength to her and plain featured."

"And yet she escaped you," Cavell said, feeling a strange need to defend his wife.

The monk acknowledged the fact with a nod but remained silent.

"Have any merchants visited here lately? She could have escaped in one of their carts?" Cavell suggested.

"Merchants rarely stop here since we need nothing from them."

"What of travelers seeking shelter for the night?" Cavell asked.

The monk stared at him oddly. "We do not accommodate travelers here."

His senses had been right. Something wasn't right about this place. Monks did not turn people in need away.

"I thought all abbeys were a refuge for travelers, the ill, the needy," Cavell said.

"Forgive me, sir, I thought you were aware of what we do here," Brother Emanual said. "We are different from other abbeys."

"Different how?"

"I think you would better understand our mission here if I showed you rather than tried to explain it," Brother Emanual said and extended his arm toward the door.

Cavell placed his empty cup on the table, then his hand went to rest on the hilt of his dagger, letting the monk know he was prepared to fight if necessary.

"I would keep my hand on your dagger. It is not safe where we go," the monk said, and instead of giving Cavell the lead, walked out the door, leaving him to follow.

***

The stench hit Cavell long before they reached the door at the far end of the abbey. Once in the narrow corridor, the foul odor overwhelmed. Several doors with square openings in the center top of the door, iron bars preventing anyone from reaching out or in, ran along the corridor. Moans of anguish and pain sounded a sorrowful melody, and Cavell could only imagine what suffering occurred there.

A sudden jolt at one of the doors had Brother Emanual jumping, not so Cavell. His training had taught him well not to respond to sudden sounds, to always be in command of himself, to always be confident and fearless.

"Help me, please help me!" a soft voice begged.

"We do help you," Brother Emanual said gently.

"I do not have the madness and no demon lives inside me. Please! Please, I beg you to free me from this horror," the woman pleaded.

"When you are well, you will return home," Brother Emanual said.

As Cavell followed alongside the monk down the corridor, those in the cells, a mix of men and women, came to their window to plead for help.

"A generous benefactor allows us to care for people beset with madness or demons. We do our best to not only care for them but to root out the madness or demons so they may eventually return home or at least die pure and whole, the monk explained and stopped by two cell doors that stood ajar.

Cavell peered inside one cell and spotted a narrow slit in the stone wall that allowed for a modicum of air and barely any light. But he did manage to see the shape of a woman sitting on the hay-covered, stone floor, her wrists shackled, and the chains attached to an iron ring in the stone wall and her head covered with a sack.

"No one can look upon her. She is beyond help. The poor soul is possessed," Brother Emanual said and closed the door.

Cavell wondered how many in the cells were truly possessed or mad or were here simply due to circumstance. That, however, was not his concern. His wife was his only concern.

The monk pushed open the other door that stood ajar. "This was your wife's quarters."

Cavell grabbed a torch from a sconce on the wall and entered the cell. It was much like the cell he'd just seen though smaller. Barely a thatch of hay with a thin blanket tossed over it served as a bed and a stench came from a wood bucket in a corner. If someone had no such madness before arriving here, they surely would acquire it after being locked away in a place like this. The obvious question was…

"Are you telling me that my wife is insane?" Cavell asked after stepping out of the cell.

The monk took a step back before he responded. "I believe so, which is why I would have opposed the marriage."

That gave Cavell some thought. "Who brought her here and how long had she been here?"

"Two men from Clan Murdock brought her here tethered, gagged, and completely out of control about a month ago."

"Since I had no knowledge of her insanity, can the marriage be annulled?" Cavell asked, seeing a possible easy way out.

"I believe so, though since she is legally your wife, you are responsible for her and it would bode well if you were to find her and return her here, then apply for the annulment which I, of course, would assist you in securing."

"That way no one learns of her escape," Cavell said, aware the monk was bargaining with him.

"Her return here would serve both of us well, and I can guarantee your freedom from the marriage."

Cavell had faced far more difficult challenges than tracking down an insane woman. "It won't take me long to find her, so make sure you have ready whatever document necessary to end the marriage when I return."

"You have my word on it, sir," Brother Emanual said with a smile. "Now, how about some more mead and some food before you take your leave?"

Chapter Two

Cavell, his face concealed by his hood, sat unnoticed as he savored ale and meat amidst the bustling market at Pinkeny Village. His search for his wife had been disappointing thus far. It had been a week since his stop at the abbey, yet he had not found her. He had begun to worry about her safety since a woman traveling alone was easy prey, and any manner of harm may have befallen her.

A swift glance of his surroundings revealed several stalls and booths busy with merchants and craftsmen hawking their wares and people haggling over prices with them. Chatter flowed abundantly, accompanied by children laughing as they ran in play and musicians performed lively songs.

A village on market day was once a source of joy for Cavell before the battle that had left him scarred. He would barter with merchants, indulge in ale and wine, stay informed through gossip, and easily find a willing woman for the night. Those days were long gone. Women no longer flocked to him. They now shunned him, turning away in disgust.

He silently cursed his situation for bringing him here, but it was one place he just might learn news about a lone woman traveler. He kept his attention focused on the conversations at nearby tables, hoping to catch at least a bit of gossip that might connect with his wife.

"No man should drink alone," a woman said and sat down opposite Cavell at the table.

Cavell raised his head enough to catch a bit of an ample-breasted woman and a pleasantly scented one at that, a flowery sweet scent drifting off her. She no doubt had readied herself to sell her wares at market day and he wouldn't mind obliging her. It had been too long since he had enjoyed coupling with a woman or even sharing a fast poke with one.

"Buy me a drink?" she asked.

He motioned the server lass with two fingers, and she was soon at his table refilling his tankard and placing another in front of the woman.

The woman wasted no time swallowing a good portion of ale, then reaching across the table to take Cavell's hand.

"I can tell you're a loner, but there's no need to spend the day or night alone," she said, giving his hand a gentle squeeze.

Her invitation aroused him and there was nothing better he would have liked than to accept it, but once she saw his face… he drew back his hood as he raised his head.

She gasped, the shock making her unable to look away.

Cavell drew a coin from the purse tucked at his waist and laid it in front her. "For sharing a drink with me."

She grabbed it and smiled. "Get me drunk enough and I'll share a bed with you."

Damn, if he wasn't tempted, especially since she was attractive and well-endowed. He enjoyed a good-sized woman that could take a good pounding from a man.

"Curdie! You promised the day to me," a man, lean and with a quick stride, called out as he approached. He stopped abruptly when he reached the table and caught sight of Cavell. "Bloody hell!"

"He's a gentleman this one, Meldon. Paid for my drink he did, then paid me for having a drink with him," Curdie said in defense of Cavell. "He's generous, unlike you."

"Come away from him, Curdie," Meldon cautioned with a wave for her to come to him. "You don't want to be with the likes of him."

People were starting to take notice and Cavell didn't need that. He grabbed another coin and pushed it across the table to the woman. "Go!"

Another coin made Curdie hesitate, thinking how generous he would be if she coupled with him.

"He's Cavell of the Gallowglass," Meldon said, his voice raised in fear.

News was spreading about the vicious and victorious battle the Gallowglass had fought and the warrior, Cavell, who had been left forever marked with its memory. Soon there would be no place where he would not be recognized.

Curdie gasped as she rushed to her feet, keeping a tight hold on the two coins, and hurried to Meldon.

"What do you want here?" a slim man asked.

"You dare ask me that!" Cavell barked at the man as he brought his fisted hand down on the table. "No one questions a Gallowglass warrior."

The man bobbed his head as he hastily apologized. "Forgive me, sir, I meant no disrespect."

"Leave me to enjoy my drink," Cavell ordered, and he was soon left alone, people drifting off, whispering and stealing glances back at him.

There was no point in staying there now. People would avoid him, and all would talk in whispers... about him. He would learn nothing. He also risked the chance of some fool trying to show he could fight and claim victory over a Gallowglass warrior, and he was too angry to fight today. He was angry that he had yet to find his wife and angry that his scars deprived him of poking a sweet-smelling woman. That much anger would have him beat someone senseless.

He downed the last of his ale and debated on whether he should have another or take his leave.

"Cavell!"

Cavell groaned low. A fool who thought to challenge him. He ignored the shout and raised his tankard to the serving lass.

She approached hesitantly.

"Leave the jug," he ordered and laid several coins on the table for her.

She quickly scooped them up and hurried away.

If he was going to fight, he intended to make sure he had enough ale to drink after he beat the fool senseless.

"Cavell!" the man shouted again.

16

He stood slowly and removed his cloak, taking his time to drape it over the bench, all the while keeping his eyes on the man who challenged him. He was big and thick, his nose crooked, which meant he had fought before and was not afraid to fight again.

Cavell walked toward him. "Are you sure about this?"

The man laughed. "A Gallowglass warrior afraid to fight?"

A curious crowd was gathering to watch, and not one of them joined the man in laughter.

"I like to give a fool a chance before I send him off bloody and weeping like a bairn," Cavell called out, and laughter broke loose.

That he was laughed at made the foolish man even more foolish, and with his face flushed red with anger, he ran at Cavell.

Cavell waited and when the fool nearly reached him, he side-stepped and delivered a blow to the man's jaw that sent him stumbling to the ground.

"Surrender while you have the chance," Cavell cautioned, seeing blood running from the man's mouth, but, of course, the fool didn't listen.

He got to his feet, spit the blood from his mouth, and charged at Cavell once again.

Cavell had already judged the man to be a clumsy fighter, charging and throwing punches randomly. He was set to deliver another blow to the man's face when he caught a flash of a dark brown robe like the ones the monks wore at the abbey. Had his wife been found and returned to the abbey? Had Brother Emanual sent someone to find him and deliver the welcoming news?

His years of fighting kept his senses alert and his nose picked up the man's foul odor before he reached him, giving Cavell enough time, though barely, to avoid his meaty fists and deliver another blow to his face.

While the man shook his head as he struggled to his feet, Cavell glanced over the crowd looking for the monk. Annoyed he saw no sight of him and annoyed that he allowed his anger to take hold and play with the foolish man like a cat with a mouse before finishing it quickly had him ready to end the fight so he could search for the monk and hopefully receive good news.

When the man finally stood firm on his feet, Cavell said, "I am tired of playing with you."

He approached the man, and the fool threw a punch before Cavell was close enough for his fist to reach him, though he ducked anyway to deliver a fierce blow to the man's gut when close enough. He delivered another punch to his face as the man doubled over, then another as his face swung up, and one last vicious blow that sent the man sprawling to land with a thud on his back.

"Get him out of here! And the rest of you get back to your business," Cavell ordered, and several men hurried to drag the man away.

Cavell glanced around as the crowd dispersed, hoping to catch a glance of the monk. He didn't see him anywhere. He took another cautious glance around and mumbled an oath when once again he did not spot the monk.

Ale. He needed ale. He turned to head back to the table and saw the monk sitting there.

Cavell sat as soon as he reached the table, hoping to see if it was one of the monks he had met at the abbey, but the hood was pulled too far down on his head.

"Tell me you found her. Tell me I am free of this marriage," Cavell said and got annoyed when he didn't receive a hasty reply.

The monk finally shook his head slowly. "Nay, but we received news that she is here in this village."

"Tell Brother Emanual that I will find her and return her and when I do, he better honor our agreement to dissolve this marriage," Cavell warned.

"I will take word to him," the monk said.

"Right away," Cavell ordered, and the monk took his leave, slipping off into the crowded market.

Cavell drank and ate, keeping his eyes on all that went on around him while keeping watch for a skinny and plain-featured woman.

The day waned and so did the market, merchants and craftsmen alike gathering what little was left of their wares, the day having proved fruitful, ready to return home and count their coins.

Cavell was surprised to see Curdie make her way toward him while Meldon waited in the distance.

"I found a willing lass for you if you're interested," she offered. "She knows about your scars and who you are, but she needs the coin to feed her starving family. She can meet you after dark at my place since I'll be spending the night with Meldon."

Cavell eyed her skeptically.

Curdie shrugged. "Give her a try. I felt bad for her since she's desperate, thin from starving herself so she

19

can feed her family. She'll be there waiting at my place. You were generous with your coin, and I wanted to repay your kindness. My cottage sits at the far end of the village, right past the smithy's place, in case you change your mind."

Cavell lingered along with some other men who kept themselves engaged in talk, too far into their cups to pay him any mind. The later it grew the more he thought about the woman who was willing to couple with him.

Desperate.

Was he as desperate for a poke as she was for food? He hated to admit it to himself, but he needed a woman. He needed to satisfy himself with one instead of relying on his hand. He wanted to feel his shaft slip into a wet sheath and tighten around him, roll his tongue across a hard nipple, taste lips ripe for kissing.

Bloody hell, he mumbled feeling his shaft respond to his wicked thoughts. Why not indulge himself for the night? With night falling, his wife was not likely to arrive.

Wife.

He was wed, though the marriage was not valid until it was consummated. Besides, he had no intentions of staying wed to his insane wife. Tomorrow at dawn was time enough to keep watch for her. And tomorrow this willing woman would have enough coin to feed her family.

With his shaft refusing to be ignored, he mumbled several oaths, dropped some coins on the table, grabbed his cloak, and took off for Curdie's cottage.

He kept alert since he considered the fellow he had fought could be lying in wait for him, even though he had heard men say that the fool was on his way home with his brother, who had given him a good tongue lashing for being an idiot. It always pays to be overly cautious, something Noble, a Gallowglass warrior he knew well, would advise, and it was advice he paid heed to.

Cavell entered the cottage without knocking to find a low fire burning in the small hearth. He saw no sign of a woman and wondered if she had changed her mind. Then he heard movement and turned toward the bed.

"I am here," came the soft voice.

"You are sure of this?" he asked, giving her a chance to change her mind.

"Aye. I am sure, this must be done," she said.

She sounded desperate and so he offered, "I will pay you extra to stay the night with me."

It was a selfish offer since he intended to make the most of the time spent with her, not sure when he'd find pleasure with a woman again.

"I will stay."

He was glad he did not hear any reluctance or hesitation in her voice. It just might turn out to be an enjoyable night after all. He rid himself of his garments, eager to feel a woman's body again, and approached the bed tucked against a wall with barely any light cast on it to his relief. It was better that she did not see his face, or she might change her mind.

"You will not touch my face," he ordered.

"Aye," she said.

"But you are welcome to touch me anywhere else as much as you'd like," he said to see how receptive or repugnant she would be to his offer.

"I would like that," she said.

Her hasty willingness had Cavell's shaft jutting out ready for pleasure as he slipped beneath the blanket, and he asked, "Your name?"

"Sara," she said, as she turned on her side to rest her face against his chest and ease her body against him.

He slipped his arm over her waist to draw her closer to him, relishing the feel of her warm, naked body. He expected her to be thin after what Curdie had said about her starving herself to feed her family, but he had not expected her skin to feel so soft. His hand slipped from her waist down over her backside and gave it a squeeze, then roamed over it relishing her slender curves. Never had he felt such soft skin and he could not stop touching her.

Her hand roamed over him as well, slowly, as if she wanted to familiarize herself with every inch of him.

"I like your touch," he said, encouraging her.

"And I yours."

"Then we shall have a good night together," he said and eased her on her back to cup her breast and roll his tongue across the hard nipple. She was far from well-endowed, her breast not even filling his hand, but her nipple was tasty, and he was happy to take his time feasting on it and her other breast as well.

Her soft moans let him know how much he pleasured her, as did her hand that gripped tightly at his arm.

He did not think twice about claiming her lips in a kiss, something he had not done with a woman since his face had been scarred. How could he expect a woman to gaze upon his hideous face when in the throes of pleasure? He was relieved that they could barely see each other. They appeared as mere shadows and shapes. Not that he would mind looking at her naked, but it was better this way... for her.

Her lips wasted no time in returning the forceful kiss and she opened eagerly to him when his tongue skimmed her closed lips. She clung to him as their kiss turned demanding and he favored the way she gasped in disappointment when his lips left hers. She enjoyed him and that she did made it even more pleasurable for him.

"It has been too long since I tasted a woman's sweet nectar and I intend to drink of your sweetness all night," he said and lowered his mouth to her breast but only to give each nipple a short nibble before moving down along her stomach.

He loved the way her fingers raked through his hair, tugging at the strands as she released a melody of moans that fired his passion.

Damn, but he wanted to slip into her, though not before he tasted her. He buried his face between her legs, brushing her tender nub with his tongue before slipping it inside her and he thought he would climax, her taste was so intoxicating.

It was not long before he heard her plead.

"Please, Cavell! Please!" she begged.

His name falling eagerly from her lips gave a strange tug to his heart, something he had never felt before with any woman.

He couldn't wait any longer. He slipped eagerly over her and ordered, "Spread your legs wide for me, Sara."

She did as he said, her hands latching onto his arms.

He maneuvered the tip of his shaft to her entrance, her wetness inviting and enticing him, and he did not hesitate, he plunged into her swiftly.

She gasped and her fingers dug at his arms, then she let loose with a series of passion-filled moans that he enjoyed hearing and that intensified as he drove in and out of her.

He had gone too long without a woman or was it that he had never coupled with the right woman that had him so eager to climax? Feeling how she met his rhythm so easily and eagerly, he did not think she would last long either.

He was right. She cried out as her release hit her and it was all he needed to let go and burst inside her in a mind-shattering release that seemed to go on forever. He did not know when her arms had slipped around him, but he liked how she hugged him with a strength that made him feel her reluctance to let him go, and he lingered a bit before he slipped out and off her.

He was surprised and pleased when she said, "I did not touch you enough."

"We have the entire night. There will be time for you to touch me more."

"I look forward to it."

"So do I," he said and wished he could keep this woman for himself, but Curdie said she had family, which meant she was not free, but then neither was he.

***

Cavell woke to her caressing his shaft. He had thought it was a dream and was glad to discover it wasn't. She was quite enjoying herself and in turn so was he. She peppered his chest with kisses working her way down to his belly as her hand took a firmer hold of his shaft and began to pump it. He feared if her lips touched his shaft, it would be over, and he not only wanted her to share in the pleasure, but he was also eager to bury his shaft inside her once again. He grabbed her beneath her arms, swung her up and under him and entered her hard and fast.

Her cry of pleasure drove him harder into her over and over and over again, and it wasn't long before they both released in a blinding climax.

Sleep claimed them soon after and Cavell was surprised when he woke later, his shaft eager to give her another poke. He woke her gently with kisses and entered her just as gently though she soon demanded more from him, and he obliged her. Once again, they found release together and once again they fell asleep, this time in each other's arms.

As sleep claimed Cavell, a sudden, shocking thought came to him.

I could love this woman.

Nay. That was impossible. They had enjoyed each other out of desperation, and he was grateful to have had the night with her and that was all there was to it. Still, the thought would not leave him, and he fell asleep denying it to himself over and over again.

Chapter Three

Cavell stretched himself awake, his body feeling anew, better than it ever had, and he turned eager to finally look upon the woman he had found such pleasure with last night. He bolted up when he saw he was alone in bed and hurried a glance around the room.

She stood by the burning-bright hearth that cast good light on the room. She was fully dressed, her back to him, her long, light brown hair lay straight to the middle of her back, and he recalled how soft it had felt to the touch just as her body had felt, soft and inviting.

Sara. He let her name linger in his mind but wouldn't let it pass his lips. Last night the darkness let them couple without thought of anything but the magic they had created. Today, however, the light would reveal the truth, and he worried how she would react to his scars.

It took more courage for him to speak her name than it would have for him to ride into battle. "Sara."

She turned slowly and looked upon him with soft blue eyes, not cringing or turning away in disgust but keeping her eyes fixed on him.

He did the same, his eyes locked on her face. She wasn't a beauty and barely pretty, more plain-featured like many women, though she did have the softest blue eyes he had ever seen. She appeared thinner than he thought, her underdress and tunic hanging loosely on her, and she did not have much height to her, something he had not even given thought to last night.

She said not a word to him, just stood there staring.

Something tugged at him, and he scrunched his brow in thought. There was something familiar about her. There should have been after the intimate night they had spent together, but it wasn't that. It was seeing her now in the light that made him think she was familiar. What was it?

She is skinny and plain-featured.

His heart slammed against his chest recalling Brother Emanual's words. It couldn't be. He could not be that much of a fool. Anger stirred in him, and he tossed the blanket off himself and got out of bed and, ignoring his nakedness, went to her.

Her head barely reached his shoulder when he stopped in front of her.

"You left me no choice but to deceive you, husband."

Cavell was ready to strangle her, though it was himself who he should strangle for allowing a desperate need for a woman to have him make such a foolish mistake.

"Our marriage has been consummated and cannot be annulled," she said.

He bent his head toward her, thinking she would recoil from his scarred face, but she did not budge. "We will see about that, wife."

Her chin went up in defiance. "You would rid yourself of a wife who could possibly be carrying your bairn?"

28

Her words were like a punch to his gut. "Bloody hell, woman, what have you done?"

"What was necessary," she shot back.

"You are insane," he accused.

"Lies! I am no more insane than you are."

His hand shot out and grabbed her chin, squeezing it. "Insanity is a requirement for a Gallowglass warrior."

He released her and, shaking his head, went to retrieve his garments and get dressed. He spotted the red mark on the bedding when he bent to snatch up his shirt. He took a closer look at it and turned to her.

"You were a virgin?"

"Aye, I would come to my husband no other way," she said proudly.

Could this get any worse? He quickly and silently cursed for even thinking it since no doubt it was about to get much worse.

He dressed quickly. "We leave here before any of this becomes known."

The door opened and as soon as Curdie stepped inside her eyes went wide. "I thought you both would be gone by now."

"Come in here and shut the door," Cavell ordered sharply.

Curdie hurried in, going to Elsie's side, and giving her a questioning look.

"I am grateful for your help," Elsie said to her, then looked to Cavell. "I promised her that I would share the coins you gave me but give them all to her."

Seeing the way anger distorted the scars on Cavell's face reminded Curdie that he was a

Gallowglass warrior, and she was quick to say, "I need no coins. You have been generous with me."

"You will take the coins," Cavell said, taking several from his purse. "A payment for holding your tongue for what went on here." He snagged Curdie by the arm and yanked her over by the bed.

Curdie's eyes widened once again, seeing the blood on the bedding.

"No one is ever to know, for if I find out you let your tongue loose, I will find you and cut it out of your mouth," Cavell threatened. "Start with Meldon, the man you spent the night with, and no doubt told that you arranged this liaison. Make certain you tell him it never happened."

"I will see it done and keep my lips forever sealed, sir. Never will I say a word. Never. You have my word on it," Curdie promised.

He shoved coins in her hand, slipped his cloak on, then went to his wife. "We cannot be seen leaving together. You will meet me just inside the woods next to the pen where those staying the night after market day sheltered their horses. I warn you. Do not try and run from me."

"I won't. I need your help," Elsie said.

"Curdie," Cavell said, turning to her. "See that she gets there without a problem."

"Aye, sir, I will."

Cavell stepped out of the cottage after peering out to make certain no one was about and made haste to fetch his horse. People avoided him, turning away or hurrying off or blessing themselves when they caught sight of him. He had not bothered to hide his face with his hood, and with wearing his anger for all to see, he probably resembled more demon than man.

He spotted a farmer hitching his horse to his cart when he reached the pen.

"You have food to sell?" Cavell asked.

"Take what you want," the farmer offered out of fear and showed him what was left.

Cavell had the man put a hunk of cheese, two loaves of bread, and a few quail eggs in a sack and startled the farmer when he gave him coin for the food.

He soon had his horse ready, and he mounted and rode away from the village and into the woods, knowing he would be fodder for gossip for some time to come. Once in the woods he turned his horse and rode to the area where his wife had better be waiting for him.

That she had tricked him into consummating their vows continued to trouble him. That she could be insane troubled him, and that she had said she needed his help troubled him. But what troubled him even more was that he continued to desire her. The memory of last night lingered far too much in his mind, the softness of her body, how easily she had responded to his touch, how she had enjoyed touching him, kissing him, surrendering to him and her own desires. He would have never thought her a virgin, and yet the proof had been there.

"We're here," a voice called out, and Curdie stepped from behind a tree, Elsie following from behind her.

He waved his wife to him and once close, he leaned down, hooked his arm around her waist, and hoisted her up on the horse to settle her in front of him.

"Curdie," he said when she went to walk away, and she turned. "Keep your word to me and you will have a Gallowglass warrior for a friend to help you if ever needed."

Curdie smiled. "Then friends we are, for I can say nothing when I know nothing."

Cavell nodded, then turned his horse and headed into the woods.

***

Elsie sat silently, gathering strength. Her heart pounded wildly, and fear set her insides trembling. But she would not succumb to fear, she would not wear it for all to see, and she would not let it stop her from doing what was necessary. She had to mask her fear as she often did and instead, keep an unwavering façade that belied the truth just as she had done last night. Only she never imagined that her husband would turn her gut-wrenching fear into desire, and she would share with him a night of pure bliss.

With no experience, she had followed his lead and it had become easy after he had stirred her body in ways she would have never imagined possible. She had thought one day to wed, hoped to wed, and have a family. Never, though, had she believed she would find such pleasure in the arms of an infamous Gallowglass warrior, nor did she think she would ever wed one.

She forced her fear aside and finally raised her head to speak with him, but her words caught in her throat. Seeing his scars up close had her heart aching for him. Some had been stitched but not by a skilled hand, while others had been left to heal on their own and could use some care.

He could see the disgust in her eyes and wondered if last night would have gone differently if she had been able to see his face.

Seeing how it must make him feel to stare at him, she looked away and asked, "Where do you take me?"

"I should take you back to the abbey, but you have made that impossible," Cavell said, annoyed that he enjoyed the feel of her nestled in his arms when she obviously found his scars appalling. "Until I know for certain no seed of mine grows within you, we avoid being seen."

And if it hadn't, would he return her to the abbey? She would not let him do that. Never would she be locked away there again.

"I am not possessed of madness," she said, something she had continually reminded herself of while at Dundren Abbey.

"Who sent you to the abbey and why?"

"I was told it was my da's decision to send us there." She shook her head. "But that makes no sense. He would have never done that."

"Us?" he asked.

"My two sisters, Leora and Sky. I need you to help me rescue them."

"First, I need to know more," Cavell said, determined to get to the truth and discover if his wife talked nonsense because of her insanity or that she was not insane and spoke the truth. If she did speak the truth, then that meant someone wanted her and her sisters locked away but for what reason?

"Ask me anything," she said, her fear abating and wondering if it was because she felt safe when in his arms as she had felt last night. Another thing she had never expected to find with a Gallowglass warrior.

"Did you agree to this marriage with me?"

"Aye, I did. My da's old age does not wear well on him. He is an ill man and does not have the strength to lead the clan. When your da, Lord Philip, proposed the arranged marriage, my da sought my counsel and realizing the benefits to our clan, I immediately agreed to it."

Cavell was blunt with his next question. "Were you made aware of my scarred face?"

"Aye, gossiping tongues carried the news to us, but I am no beauty for you to look upon, so we are equal when it comes to that. Besides, with some care to those wounds many of them will fade with time and your fine features will return to you. My features will not change. Does that matter to you?"

"You're not bad on the eyes," he said, her soft blue eyes capturing his attention along with her long eyelashes that were a shade darker than her light brown hair and framed her eyes perfectly, and the way her eyebrows, the same color of her eyelashes, arched slim and graceful above her eyes.

Elsie couldn't hide her shock. "Never has anyone complimented my features."

Only someone who never received a compliment on their features would know that was not much of a compliment and he felt something he had thought he'd lost long ago… empathy. He dismissed the thought, thinking it would not serve him well.

"There is a place where we can shelter until you learn if you are with child," he said, the thought troubling him. He wanted bairns, a slew of them, but not before he had a good place—a home and wife of his choosing—to raise them properly.

"We cannot wait to rescue my sisters. I will not leave them to suffer any longer," she argued. "Did Brother Emanual bother to show you how he treats the captives he keeps there in the pretense of helping them?"

Cavell felt her upset with the way her body tensed in his arms and he eased her a bit closer against him. "He did and it was disturbing, but how many there actually do need help?"

"Not as many as you would think, but I know for certain my sisters should not be there and I fear that—" She stopped, tears threatening her, and she did not want to show weakness in front of her husband.

He could hear in her voice that she was on the verge of tears. His training as a Gallowglass warrior had taught him to be impervious to a woman's tears, so why with his wife, with not a tear shed and only on the verge of tears, did it disturb him?

"The way they treat my sister Sky is horrendous. They keep her chained and with a hood over her head. She cannot last much longer. I must free her."

Cavell recalled seeing the woman. "Brother Emanual claims she is possessed by a demon."

"No demon possesses Sky. She is the sweetest person you would ever meet, and she has the kindest heart, and she is the most beautiful woman you would ever lay eyes on."

And yet she was chained to a wall and a hood kept over her head. There was something about her sister she wasn't telling him, and how did he know if the woman was truly his wife's sister? If she was that beautiful, then why was Elsie so plain featured?

"And what of your other sister? There was a woman who begged for help to free her, and Brother Emanual assured her she would be freed once she got well."

"Leora would never beg. Out of the three of us, she is the most strong-willed one. She would have reasoned with you to convince you to help her. That woman who begged was probably Edith. She does not know why the chieftain of her clan sent her there, but without his permission she will never be freed. I will not let that happen to my sisters."

"That is the problem for us," Cavell said.

"How so?" Elsie asked, worry in her voice and unshed tears lingering in her eyes.

"I am your husband and that makes me not only responsible for you, but it also permits me to make any and all decisions for you, not so your sisters. Your father is the only one who can get them released. So, if your plan is for us to go to the abbey and demand their release, it will end in defeat."

"I did not think Gallowglass warriors ever accepted defeat," she challenged.

"We don't, but we also don't ride into battle blind. We get to know our enemy and often use what we learn about them against them."

Elsie shook her head. "I didn't even know we had an enemy."

"Presently, your enemy would be the person who sent you to the abbey."

Elsie shook her head again, more strongly this time. "My da is not our enemy. He is a good and loving father. He would suffer before he would see any of his daughters suffer."

"Yet he sent the three of you there," Cavell reminded. "It is his help you need to free your sisters."

"Then I will return home and speak with my da."

"Nay, you will not," Cavell ordered and pressed his finger to her lips when she went to argue. "Your da presently is the enemy until we can prove differently. That means we find out why he sent you and your sisters to the abbey before we do anything."

It also gave him time to find out if she was telling the truth or, if as the monk said, she was insane. Although, from their conversation she appeared to have her wits about her. But then he had seen men who had appeared the same as her only to find out too late that they were raving madmen. And he would not stay wed to an insane wife, no matter how pleasurable she was in bed.

"Does it not strike you as odd that my da would send all three of his daughters to an abbey that cares and treats the insane?" she asked.

"The thought has not been lost on me," he admitted. "And it also proves an excellent reason why we need to discover the reason he did so before we do anything else. Need I remind you about the part of being a husband where I make all the decisions for you?"

Fear prickled her skin when she thought to voice her opinion on a husband's dictate but worry and limited freedom had her wanting to speak up. "What if your decisions prove wrong?"

"I am never wrong."

That he spoke with such confidence about an obviously flawed thought had her smiling. "No one is that perfect."

There was a prettiness to her face when she smiled, and he couldn't help but smile in return which unexpectedly caused him to rediscover his once effortless charm.

He continued smiling as he proudly announced, "I am cursed with perfection."

Elsie laughed. "I do not know if I am blessed or cursed to have such a perfect husband."

The sound of her genuine laughter poked at his heart. It seemed like forever since he had heard a woman laugh in response to his charmingly, teasing manner and he realized how much he had missed it. It also made him realize that Elsie might just make him a good wife as long as she wasn't insane.

Chapter Four

Elsie was so hungry that she had to clasp her hands tightly together to keep from reaching out and snatching a piece of bread and cheese that her husband had pulled from a sack and placed them on it. It had been a whole day since she had eaten or had it been longer, she could not recall. She had found some silverweed and eaten the roots. Before that, and having no choice, she had dared to eat a small amount of blackthorn berries, knowing too many could make her seriously ill. But she had had no good, solid food since leaving the abbey and her stomach gurgled, reminding her of that.

"When did you eat last?" Cavell asked, hearing her stomach protest, and ripped a piece of bread off the loaf and snapped off a hunk of cheese to hand to her.

Her mouth watered for both, and she wanted to shove both into her mouth and finally silence her complaining stomach. But she didn't. She took a small bite and finished chewing before she answered him.

"A day or more."

"Eat," Cavell said, imagining how harrowing her ordeal must have been and wondering how she had survived it.

Elsie had no problem doing as he said, her stomach grateful as she began to fill it and chase away the gnawing emptiness that she had had no choice but to ignore.

Cavell waited while she got some food into her then asked, "How did you ever escape that place?"

"I watched the daily habits of the monks and listened as they talked in our presence as if we did not exist. It was when I heard one monk complain that he believed another monk had stolen his robe after it had been washed, something they did not do often enough, that I knew if I could snatch one of the monks' robes then I could easily walk right out of the monastery and be free to find you and have you help me free Leora and Sky."

Curious to know how she had accomplished that, Cavell asked, "How did you get the robe?"

"It wasn't difficult. I learned quickly upon arrival what happened when you didn't stop protesting your internment there." Her glance strayed in the distance from where they sat on the ground, past the stream that flowed busily nearby, it all disappearing as the image of that day returned to her. "Several monks tossed me into one of the large vats where their robes are washed. Thankfully the water had not been recently refreshed or it would have been scalding hot. It was barely warm. They dunked me beneath the water repeatedly, holding me under until I finally stopped fighting. Then they dumped me in the chapel and forced me to kneel in front of the altar and ordered me to pray for my madness to be forgiven. I was left alone for hours, no strength left in me to do anything but comply with their demands. I realized if I could be left alone again like that, then I could manage to steal one of their robes from the baskets the monks dropped their soiled or worn robes in to be washed or repaired. It sat just outside the washroom. I could grab one and make my escape. I managed to alert Leora to my plan and told her I would return with help and prayed she would relay the message to Sky so she would not lose hope."

"You willingly suffered another torturous dunking so you could attempt an escape?" he asked, a bite of anger in his voice at what she had been made to suffer. Insane or not, he could not allow her to suffer that agony again. But what would he do with her if she was insane?

"It was not an attempt. I intended to succeed. I had to. My sisters' fate rested with me, and I would not fail them."

"Did you not consider the water might scald you?" he asked, almost cringing at what might have happened to her, and the thought fed his annoyance.

"I did consider that, which was why I did it later in the day when I knew the water would be cool. This way I would be left forgotten in the chapel until near dusk, or possibly the entire night, which would not only make my escape that much easier, but it would give me a better chance of succeeding, and it did."

"Did you even once consider the dangers you would face once free, a lone woman traveler?"

"You mean a monk traveling alone," she reminded. "You gave no thought that I was anything other than a pious monk when I joined you at the table."

"Bloody hell! That was you at the market?" he asked but already had his answer. He had been so consumed with the possibility that his wife might have been found that he allowed good judgment to elude him. His wife had robbed him of his common sense and warrior ways before he had even met her.

"I had no choice. I had to do something, or I feared what my sisters' and my fate might be," she said, dusting off her hands.

"You took a dangerous chance," he scolded, annoyed at himself for not paying more heed to the situation that was more complex than he had first thought.

She had not only finished the bread and cheese he had given her but a second piece as well and he broke off more to hand to her. He was not surprised that she took it since hunger still showed in her blue eyes that he found so appealing. Somehow there was a comfort in their soft blue color, and he enjoyed getting lost in it.

Elsie raised the bread to her lips then stopped. "I should not eat so much of what little we have. We will need it."

We. That she thought of him, cared that there would not be enough food for him when she was still hungry, told him that she was thoughtful. Or was she being deceitful, trying to win his favor?

"If there is time, I will hunt for food tonight. If not, there is sufficient food left to feed us later. Once at the shelter, I can hunt for fish or meat."

A smile hurried across her face. "That would be wonderful."

Her smile did not change her plain features substantially, yet there was something about it that captivated.

Genuine.

Her smile was honest, not forced, not trying to win favor with him, but then she was hungry, so such news would please her, and yet… her smile pleased him.

"Where do you take me?"

"There is a shelter that sits on a small area that borders McCabe and Murdock land. It is ignored by all but me, which keeps people away from it, never knowing when I will occupy it. I think my father prefers that I reside there when I return home. So, no one will disturb us there."

"That will give us a chance to see what goes on with my da."

She glanced away for a few moments and Cavell began to understand that was her way when contemplating an issue.

"Once we can confirm that my da did not send my sisters and me to the abbey, then we can have him get them released from that horrible place." Her brow suddenly wrinkled with concern. "When seeing the cell where I was kept, did you and the monk speak my name?"

"Aye, we spoke freely about you." That her brow wrinkled more with concern had him asking, "Something troubles you about that?"

"If Leora heard my name, she would have attempted to speak with you if she was there. It worries me that she may have been suffering one of their painful tortures that were meant to drive the madness from us."

Cavell recalled the agonizing scream he had heard upon entering the building but thought better than to mention it and cause her more worry. The more she told

43

him, the more he began to wonder over the strange situation and possibly his father's part in it. Why had he suddenly arranged a marriage for him when his father's only concern had been that he join the Gallowglass?

"We will see your sisters freed," he said, knowing too well the feeling of being imprisoned, though his prison had no true walls, only endless battles.

Elsie reached out to rest her hand gently on his arm. "I am most grateful, husband, for your help."

The sincerity in her voice, the gentleness in her soft blue eyes, and the tenderness of her touch hit him like a punch to his gut. A punch, as insane as it may seem, he favored.

"We need to be on our way," he said, shoving the remainder of the food back in the sack, then standing. "Go drink your fill from the stream before we go."

He turned away from her, troubled by his thoughts.

Elsie got to her feet and went to the stream, wondering why her gratefulness seemed to annoy her husband. Perhaps referring to him as her husband caused him to get upset and she should refrain from doing so. After all, he did not wish to be married to her, but she needed him to remain married to her. Fear and worry that she would fail her da and sisters churned her stomach, but she could not let either slow her down or stop her from doing what must be done.

She lowered herself by the edge of the stream and scooped up handfuls of water to quench her thirst. She took one last handful, after several, and brought it to her mouth when something had her glance across the stream.

A man stood there staring at her and in his hand was gripped a battle axe.

Instinct had her scrambling to her feet and shouting, "CAVELL!"

He caught her with one firm grip around her waist as she stumbled toward him.

"A man with a weapon across the stream staring at me."

He held her close as his eyes hurried a glance that way. He saw no man, though he could easily have taken refuge in the forest that was lush with trees and foliage.

"What did this man look like?" he asked, keeping his eyes on the opposite bank while also keeping a firm hold of his wife.

She shook her head. "I'm not sure. It happened so fast and the weapon he carried is what got my attention."

"What was the weapon he carried?"

"A sizeable battle axe with a long handle," she said and shuddered, fright welling in her eyes. "He may not be alone. There could be a whole group of them."

"Or he could be a single warrior waiting to see if the pretty woman drinking from the stream was alone."

Pretty. He called her pretty. Had he meant it or was he trying to distract and ease her worry? If so, it worked since she focused on that rather than anything else.

"It is best we leave and get on with our journey," he said and hurried her to the horse.

They were soon on their way, Elsie keeping herself snug against her husband and her eyes alert to her surroundings.

Cavell did the same, though it was possible she had seen a Gallowglass warrior, a long-handled battle axe, a weapon of choice for many of the Gallowglass who learned to wield it with skill. But he could not be sure since a rare, few renegade warriors had taken to using it as well, though not as skillfully as Gallowglass warriors. He would keep a watchful eye and be ready to fight if necessary.

***

"We can finish the food you brought with you tonight," Elsie said, gathering sticks and broken branches for firewood shortly after they had found a place to stop for the night. "Tomorrow when we reach the shelter is time enough for you to hunt."

She hoped she didn't sound fearful or desperate, but she rather not be left alone after seeing the warrior with the battle axe as if ready to attack. She had managed to avoid people on her quest to find her husband and when it hadn't been possible, the monk's disguise served her well. Few if anyone troubled a monk. She also now had her husband to rely on and she had no doubt of his ability to protect her. The Gallowglass reputation alone would keep people at bay, but only if he was in close proximity. Otherwise, she would need to rely on herself.

"I will see you kept safe," Cavell said, realizing that the battle axe wielding warrior had left her feeling uneasy.

A soft smile touched her lips. "I appreciate that, husband." She tilted her head and turned a questioning eye on him. "Do you mind if I call you husband?"

"Though a shock to hear, it is an accurate description," he said with a smile that meant to tease, then realized his scars might signal differently.

That her smile widened meant she understood that his response was meant to be humorous but more importantly, she had not cringed at the change in his scars his smile produced. They made no difference to her, and he felt the tautness that constantly pervaded his muscles begin to ease.

Cavell got a fire going, the spring night chilly.

"How far is this shelter from my clan's keep?" Elsie asked and dropped her hand down on husband's shoulder for support while she lowered herself to sit on the ground.

She cried out in fright when his hand clamped around her wrist and yanked her down into his lap. "I am sorry. I thought it was permissible to touch you since we have already been intimate."

"It is unwise to unexpectedly touch a Gallowglass warrior, especially from behind," he warned, his reaction having been instinctive, but it was that she did not hesitate to touch him as if it was something familiar for her to do that so shocked him. And having her nestled in his lap, her backside pressed snug against his manhood, stirred more than memories of their intimate night together. It stirred his passion for her, and unwisely and selfishly he kept her there.

"That was rather foolish of me," she said softly, her fright dissipating and replaced by the enjoyment of his closeness and the way, to her surprise and pleasure, it aroused her. She wondered if it was her imagination or her own desire that made her think she felt him hard against her backside. Or did he desire her as she did him?

She chased the thought away, fearful of the next time they coupled. There would be at least a modicum of light and he would see that her thin body was lacking and turn away from her in disgust and it would pain her.

Cavell shifted her to adjust her more comfortably in his arms and to remove her all too alluring backside off his growing shaft and wondered over the sudden sadness he saw in her lovely eyes.

He ran his finger gently beneath her eyes. "Why the sadness in your eyes?"

It troubled him to see it there. He preferred seeing her smile.

How did she tell him she would have preferred to remain as she was, enjoying the feel of his rising manhood or how the simple touch of his finger to her face was magical with the way it flared her body in desperate desire for him? Unfortunately, she did not have the courage to say any of what she felt. What he made her feel. Or was it that she was too fearful he would not find her words welcoming?

Her response could only hint at what she felt. "I wonder how we will fare as husband and wife. I hope well, for I would make a proper and worthy wife if given the chance."

"I would not make a good husband," he said, continuing to hold her with no thought of letting her go.

"How about a tolerable one?" she asked quite seriously.

Cavell laughed. "Isn't it the husband that must tolerate the wife?"

She smiled as she proclaimed the problem solved. "We can tolerate each other."

Not able to keep from touching her, he ran his finger along her cheek and marveled at her softness. "You deserve more… more than I can give you."

"But I need you, Cavell. I need you to remain my husband," she pleaded softly, thinking her clan did need him, but she, herself, needed him much more.

I need you. Her words resonated in his head. If only she needed him, just him. It would make a difference.

He ignored her plea and recalled her question that he had yet to answer. "You asked how far from the shelter to your clan. It is a morning's ride."

That he changed the subject was a clear sign that he would no longer talk about their marriage. He could not ignore it for long, but for now she would let it be.

"Then we should waste no time going to speak with my da after spending the night in the shelter."

"Did you forget I told you that until we find out if your da is truly responsible for sending you and your sisters to the abbey that you will stay away from him?"

"I did not forget. I will not go, but the monk will," she said with a smile and tugged at the robe she wore.

"Nay, you will not take such a chance," he ordered, the thought of the problems it could create and the danger it might put her in not to his liking.

49

"What chance do I take if discovered? I am with my husband, a mighty warrior who no one would dare challenge. Besides, my da is ill and would welcome a visit from a monk."

It would settle his worry about leaving her alone while he visited with her father, and the robe would provide some protection, but he wasn't ready to commit to it yet.

"We shall see."

"At least you do not dismiss it completely," she said, relieved.

"We will eat, then sleep so we may rise with the dawn and be on our way," he said, not ready to let her go but knowing it wise.

"Aye," she agreed but did not move, finding pleasure in his arms.

A crack of a branch sounding like thunder to their ears had Cavell rushing her off his lap to bring them both to their feet, then he drew his sword and shoved his wife behind him.

"Who goes there?" he shouted.

Elsie's legs went weak when she peeked around her husband's wide shoulders and saw the man with the battle axe step out of the woods.

Chapter Five

"I have a message."

Cavell recognized the man… Melvin, a Gallowglass warrior. He was short in height, thick in body and kept his hair sheared to the scalp, insisting it benefited him. Perhaps it did, but more likely what benefited him was his amazing skill with a long-handled battle axe that had left many a warrior dead on the battlefield.

Cavell sheathed his sword, then scooped up the sack of food and handed it to his wife. "You will eat while I talk with this man."

"He is a Gallowglass warrior?" Elsie asked, taking the sack, and hugging it to her chest.

"Aye, and there is nothing to fear from him," Cavell assured her.

"I trust your word, husband," she said and caught a brief glance at the man to see if he showed any surprise that she referred to Cavell as her husband. His expression did not change. So, either the news had reached the Gallowglass, or it mattered not to them.

Cavell took hold of his wife's arm to help lower her to sit near the fire and stay warm while she ate. He took the opportunity to inform her—"A wife stays out of Gallowglass matters."

She saw the warrior nod in agreement with Cavell.

"As you say, husband," Elsie said, behaving as expected, though ready to follow them, unnoticed, to hear their every word.

She was glad it wasn't necessary to trail them when her husband approached the man and remained where he stood to speak with him.

"What is the message and who sent it?" Cavell asked, prepared to decipher it since the Gallowglass spoke in ways that only they would understand.

"A situation brews and Lord Slayer wants his warriors aware of the impending problem and prepared for what might come."

"Tell Lord Slayer that I am always prepared," Cavell said, concerned by what he heard.

"Lord Slayer will be pleased to hear that, and he extends congratulations on your marriage that brings substantial benefits and will serve you well. Noble also extends his well wishes for a long and fruitful marriage."

His concern grew hearing that and his response confirmed he acknowledged the message. "My appreciation to his lordship and Noble."

"You should also be aware that unfettered renegades prowl the area for work."

"I will keep watch," Cavell said, the message disturbing and a signal that something substantial was brewing. "You are welcome to camp with us for the night, Melvin."

Elsie was not surprised by her husband's invitation. Gallowglass warriors were known for their close ties.

"I am grateful and pleased to accept your offer," Melvin said.

Elsie tore what was left of the bread and cheese into several pieces for them all to share and laid out what quail eggs there were. That the man ate sparingly was not something she expected. Warriors who visited her clan often gorged themselves on food and drink, not even thinking food might be sparse for the clan members.

Elsie held her tongue as the two men talked, thinking she might learn something, but their conversation remained light, and it was not long before the small meal was finished and blankets were made ready for sleep.

Her husband curled himself around her when he joined her on the blanket, hooking his arm over her waist to draw her back snug against him and drape his cloak over her to keep the chilled night air at bay.

The heat of his body soon worked its way into her, comforting her, and with her worries waning, sleep soon sneaked up and claimed her.

Cavell found himself content wrapped around his wife while he waited for her to fall asleep so he could talk privately with Melvin. His thoughts, however, remained troubled. He needed to confirm with Melvin what he had deciphered the message to truly mean. That by referring to Slayer, a feared and mighty leader of the largest and most powerful Gallowglass group of warriors in the area, as Lord Slayer meant not only his father had died, but his older brother who would rule the clan upon their father's death had also died, leaving Slayer to rule Clan Ravinsher. That both men were dead was suspicious and Cavell wondered what happened to them. Their deaths also meant that Slayer would no longer rule over his troop of warriors since it would be more important that he lead his clan.

Cavell heard Melvin stir and he looked past the campfire's flames and saw the man was awake and waiting to talk just as he was, and he gave him a nod. Relieved exhaustion had claimed his wife and she slept soundly, he eased himself off her, taking his cloak off and tucking it around her to keep her warm. He joined Melvin where he sat on the opposite side of the fire.

"How is it that his father and brother are dead?" Cavell asked, keeping his voice to a whisper so as not to wake his wife.

Melvin did the same when he spoke. "He was and remains beyond rage when the news reached him. His brother, Warrand, died from an attack on him and his troop as they returned home from a visit to," —his eyes strayed past the flames to Elsie— "Clan Murdock, and his father, Lord Bannaty, was poisoned a week later. He died in Slayer's arms."

"I assume that Slayer believes my marriage into Clan Murdock could be beneficial for him and Noble warns me to remain in it until they can garner something fruitful from it. And the problem that brews is battle with whoever is responsible for Slayer's father and brother's deaths."

Melvin nodded. "Lord Slayer will hunt down who did the killing, but he will go to war with the person who ordered their deaths and decimate him and his clan. Lord Slayer is well aware that he freed you of the Gallowglass, but as a once Gallowglass warrior, he requests your support and in return when all is done, he will see you freed from your marriage if that is what you wish, and he will also pay the debt you owe Lord Cree, freeing you of any obligations so you may live your life as you choose. It is a generous offer, Cavell."

"And one that I might not live to enjoy if someone sees me as being in the way."

"There is that possibility, but Lord Slayer thought that once you took control of Clan Murdock you might find it to your liking and—"

"And become chieftain of the clan and claim fealty to him."

"There is that."

"I do not want to lead. I want to live in peace."

"Something most people want. Me, I prefer battle," Melvin said and once again glanced at Elsie. "You might want to consider your wife. Whatever trouble is brewing involves Clan Murdock, which means her life could be in danger."

***

Clouds filled the sky the next morning and along with them came a chill. Elsie stayed huddled against her husband as they continued their journey, his body heat keeping her warm as it had done last night.

"You talked with Melvin last night," she said, having waited until they were alone, Melvin having left just before they did at dawn this morning.

"What makes you think that?" Cavell asked, wondering if she had heard them.

"Men like to talk alone with other men just as women like speaking privately with other women," she said, letting him know that men and women both kept secrets.

"We talked some," he said and thought it the perfect time to see what she might know, if anything, of Slayer's brother Warrand's visit to Clan Murdock. "He mentioned Slayer's brother Warrand paying a visit to your clan." He saw that she was surprised by the news, her brow arching slightly.

"Not when I was there, though I do recall my da being upset after a visit from Lord Bannaty and grumbling that there was no pleasing nobility. But he never told me what they discussed."

"Was that before or after my father arranged our marriage?" Cavell asked, trying to see what events might tie people together and give clues to the culprit behind it all.

"It was after our marriage documents were signed, so perhaps Lord Bannaty was not pleased that my father would pledge his allegiance to your clan," she suggested, and her brow wrinkled in question. "Is there something you are not telling me?"

He saw no reason to keep the news of the two deaths from her since she would learn of it soon enough. "Warrand was killed in an attack on his return ride home after visiting with your da and Lord Bannaty was poisoned and died a week later."

"Good Lord!" Elsie said and fear suddenly filled her eyes. "Lord Slayer isn't blaming my da, is he?"

"Is there any reason he should?" Cavell asked.

"None!" she snapped, defending her da. "My da is a chieftain who cares well for his clan and his daughters and asks nor expects anything of such powerful men."

Her worry grew. "If you think of asking such a question of my da, then Slayer will as well. I need to return home now and see that no harm befalls him."

"And what if your da does plot and he is using you and your sisters as pawns in that plot? Any one of you could be in danger."

Elsie shook her head, angry that he could suggest such an outrageous thing. "Never! Never would my da do that. Whoever plots this scheme also plots against my da and since he is too weak to defend himself, it falls to you, next Chieftain of Clan Murdock, to protect him."

"Not until I make sure he poses no danger to you," he said and shook his head when she went to protest. "You waste your time objecting. It is my decision to make, and I have made it."

"If anything happens to my da, I will blame you," she threatened and a weak threat at that since she had no recourse if her da fell to Slayer's rage.

"And if your da is the good man you claim him to be, he would blame me if I failed to keep you safe. And as for Slayer, he may want to rush into seeing whoever is responsible for his father and brother's deaths suffer for the horrific deed, but what he wants more is to make certain the people truly responsible fall to his sword. He will not rush into anything, but his rage will grow and when it bursts… hell will be a safer place than here."

Cavell thought his wife would resort to silent anger or sulk because she did not get her way and though she remained silent, he felt the tenseness that had gripped her body begin to ease and fade until she fell limp against him drained of all anger or fight.

Elsie raised her head to look at her husband. She disliked his scars, not for how they had robbed him of his fine features but because of the pain he must have suffered when slashed and continued to suffer every time someone turned their eyes away from him. He was courageous in his suffering, she feared she would not be in hers.

"There is only you, husband. Without you there is little I can do to help my da or my sisters," she said and stopped, leaving the rest of what she wanted to say in her thoughts… *and if you should walk away from our marriage, I fear what the consequences will bring, and it would be no chore to care for you since I already do.*

***

They arrived after midday at the shelter. It sat nestled among towering trees as if through the years they had embraced the humble dwelling as one of them. A thatched roof topped the place while a lone window was firmly shuttered, and the thick wood door appeared impenetrable. It was a place of solace and Elsie would not mind spending time here… if things were different.

"I will get a fire going, then go hunt," Cavell said after lowering his wife off the horse. "You will not step a foot outside the door until I return."

That he turned and walked to the door, not waiting for a reply, told Elsie that it was an order intended to be obeyed without question.

Elsie smiled when she entered the dwelling. It was cozy. A single bed and small table with a chair occupied most of the limited space. Her husband soon had a fire going in the small hearth that heated the room sufficiently.

"Do not take a step outside that door while I am gone," Cavell reminded.

"Then let me fill a bucket with water, for I will take the time to wash while you are gone," Elsie said, and spying a bucket faintly covered with dust from lack of use near the hearth scooped it up.

"Mind my word, wife," he reminded once again and left as soon as she returned from filling the bucket from the rain barrel by the corner of the dwelling.

Elsie was glad for some time alone to wash and gather her thoughts and to try and make sense of things, though she feared that might take time. Time was not something her two sisters had, not locked away in the abbey, especially Sky. Her da's illness was another thing that concerned her. She did not want to lose him. No matter what her husband might think about him, he was a good man, a good da, and if he should die before freeing his two daughters, she feared what problems it might cause.

She slipped off the monk's robe, wishing she could give it a much-needed washing but fearful it would not dry before tomorrow when they would travel to see her da. Curdie had jumped at the chance to collect most of the coins she got from Cavell if she agreed to let Elsie wash at her cottage and provide her with clean garments. They were far too large for her but at least they did not smell like her other garments had. Never would she have gone to her husband filthy and with a stink about her.

She dropped the robe on the bench and dust floated everywhere, causing her to cough. A quick wash would have to wait. First, she needed to make the dwelling habitable.

She spied a broom tucked in a corner and her husband's warning rushed into her head.

Do not take a step outside the door.

She frowned, then her glance fell on the window, and she smiled. She hurried to it and with some effort got the board that kept the shutter closed free of its latch and pushed the shutters open, flooding the dwelling with light. She then opened the door, remaining inside, and began to rid the small room of dust, dirt, and cobwebs.

***

Cavell refused to let his mind drift. He intended to snare something for supper and hurry back to the dwelling. With renegades in the area, he did not want to leave his wife alone for long. He shook his head. Gallowglass were renegades but they were elite renegades, men from noble and influential families who fought to keep their lands, fought to keep the Highlands under their rule and they were ruthless in their endeavors, even savage at times. Why unfettered renegades would dare enter Gallowglass territory was a puzzle. But then everything about this situation puzzled him and as much as he would prefer to walk away from it, he had no choice but to stay.

He could convince himself that it was because of Slayer's generous offer to see him freed of all obligations. He could walk away and live life anywhere he pleased. Or tell himself that he owed Slayer to help him as a fellow Gallowglass warrior. But the truth was that he could not leave his wife—just yet. Though a thought had been nagging at him that he might not want to leave her at all.

It could be because she did not mind looking upon him. She always looked him straight in the eyes, though he had seen her glance drift to his lips on occasion and he wondered if she thought of kissing him again. He certainly thought of kissing her again.

His manhood perked up.

"A kiss no more than that," he mumbled glancing down at the slight rise between his legs.

He could not let it go any farther than that. Not until he knew for certain that she wasn't insane. But if she carried his bairn, whether insane or not, he would not leave her for the child's sake.

He grumbled beneath his breath. First, his father insisted he join the Gallowglass, then he arranged this marriage without informing him until it was done. Never again would he allow his father to dictate to him.

The rabbit hopped into his line of vision, getting his attention, and it was not long before Cavell caught their supper.

He had it cleaned, speared on a stick, and ready to roast over the fire in the hearth, his mouth already watering for it, when he returned to the dwelling. He stopped abruptly when he spotted the shutters open and a plume of dust rushing out the open door as if being chased.

"ELSIE!" he shouted, his temper flaring as he kept his distance so that he and the cleaned rabbit would not get consumed by the dust.

His wife suddenly appeared at the door, her eyes wide, her lovely hair braided and patches of dirt on her face.

"What is it? Do we need to flee?" she asked anxiously, brandishing a broom as if it were a weapon.

He had to hide his smile, for at that moment he thought his wife was the most beautiful woman he had ever seen, and his temper faded.

"What did I tell you about stepping out of the dwelling?" he reminded, forcing himself to sound annoyed.

"I paid heed to your word, husband. I did not step out of the dwelling. I never crossed where I stand now just as you ordered," she said. "The inside was far too dirty and dusty for us to dwell here comfortably, so I did what any good wife would do—I cleaned it."

How did he argue with that?

"Besides, if I heard any noise foreign to the forest, I would have closed the shutters and door immediately. I also assumed you would be in calling distance if necessary, so I felt safe." She smiled suddenly and pointed. "You got a rabbit, and I found some pot herbs that will make a fine broth. We shall eat well tonight. Hurry and set the rabbit to cook."

Cavell stared for a moment at the open door where she no longer stood, having returned inside. She cared enough to make the dwelling comfortable for them. Bloody hell, but he really could care for this woman.

Her face suddenly appeared by the open window. "Hurry, husband, the sky does not look promising."

He shook his head, clearing it as if from a trance and glanced up. She was right. Dark clouds had moved in overhead and a wind had swept in. One sniff of the air and Cavell knew rain was not far off. He hurried inside, looking forward to the night, though not too much, for fear he would do something regrettable. Or would he regret enjoying intimacy with his wife once again?

While the rabbit cooked and the pot herbs bubbled in the cauldron, Elsie decided to freshen herself the best she could now that her husband was present. She continued to worry what he would think, say, react when he saw her naked and she was not ready to face any of the possibilities just yet.

She grabbed the bucket, the water now dirty from seeing to the room, and went to the door.

Her husband was in front of her, blocking the door before she reached it.

"Where do you think you're going?" Cavell demanded.

Worry rather than anger sparked in his eyes and seeing that calmed the fear that had rushed through her when he suddenly loomed over her, sounding angry.

"I need fresh water to wash," she said.

Cavell grabbed the bucket from her hand. "I will get it for you."

As he left the dwelling, he cursed himself for being so abrupt with her upon seeing the fright in her eyes. Then cursed himself again for worrying about it. Damn, if his wife did not have him confused.

He stopped a moment upon his return, seeing that she had removed her tunic and stood in her shift that hung loosely on her and he wondered aloud, "You got those garments from Curdie, didn't you?"

"I did," she said and went to the water-filled bucket he had placed on the table, anxious to wash quickly and be done with it.

"You were not allowed to wash at the abbey?' he asked, taking a seat on the bed a short distance away from her, for his own sanity since he was hit suddenly with the need to see her naked and talking with her kept his mind from dwelling on it.

"Barely," she said and lowered her head over the bucket and scooped up a handful of water to splash over her face. It felt good, especially since her cheeks had suddenly heated when the thought had popped into her head of sharing the narrow bed with her husband tonight.

Cavell watched the water trickle down her slender neck inviting him to taste it, and he shook his head. He almost stopped her when she grabbed the cloth she had set on the table and wiped her neck and face dry.

Keep talking with her, he silently warned, but he was too enthralled with her movements to pay himself any mind. He watched her slowly ease her arm into the bucket of water and splash water over it repeatedly, washing away the dust and leaving her arm glistening. Her innocent actions brought back memories of the way her hands had caressed his body, explored it, having never touched a man before him and the thought further aroused his already stirring manhood. Her touch was meant for him and him alone, as his touch was for her.

That night had been magical with her. Never had a woman satisfied him as Elsie had. Never had he felt so content with a woman as he had with her. Never had he found such pleasure in sleeping wrapped around a woman as he had with Elsie. Never had he thought one night with a woman could have him caring so much for her as he did now for Elsie, and never had he hungered for a woman as he did now for his wife.

Cavell moved his glance off his wife's arm and looked upon her puzzled expression as she stared at him. He realized then how potent his desire must be in his eyes, and how unfamiliar it must be to her since they had coupled in the dark, only able to touch and feel but not see each other.

When he saw desire spark in her eyes, he tried to ignore it. But when she simply stood there continuing to stare at him as if she was lost, not sure what she felt, what to do, he mumbled a curse, stood, and went to her.

His hand hooked the back of her neck, his arm rushed around her waist to yank her to him, and his lips came down on hers in a kiss that demanded.

Chapter Six

Bloody hell, but he loved kissing his wife. While her body was soft and inviting, her lips were strong and eager to return his kiss. They not only matched his demand but demanded more from him and he did not hesitate to give her what she wanted, what he himself wanted… every bit she could give him and all he could give her.

He tightened his arm around her waist, lifted her so that her feet didn't touch the floor, and walked to the bed. He dropped her down on it, his body following along.

His hand instantly went to her small breasts, and he stopped himself from ripping her shift off her so he could cup her breast naked in his hand. Her hips rose to rub against his hard shaft, invitingly, and her arms locked around his neck, not letting him go.

Her wet arm shocked him enough to make him realize what he was doing. He was yet to know if her story was true, if she was or wasn't insane, if she already harbored his child within her. He could not let his manhood rule him. It had been what had gotten him into this position in the first place. But damn if he didn't want to surrender to the passion that soared between them.

Reluctantly, he pulled away from her, stood, and went to the door and stepped outside. He went to the rain barrel and splashed handfuls of water in his face, not once but three times. Then he stood there, hands braced on the rim of the rain barrel, water dripping from his face, silently cursing himself.

***

Elsie sat up, staring at the closed door not knowing what she had done wrong. Or was it as she feared that seeing her, kissing her, touching her when he could clearly see her made him realize that he did not favor her after all? That the one night they had shared together was magical because he could not see how plain she was and did not care if she felt thin, his need for a woman too great, but now that he could see her clearly, he desired her no more.

"It does not matter," she said to the empty room and took a deep breath to push back tears and got to her feet.

Her only concern was for her da and sisters. She would make certain he helped her and if when all was done, he wished to end their marriage, she would not object. The only problem she did not know how to solve was the hurt she felt in her heart, and she admonished herself for caring for a man she barely knew and who would never care for her.

She hurried to don her tunic, promising herself she would always remain fully dressed in front of him. Never, not ever, would she stand naked or even partially dressed in front of her husband.

The door opened as she was moving the bucket off the table and her husband quickly took it from her.

"Are you finished? Do you need more water?" he asked, annoyed at seeing the upset in his wife's eyes and her changed demeanor and knowing it was his fault.

"Enough to wash our hands after we eat," she said and turned away to stir the contents of the cauldron even though it didn't need it.

"Elsie," he said.

"Aye," she said but did not turn to look at him.

"Look at me!" he snapped.

She turned, her heart thumping madly and her stomach roiling, hearing the annoyance in his voice. He would tell her now, tell her that he had no interest in her.

"I will not chance getting you with child."

"Aye, so you have told me," she said and wondered if he spoke the truth or if it was an excuse so he need not speak the truth.

"Then stop tempting me," he warned, annoyed at himself again for blaming her and went to the door, shutting it so hard it rattled.

Elsie stared dumbfounded at the door. Whatever did he mean that she tempted him? She had no idea how she tempted him, but if he believed she tempted him, and he surrendered to the temptation, then could it possibly mean that he found her appealing? Or was it nothing more than a need that rose to torment him and being his wife, she was available to him?

She shook her head. She could not be any more confused than she felt now or what to do about it. She reminded herself that there were more important matters to dwell on and she would leave this be for now, not wanting her heart to hurt any more than it already did.

***

"You barely ate anything, no wonder you are so thin. You need to eat," Cavell said and handed her a piece of meat.

She waved the meat away and turned her head. "I had enough. I can stomach no more."

She had lost her appetite after the incident between them, and she had to force herself to eat the little she had eaten. It also did not help to hear him say what many had said to her since she was young about her being thin because she did not eat enough. Those who knew her well knew she possessed a hardy appetite, but no matter what she ate she remained thin.

She was still upset, and he knew full well that she had been looking forward to tonight's meal and that it was his fault she did not eat. But what should it matter to him? He barely knew her and yet he enjoyed getting to know her, learning things about her, something he had never cared to do with a woman.

Feeling the need to lighten her spirits, he gave her a casual poke on the arm and smiled. "At least it won't take much to feed you."

She snapped her head around ready to glare at him only to see a teasing glint in his eyes and tossed her chin up a notch. "I need no one to feed me. I can take care of myself."

"You would deprive me of my duty, wife?" he asked as if affronted yet continuing to smile.

She liked it when he wore a teasing smile. It lit her heart and fluttered her stomach, and she wondered if his teasing was his way of trying to make amends.

She shook her head. "I doubt anyone could deprive you of anything, husband."

He chuckled. "You have come to know me well in a short time."

"How well have you come to know me?" she asked and was surprised by his quick response.

"Not well enough." He leaned toward her. "But I will learn much, on that you have my word." He leaned back and reached for a piece of meat and handed it to her. "Now appease your husband and eat at least one more piece so you are not hungry on our journey to your home tomorrow."

Her husband's teasing manner had settled her stomach and she would be wise to eat a bit more since they probably would not eat until they arrived at her home.

She took the meat from him and took small bites, chewing slowly.

Relieved she ate a bit more, Cavell reached for more himself. "Now tell me, is there anything I need to know about your home before we arrive there tomorrow?"

Elsie detailed the village and the small keep, talked about the various people, and suggested he see their healer.

"May is a skilled healer, you should have her look at your scars."

"My scars are what they are. Nothing can be done about them," he said.

"Not if you don't try, but it is your decision to make," she said and went on talking about her clan.

That she did not pursue it or try to persuade him made him think that his scars truly did not bother her, though how so amazed him. They slashed through his face making him look as though he'd been pieced together. He turned his concentration back on his wife, not wanting the memories of that day he got the scars to take hold.

It wasn't long after that Cavell announced, "Time to sleep. We need to get an early start in the morning. We'll let the fire die so it will be nothing more than a few embers by the time we wake."

Elsie nodded and looked at the narrow bed. "We'll never fit."

"I will brace my back against the wall, and you will stay tucked against me so we will keep warm, and both get the sleep we need," he said and got into bed, tossing the blanket back before bracing his back against the wall. He then reached his hand out to her. "Tuck yourself in, wife, with your back to me."

Elsie did as he said, though tried to avoid tucking herself too close. She had no choice when his arm settled around her and pulled her tight against him then he tossed the blanket over them both.

She feared she would never sleep, her mind going to the intimate night they had spent together, but the warmth of his body soothed her, and she was soon asleep.

Not so, Cavell. He knew he took a chance getting in bed with her, but the room would chill as the fire died and he wanted to make sure his wife stayed warm.

71

Besides, he had upset her once already tonight. He was not about to do it again. They both had enough to consider without adding coupling to their problems.

One thing that he was glad to see thus far was that his wife had shown no signs of madness. She actually seemed more reasonable than most women he had met. But he intended to learn more about her from others once they reached her clan, and he would also see what he could find out that would help Slayer discover who killed his father and brother since Melvin would be lurking about waiting for news to report to Slayer.

He yawned, and feeling content and comfortable wrapped around his wife, he fell asleep.

***

"Keep your hood pulled down," Cavell said as they approached the Clan Murdock village. "If all proves safe, we can reveal your identity."

"Then we can remain here," she said, sounding hopeful.

"Aye, we can," he said.

He hadn't planned on it, but then he hadn't planned on hearing the news about Slayer's loss or that his help was needed with it. It was wiser that he remained here and discovered what he could, not only for Slayer but for his wife.

"We will speak to my da immediately," Elsie said, anxious to see her da and know how he was doing, and for her husband to hear the truth so she could finally discard the monk's robe.

"You knew of my scars, so I assume your clan is well aware of my appearance as well."

"They are and care not about the scars since they are pleased that they will have a courageous warrior as their chieftain," Elsie said with pride and hope that he would choose to remain in the marriage.

Cavell wondered if they would feel that way once they looked upon him.

He shoved his hood off his head. "Then they will have no doubt as to who enters the village."

Elsie was glad to see the clan greet him with welcoming shouts, generous smiles, and firm nods. Though it also worried her. It could mean her da's illness had worsened and the end was close for him, and just the thought of losing him sent a dreadful pain to her heart.

"What's wrong?" Cavell demanded, feeling her body tense as she tucked her arms tight against her chest.

"I worry over my da," she said softly.

He offered what comfort he could. "You will see him soon."

He only hoped she would not be disappointed.

A young lad, thin and tall with a tuft of flaming red hair and barely past ten years, hurried toward them when they stopped in front of the small keep.

"I am Rory, sir, and I would be pleased to see to your horse for you."

With an arm around his wife's waist, he lowered her to the ground, then dismounted and looked the lad over. "Are you strong enough to handle the likes of my steed?"

"Aye, sir, I am stronger than I look," Rory said, drawing his slim shoulders back and lifting his chin with pride.

"You best be, or Quinn will show his displeasure," Cavell warned and handed the reins to the lad.

"Come with me, Quinn," Rory encouraged the horse with a slight tug on the reins. "I will give you a good rub down and feed you."

The stallion snorted and followed along with the lad.

"Rory will take good care of Quinn. He is excellent with horses," Elsie assured him.

Cavell was glad to hear it. The lad had impressed him by keeping eye contact and not once staring at his scars.

The door to the keep opened and a buxom woman with gray hair piled atop her head haphazardly stepped out.

"I am Cavell, Elsie's husband, and I have come to speak with Chieftain Norris. I have brought a cleric along with me to comfort your chieftain."

"Welcome, sir, I am Alda. I oversee the keep servants. Chieftain Norris will be pleased to see you and he will also be pleased that you have brought a cleric with you." Alda stepped aside for the two to enter.

Elsie had detailed everything so clearly about her home that he felt as if he had already been there. The Great Hall was small as she had said, room enough for only four trestle tables with benches and no dais, no distinction that anyone led the clan. A low fire burnt in a fair-sized fireplace and wall scones with burning torches circled the room lighting it well. It was also the cleanest Great Hall he had ever been in.

"Take us directly to Chieftain Norris," Cavell ordered.

"Your visit with him will have to wait."

Cavell turned to see a stunningly attractive woman, tall, shapely, and with her dark-haired braid resting on her generous chest.

"I am May, the clan healer," she said, introducing herself. "Chieftain Norris had a difficult night, and he finally sleeps. It would be best if you waited a couple of hours before speaking with him. You must be hungry and thirsty after your journey. Why not partake of food and drink while you wait."

"An hour, no more," Cavell ordered and saw that servants were already placing food and drink on one of the tables.

Elsie went to the table in hopes that he understood that she preferred to give her da time to sleep, and she was relieved when he followed her. She was not surprised to see May follow as well and join them.

Cavell took one of the filled tankards and drank. The ale was tastier than others he had had, and he drank nearly half of it. He was glad to see his wife reach for a piece of bread and cheese, and he did the same.

Cavell asked what he knew was on his wife's tongue. "Has Chieftain Norris improved at all?"

"He has not grown worse, but he has not grown better either," May said. "I thought by now he would rally and improve, but he lingers as he is, and it perplexes me. I have started him on a different brew in hopes that it will help him."

"I hear you are a skilled healer, so I am sure you do well by him," Cavell said.

"I do my best. My mum taught me much and I continue to learn." May pointed to his face. "I can heal most of your scars if you let me."

Skepticism flared in his eyes. "How can you do what others claim cannot be done?"

"I can do it because I know more than those fools," May said. "The question is will you let me, or will you continue to hide behind your scars?"

While Elsie did not sit that close to her husband, she could see and almost feel his body grow taut with anger. She wanted so badly to toss her hood back and reveal herself so she could speak up, but it would only serve to make her husband angrier.

"I would watch your tongue with me, woman," Cavell warned.

"I meant no disrespect, sir, but scars like yours often hide more scars and healing a few helps heal the others until they are all finally healed or very few remain. I am here to help you when you are ready," May said calmly, not at all perturbed or fearful of his anger.

Cavell stood. "I go to see how Rory fared with Quinn. When I return, I expect to be taken to Chieftain Norris." He jabbed a finger toward Elsie. "You, cleric, stay here until I return." He looked at the healer. "And you will take your leave so as not to disturb him while he eats and prays."

"Aye, sir," May said, sliding off the bench.

Cavell turned away and angry strides took him to the door. He turned when he reached it to see May disappear through a doorway, then he turned and left.

Elsie sighed, relieved to have been left alone, though debating whether or not to sneak to her da's bedchamber and speak with him alone. She was eager to see him and worried when May said he had not improved, though relieved he had not grown worse. She recalled her da telling her something about his father having suffered the same as he did and how he had died from it. So, she worried he would meet the same fate. Her only hope was that May could save her da from the same fate as his father.

She heard someone enter the room and made sure to keep her head down. She had given her husband her word this morning before they left the dwelling that she would not reveal herself to anyone until he said otherwise.

The footfalls stopped at the table, and she prepared herself to speak with a deeper tone if necessary. She was shocked when the person spoke.

"Why do you hide under a monk's robe, Elsie?"

Chapter Seven

Elsie raised her head and smiled at May, trusting she never would have approached her and spoken if anyone else was about. "I should have known I could not fool you."

"Your determined walk and the way you move your hands with distinct purpose make it obvious to me. How anyone doesn't realize it is you beneath that robe puzzles me," May said, shaking her head as she joined Elsie at the table.

"People always paid little mind to me. It was Leora who got their attention."

"Because she demanded it," May said.

"Her fine looks also helped," Elsie said with no animosity or envy. "She can get a man to do anything when she smiles."

"Maybe so, but the one who is the most beautiful of the three of you is Sky. She could command any man if she had not been unfortunate to be born as she was. I keep hoping she will find a man who values her for who she truly is, a gentle, unselfish woman. But tell me why you hide and who you hide from? And where are Leora and Sky? When the three of you left here to go meet your husband, all was well. What happened?"

"I wish I could confide in you, but at the moment I can't," Elsie said. "There are things I must find out before I speak of what happened."

"I hope you know you can always trust me."

Elsie nodded. "I do, but for now I must hold my tongue."

May lowered her voice though no one was around to hear her. "Your husband, can you trust him? He is Gallowglass," May said as if that distinction somehow made him untrustworthy.

"It is precisely why the clan needs him. He will see us kept safe, align us with clans that will serve us well, especially now with my da so ill. A clan less than honorable could attack and lay claim to our clan and our land. My marriage to Cavell prevents that."

"Then it is good he is receptive to the marriage," May said.

Elsie was not about to let anyone know that her husband was anything other than accepting of their marriage. That was a matter between Cavell and her.

"I would love to talk more with you, but you should go before my husband returns," Elsie urged. "I promised I would not reveal myself to anyone until he says otherwise."

"I gave you no choice," May said, "but I understand and look forward to when we can talk openly without worry." She stood. "I will go fix the new brew for your da and will return when notified that your husband is once again in the keep."

"I am grateful, May," Elsie said, and after she took her leave, Elsie pulled her hood down far enough so no one could see her face and waited impatiently.

***

Cavell was pleased with the way Rory had cared for Quinn, though surprised he had little to say about Elsie and even less about Sky. Leora, however, he had no trouble praising.

He found the same with other people he spoke with, telling him how pleased they were that he would become chieftain, and said little of Elsie. And when he did mention her, all agreed that she was a dutiful daughter, and she would make him a dutiful wife. None had the courage to ask him why Elsie was not with him.

The people he talked with did not stare at his face, they smiled, pleased to meet him, pleased he was there, and after a while he was no longer conscious of his scars.

He was about to return to the keep when he felt a tug at his cloak. He was surprised when he turned and saw a young lass no more than seven or eight years standing there. Her dark hair was braided neatly, and she had pretty features.

"When will Mistress Elsie return home?" the lass asked.

Cavell was even more surprised that the lass had the courage to ask what no one else would and that she didn't run in horror when seeing his face.

"Soon," he said.

"How soon?"

"Soon enough," he said surprised she continued to ask.

"That's not an answer," the lass said.

"It is the only answer you are going to get," Cavell said, impressed with her tenacity but letting her know she was to ask no more of him.

80

"Why? Don't you know?"

He was struck silent for a moment, expecting the young lass to be too fearful of him to continue to question him.

He crouched down in front of her. "Do you not fear me?"

"Why would I?" she asked, scrunching her small nose as if the question confused her.

"What is your name?" he asked, curious as to why this young lass was so curious to know when Elsie would return home.

"Kara."

"Why do you ask about Mistress Elsie, Kara?"

"I miss her. She was teaching me about numbers. I love numbers," she said and counted to ten on her fingers. "And if I go twice, I reach twenty. Mistress Elsie knows a lot about numbers, and I want to learn all that she knows so I can keep count like she does."

"Keep count of what?"

"Everything," Kara said, her inquisitive eyes turning wide as if surprised he didn't know. "If you don't keep count, how do you know if any animals go missing or if enough crops are planted to feed the clan or if too much coin is spent? Knowing numbers is very important. So, soon enough is not an answer. I need a number."

Cavell had to keep himself from laughing, the lass seemed as logical as Elsie.

"Kara!"

Cavell saw a woman, her features similar to Kara's, racing toward them, and he stood.

"I am sorry, sir, so sorry that she troubled you," the woman said.

Cavell defended the little lass. "Kara is no trouble, just curious."

"Too curious at times, I fear," the woman said and turned a scolding eye on her daughter. "Bless you, sir, for being understanding and bless you for leading our clan. Kara will disturb you no more." She grabbed her daughter's hand.

"But he didn't answer my question," Kara protested as her mum tugged her along.

When Kara turned her head to look back at him, he held up two fingers.

"Sunrises or moon cycles?" Kara called out.

Cavell didn't get a chance to respond, Kara and her mum both disappearing around the corner of a cottage. He turned and headed to the keep, pleased he had learned two things about his wife. She was skilled when it came to numbers and she had been right when she had mentioned that people paid her little heed, though he had not expected that from her clan.

"Your people are very accepting of me," Cavell said when he joined his wife at the table in the Great Hall a short time later.

"They respect and appreciate your strength and courage, fearful of what could befall them with my da being so weak."

"Of course, they accept me out of need," he said, "just as you do."

"They accept you for who you are, a great warrior, and I accept you because I care—"

Cavell grew angry at the voices growing closer, causing his wife to hold her tongue.

I accept you because I care—

What would have followed her words? he wondered. Would she have said I accept you because I care for you? I accept you because I care to? I accept you because I care for my clan? And why did it matter so much to him?

May stopped in front of the table while Alda stood behind her with two servants. "I will take you to Lord Norris, sir, but I ask that you please wait a few moments outside Chieftain Norris's bedchamber while I wake him and let him know you are here."

"Do not take long. My patience wanes," Cavell warned, wanting an answer today.

He stood and almost reached out to help his wife to stand, but caught himself, then followed the healer up the stone staircase to wait with Elsie outside her da's bedchamber. He watched her move from foot to foot, anxious to enter the room, to see her da and learn the truth.

Cavell was growing more impatient, May taking too long, and was about to enter the room when she finally returned.

"He is far too weak to speak to anyone. I am hoping with more sleep and the new brew he will be rested enough to speak with you tomorrow. There is no rush for you to leave is there?" May asked.

Cavell stared at the woman. Why would she say that? He realized why fast enough.

"You know," he said and turned to his wife.

"It isn't Elsie's fault," May said quickly. "I recognized her walk and the familiar movement of her hands when she speaks."

Elsie drew her hood back relieved to be recognized.

"It is good to have you home, Mistress Elsie," May said with a welcoming smile.

"I am so happy to be home and eager to see my da."

Cavell would have preferred to keep her identity a secret until he got a chance to find out who was responsible for her and her sisters being sent to the abbey and why they were sent there. At least then he would know the name of his enemy. He also could not delay in providing Slayer with information that might prove helpful to him. And after talking with the clan members and finding them accepting of his appearance, even if it was out of need, he found it a relief that while here it was not necessary to conceal his face.

"Your da will be happy to see you as will others, knowing you have secured the safety of the clan with your marriage," May said. "But how will you hiding beneath a monk's robe be explained?"

Cavell did not hesitate to take command of how that would be handled. "The monk will retire to a bedchamber to seek solitude and prayer for the night, when actually Elsie will be in my bedchamber. I will take my supper there and retire early. The next morning Elsie will be here, and the monk will be gone. All would be told that she arrived before dawn, earlier than expected, and the monk returned with the monks who saw her safely here."

"A plausible explanation that no one will question," May said and returned to Chieftain Norris's bedchamber to leave the couple to make ready for tomorrow.

Elsie sighed with relief. She was finally home and would remain so, though her relief was short-lived when thoughts of her sisters' suffering rushed into her mind. Her first words were of them after being left alone with her husband in a small bedchamber while her bedchamber was made ready for him.

"Right after we speak with my da, we must immediately go and rescue my sisters."

"I will see it done," Cavell assured her.

"*We* will see it done. I am going with you." Elsie had no intention of being left behind. She would see with her own eyes, that her sisters were freed, safe, brought home.

"I will not argue over it, wife. You will do as I tell you," Cavell ordered sternly. "It could prove dangerous, and I will not take a chance with your safety."

Elsie placed her hand on his arm. "I understand the danger, but they will need me there to help them. I must be there for them. Please, at least consider it."

He had only known the touch of a woman when she was plying her trade or when coupling. It was different when his wife touched him with ease and no thought of pleasure simply to connect, be close, rely on him, and he favored it.

"I will think on it," he said, and she smiled with appreciation. "You will remain here until I come for you."

Elsie cast a hasty glance around the small room and gave his arm a squeeze as she said, "Please do not leave me here alone for long."

Cavell saw the fright in her eyes and realized the cell-like room was a reminder of the cell in the abbey where she had been kept and where her sisters now languished.

"You have my word," he said and without thought, he lowered his head and kissed her lips gently and she returned his kiss just as gently.

His arm went around her waist to hold her close as they both lingered in the delicate kiss that neither turned demanding. He enjoyed the soft play of their lips, the tenderness they shared, the lightness of their touch that it somehow tempted so much more than a kiss filled with hunger.

Footfalls broke them apart, though their eyes locked as they did.

"I will return soon," he said and left the room, closing the door behind him, trying to chase away the image of the swirling passion he had seen in his wife's eyes and his own passion that displayed itself in his aroused manhood.

"Bloody hell," he mumbled and thought of tonight when once again they would share a bed.

Did he give in to his need for his wife? Secure their marriage once and for all? Make sure to fill her with his seed, so that she would grow round with the first of many bairns they would have together?

Wait!

He did not care to hear that warning in his head, but knew it was a wise one. He needed to know his wife better. He needed to know what went on here. He needed to know why Slayer's brother visited Chieftain Norris and if Norris was in any way involved with the death of Slayer's father and brother, for if he was, hell would rain down on Clan Murdock and he would not be able to do anything to stop it.

***

Elsie had been relieved when her husband had kept his word and returned quickly and retrieved her from the cell-like room. She was overjoyed when she found herself in her own room, Alda having had it prepared for Cavell. It wasn't large like her da's bedchamber, but it was a good size. She was surprised to see that her narrow bed had been replaced by one that would hold two people, otherwise all was the same. The chest that held her few garments sat against one wall and a small table, a bench beneath, sat against another wall. A crock of small pebbles sat atop it where she had left it. She used them when counting, though only when necessary, her mind quick with numbers since she had been young. The spring nights still held a chill that seeped through the stone walls, so a fire was still necessary to keep the room warm. Several candles added low light to the room and left it feeling comfortable and cozy and was the reason she had enjoyed retiring there at night.

Alone for only a short time, her husband having gone to speak with May for a moment, Elsie hurried to shed the oversized garments she wore and don her own garments. She rushed, so her husband would not catch her half-dressed. She did not worry that anyone else would enter since Cavell had assured her that he made it clear that no one was to enter his bedchamber until he gave permission.

She sighed when she slipped on a flax-colored, soft wool dress that fit her thin frame perfectly, and she hurried a deep green tunic over it that had a lovely design Sky had embroidered along the edges. She tied a cloth belt around her waist and sighed again when finished. Finally, she felt herself.

She undid her braid as she walked to the table to retrieve her comb and pulled her long, light brown hair to rest over her shoulder onto her chest, so she could comb it more easily.

The door opened just then, and her husband walked in.

Cavell stopped upon seeing his wife, her lovely, long hair free of any constraint and wearing garments that fit her. His thought was that he never saw such an appealing woman and his manhood agreed, giving a slight salute.

"Did May agree?' Elsie asked anxiously and did not notice the flare of passion in her husband's eyes until she got closer to him.

"She had no choice. It was an order not a request. She will alert us if your da awakes no matter the time," Cavell said, his eyes continuing to roam over his wife. "Those garments fit you well, unlike the ones you were wearing."

Was that a compliment? She didn't hesitate to accept it as one since it caused her stomach to flutter.

He reached out and lifted several strands of her hair that lay on her chest to rub between his fingers. "Your hair is so soft and such a beautiful color."

That definitely was a compliment, and it sent the flutters in her stomach soaring and more than sparked her passion. But as much as she would love to couple with her husband again, she still feared him seeing her naked. Several women had warned her that her small breasts would never hold enough milk to feed a bairn sufficiently and her hips were too slender and could cause her problems when birthing a bairn, not to mention if any man could fit inside her, or so they whispered.

But Cavell had fit inside her, comfortably so, and his manhood was sizeable, and he had quite enjoyed her as she had him. Now if only they could do so again and not in total darkness.

Cavell released her hair and walked around her to go to the table the servants had brought to the room earlier and piled it with food and drink. He filled a tankard with ale and took a generous swallow, hoping it would calm his racing heart and the passion that flared inside him.

His wife was growing more and more attractive to him, especially now seeing her in garments that actually fit her. And her lovely hair only added to her appeal.

Bloody hell, if he didn't find her tempting, far too tempting.

How was he ever going to sleep beside her in bed tonight and not touch her when he had every right to and that it was his duty as a husband to produce an heir to the clan? He needed to avoid thinking about it. But how did he do that when he was tempted every time he looked upon her?

"I meant to tell you that Kara misses you," he said, thinking of his talk with the little lass, which helped to distract from the tempting thoughts of his wife. "She says you were teaching her about numbers. Have you always had a skill with numbers?"

"Aye, since I was young," Elsie said.

"Kara claims she wants to keep count of everything like you."

"It is important to keep count of things in the clan. It helps the clan thrive and often survive. Kara is bright for her age, and it is good to know she enjoys learning about numbers. She can be an asset to the clan as she grows."

Cavell kept the talk safe, away from anything intimate and did not realize the time that past he was so enjoying speaking with his wife, until she yawned. He noticed then the candles had burned down low and the fire in the hearth had dwindled.

"You are tired. You should sleep," he said.

"And you?" she asked.

"I will join you soon enough," he said and went to the hearth to add more logs to the dwindling flames.

Elsie attempted to understand her disappointment that he would not join her right away. She feared him seeing her naked and yet she had the urge to couple with him. Or was it that she wanted to make love with him, having far more feelings for her husband than she cared to admit?

A knock on the door sounded before Elsie reached the bed.

It could only be one person and Cavell opened it to find May standing there.

"Chieftain Norris is awake, though I do not know for how long or how alert he will be. But you said to let you know."

"We will try and speak with him," Cavell said and stretched his hand out to his wife.

Elsie hurried to latch onto his hand, and he led her out the door.

The little light that was in her da's bedchamber came from the hearth, but Elsie didn't need much light to see her da's bed. It loomed large in the shadows, and she rushed to her da's side.

She fumbled to find her da's hand and was grateful to May when she tipped the candle she held for the flame to catch the wick of the candle on a chest that sat beside his bed.

Elsie was glad to see her da had not gotten any thinner than when last she saw him, though he was still too thin. She dropped down beside the bed and took hold of his hand. It was far too frail to the touch, and she kept it cradled gently in hers.

"Da. Da, it's me, Elsie. I'm here," she said softly and repeated it when he opened his eyes and looked confused.

"It's Elsie, Da. I've come home," she said.

Her da's eyes suddenly went wide. "Nay! Nay! The abbey. You should be at the abbey where I sent you and your sisters."

Chapter Eight

Elsie stared at her da shocked at his words.

"Nay! Nay!" her da said, tossing his head from side to side. "Go back to the abbey. Get back there now!"

A pain twisted in Elsie's heart and she grew more upset when he yanked his hand out of hers and waved his hand at her, shooing her away.

"Go! Do as I say! Now!" her da ordered.

Cavell clamped his hands on his wife's shoulders and brought her to her feet, moving her away from the bed. Her da's unexpected remark had obviously shocked her since she was expecting the opposite of what he had said.

"Pay him no mind, Elsie," May urged. "His illness rules him. This is why I did not want you to speak with him until he was lucid. When he heals, he will not talk so foolishly."

"And if he doesn't heal?" Cavell asked and did not wait for an answer. He let the consequences hang in the air unspoken as he hurried his wife out of the room.

He took her straight to their room and eased her down on a bench in front of the hearth, then filled a tankard with wine and handed it to her, resting his hand over hers and holding it there until the tremor in her hand calmed.

"Drink," he said, seeing that she had paled, and his heart ached for her. He knew the sting of disappointment from a parent. It truly could damage or even worse, scar the soul.

Elsie was too shocked to speak and so she did as her husband said and drank. The warm liquid stung as it traveled down her throat and spread through her insides. Surprisingly, it settled her churning stomach and it also chased away the sudden chill that had come over her upon hearing her da say he had sent her and her sisters to the abbey. Never had she expected to hear that.

"Why? Why would he do such a thing?" she asked more of herself than her husband, trying to make sense of it. Her da would never want her and her sisters to suffer as they had at the abbey. Something was amiss.

Cavell offered the most obvious answer. "To be rid of the three of you."

Elsie shook her head and kept shaking it as she spoke. "Nay. There is no denying he loves us. This makes no sense. Something is not right."

"You may be right but until I can find out for certain what goes on here, you are not allowed to be alone with your da."

That sparked her anger. "You will not stop me from seeing my da."

Cavell brought his face close to hers. "Try me."

He watched as anger flared like a mighty flame in her eyes before dying out as if doused with a splash of water. That's when he saw a glisten of tears in her eyes.

"I know my da well and I know without a doubt that he loves all three of his daughters equally, though he worries over Sky the most. He would give his life for any one of us. I will repeat again and again that none of this makes sense and I believe once he is lucid, he will explain it all."

Cavell was not as sure as his wife, but then he did not know the man, but he also could take no chances with her safety.

"Then you will wait until he is lucid to speak with him."

She sighed with frustration. "Lucid or not, I will see my da."

"Not alone or without my permission," he said firmly.

"I do not need your permission to visit with my da," she argued.

"You need my permission for most things, or do you forget I am your husband?"

"Sometimes I wish I could forget," she snapped.

Damn if her remark did not sting, though why it should, puzzled him. Wouldn't he be happy to be free of her? Wasn't that what he wanted?

Elsie regretted her spiteful words as soon as they passed her lips, and she would not let them linger between them.

"I am sorry. I did not mean that. I have never wished you were not my husband, and I wish you to remain my husband, though I would prefer you did not dictate to me. I am not a foolish woman, nor am I an insane woman. I am quite sensible."

"Sensible you say when you made a daring escape from the abbey, then disguised as a monk traveled all on your own to find me?"

"And I succeeded," she pointed out. "It was not only the sensible thing to do but the necessary thing to do."

"Sensible. Necessary. Your words perfectly describe the reasons I take precautions that you are not left alone with your da," he argued, thoughts of numerous horrific things that could have happened to her when she escaped the abbey and went looking for him, tormenting him, tearing at his gut and twisting at his heart.

Her brow went up. "You saw my da. What possible harm can he cause me in his condition?"

"Most people would assume that, but I am not most people. I have the distinction of being a Gallowglass warrior and with that distinction comes experiences that few if any will ever face. I have witnessed a chieftain, weak from a wound, on his deathbed who refused to surrender to his foe unless he stood in front of him. The foe, secure in his victory, obliged the old chieftain. Once the fool stood in front of him, the dying man remarked that the best man left alive claims victory and his foe agreed with a laugh believing he was the victorious one. The old chieftain stretched his hand out from where he lay in his deathbed and once their hands joined, acknowledging the fact, the old chieftain shoved a dagger through his chest, killing him quickly. The old chieftain clung to life for two more days so that his clan was ensured victory. So do not ever underestimate the will of a man seeking victory."

This time her brow scrunched. "Are you saying my da is trying to secure some sort of victory?"

"He is an ill man who still manages to manipulate."

"For what reason?" Elsie asked, confused and finding it difficult to believe that her loving da was manipulating anything. Unless… she glanced at the flames in the hearth, remaining focused on them.

Something caught his wife's thoughts and he let her be, though wondered where her thoughts had taken her. She was right about being a sensible woman. With no other recourse, her escape made sense and that she had not let any fear or doubt stop her spoke to her courage. Though some might think her foolish or even proclaim her insane for taking such a dangerous chance.

To him, she had been courageous though maybe a bit insane.

Elsie turned to him. "There is only one reason I can see why my da would send his three daughters away… to protect us. The question is, from what?"

And did it connect in any way with Slayer's father and brother's deaths? Cavell wondered. It seemed Clan Murdock was full of secrets, and he intended to uncover every one of them.

***

The news of Elsie's arrival home traveled fast the next morning with not a single person questioning it. Though word was asked about Leora and even Sky and they were told that both women would be returning home soon.

"Who did your da seek counsel from the most, I wish to speak with him to see if he has any information that may help us?" Cavell asked, after finishing the morning meal in the Great Hall.

"That would be Leora. She is skilled at seeing the truth in situations and either adapting to them or finding ways around them that would best benefit the clan," Elsie said.

"An unusual position for a woman," Cavell remarked. "Was there no man he confided in?"

"Aye, Morton, a close and dear friend since they'd been young. He's been dead almost a year now and my da still grieves his passing almost as much as he continues to grieve for my mum, Terena, gone five years now. My da says Morton was lucky to follow his wife in death, dying a month after her. My sisters and I were glad he didn't do the same, losing our mum had been difficult enough it would have been unbearable losing our da shortly afterwards."

For a moment, Cavell felt a jolt at the thought of losing Elsie, not seeing her smile, not feeling her touch, not kissing her ever again, not waking to her warmth snuggled against him as he had this morning, though wisely leaving the room before she woke.

The shock of his thought made him realize that he cared for his wife and that concerned him. What he would or could do about it, he didn't know, and he decided with all that presently needed his attention, it was best to let it be and see what came of it on its own.

"I have little memory of my mum except that when she spoke to me it was as if I could hear her love for me. I remember being at market one day, years after her death, and hearing what I thought was her voice. I ran to the woman only to hear a far different voice." He shook his head. "I never told anyone that. I worried they would think me foolish."

"You missed your mum and thought you heard her. There is nothing foolish in that. Not long after my mum passed, I thought I heard her call out to me several times. I like to think it was her and that she wanted to let me know she was there with me."

Why was it his wife made it sound reasonable? That it actually was his mum he had heard even if it had only been in his mind. He would like to think it was, for she had truly made him feel loved and he still missed her.

The thought hit him again how he would miss Elsie if she was no longer in his life, and he wondered over it.

"I am not ready to lose my da yet, so please do not deprive me of my time with him."

That she rested her hand on his arm did not surprise Cavell. It was something he had not only gotten used to but looked forward to since it seemed such a natural thing for her to do. Also, that she reasoned rather than argued with him was another thing he favored about his wife. And it was another reason to prove she was not insane. Insane people did not reason. He had seen that himself before and after many battles.

"We will visit with him," Cavell said.

"I must speak with him sooner rather than later. My sisters' lives depend on it. We cannot delay freeing them from the abbey."

"You do not make things easy for me, wife," he said, and her face lit in a soft smile that poked at his heart.

"I do nothing, husband. It is your rules that make things difficult."

"You are far too wise—" He paused a moment, his eyes drifting to her generous smile, and he lowered his head as his arm slipped around her waist. "And your lips are far too inviting to ignore."

Shocked that he would kiss her in front of the servants, she almost did not respond, but then desire flared, and her lips welcomed his eagerly.

Chuckles and rushing footfalls interrupted the kiss and he realized that he and his wife had an audience. He rested his brow to hers after ending the kiss reluctantly.

"I do enjoy kissing you, wife," he whispered.

"And I you, husband, more than I ever imagined I would."

"You imagined kissing me?" he asked, lifting his head to sit straight but leaving his arm to linger around his wife's waist.

"Many times," she admitted. "I feared I would do it wrong having no experience with it, and you would not find it enjoyable with me."

"You worried I would not enjoy kissing you, yet you did not worry about the scars on my face and how they might disgust you?"

"Oh, your face," she said and called out to a servant. "Fetch me a small crock of honey." She focused on her husband's face. "The honey should work on the ones not fully healed yet."

He almost pulled his face away from his wife when she reached out to gently touch one of his scars, but he stopped. He hadn't allowed anyone to touch his face after the healer had finished tending it once the battle had ended. However, his wife's touch was different, and he ached to feel her caring and gentle touch on his face.

She gently probed around the two scars with her finger. "The larger one may prove difficult, but I believe May will have something to help with it, though you might be left with a small remembrance of it. Nothing like it is now, though."

That she touched his scars without hesitation answered his question, but he could not help but ask, "I find it puzzling that my scars truly do not bother you?"

"They bother me very much," she said.

He almost pulled away from her but was glad he waited since she continued to explain.

"When I look upon them, it hurts me to think about the pain you must have suffered and continue to suffer when people turn away from you. It is not right. You are a courageous warrior and people should honor and respect you for that, especially with all the scars you carry."

Cavell did not know what to say to her. He had known no such compassion after the battle. Some of his fellow Gallowglass warriors told him to wear the scars with pride, while most people cringed when seeing him, including the women who had once welcomed him eagerly to their beds. But not Elsie, her thoughts were for him and what he had suffered, not how he looked.

In his father's zealousness to wed him to a daughter of a local clan chieftain to grow his own power in the area, his father may just have found a woman who would make him a good and loving wife.

Cavell sat still as his wife applied the honey to his scars. She did so with care, her brow scrunched in concern as she asked repeatedly if she was hurting him. He assured her repeatedly that she wasn't, her touch far too tender to cause him any pain.

He closed his eyes and allowed himself to relax under her gentle care. He enjoyed it so much that he didn't want it to end, but good things always came to an end.

"I will cleanse your face and reapply a fresh coat of honey before bed," she said.

He looked forward to it though worried what it might lead to, but for now he would wisely not continue to think about it.

"I would like to sit with my da for a while," she said.

"You treat me kindly to win favor with me and get what you want?" he asked bluntly, the prospect it could be true annoying him.

"Do you always think the worst of people?"

"Do you avoid answering me?"

She wiped the honey from her hands, shaking her head. "I tend you because I want to, not because it is my duty as your wife. Is it so hard for you to think that I might care enough to tend to my husband?"

"It is your duty to care," he reminded, though wished it was otherwise, wished duty had nothing to do with it.

"Nay. It is my duty to tend to you, but it is not my duty to care for you. That choice is mine," Elsie said.

Had she made that choice? Did she care for him?

"I beg your pardon, sir."

Cavell turned his head to see Alda standing near the table. "What is it?"

"A man who claims to be a Gallowglass warrior is at the kitchen entrance and requests food and to speak with you."

"Bring him here and food and drink as well," Cavell ordered.

Alda bobbed her head and left.

"Melvin," Elsie said. "He lingers to see what you can find here that might help Slayer."

"It is either that or Slayer will descend on your clan, and you will not like what he does," Cavell warned.

"I will sit with my da," Elsie said and waited for him to deny her.

"I won't be long since there is little to tell him. I will join you shortly."

"There is a small, unoccupied cottage not far from May's cottage. Melvin is welcome to make use of it while he is here."

"That is kind of you."

"It is the sensible thing to do since he will see that Clan Murdock has nothing to hide and report such to Slayer so that he leaves our clan in peace."

The more he came to know his wife, the more obvious it became that she was not insane, so why had her da sent her and her sisters to the abbey?

Melvin was shown into the Great Hall shortly after Elsie left. With not much to tell him, Cavell planned on keeping their conversation short.

"My wife offers you a cottage to stay in while waiting for news about her clan," Cavell said as soon as Melvin joined him at the table.

Melvin stared at him perplexed. "No one must know I am here gathering information for Lord Slayer."

"I will make it known that you are a fellow Gallowglass warrior in need of a place to stay for a while. I doubt anyone will think anything of it. Besides, another pair of eyes and ears would prove helpful."

"I suppose you are right." Melvin enjoyed a generous swallow of ale from the tankard in front of him on the table. "Have you found anything helpful so far?"

"Not yet," Cavell said. "Chieftain Norris is not lucid enough for questions."

He did not see any reason for telling Melvin about Chieftain Norris sending his daughters to the abbey, at least not yet. He wanted to find out more before sharing that bit of news.

Melvin leaned across the table and kept his voice to a whisper. "A warning, my friend, remain a detached Gallowglass warrior while here, for if it is discovered that Clan Murdock is involved in any way with Slayer's loss, he will decimate the clan."

Cavell needed no reminding about that, it weighed on his mind since learning of it. What weighed even more heavily on his mind was how he could protect his wife against Slayer's revenge if necessary.

Cavell left Melvin to eat and with instructions to Alda to show him to the empty cottage near May's place and while the woman appeared surprised, she held her tongue and nodded.

He heard voices as soon as he reached the partially open bedchamber door and hurried into the room.

"You will obey me, daughter, and return to the abbey," her da said, waving his frail hand at her.

"My wife is not going back there," Cavell said, approaching the bed.

"Cavell?" her da called out, lifting his head off the pillow to look for him. "You are here with my daughter?"

"Aye, we are home," Cavell said, moving closer to the bed so the old chieftain could see him.

"Finally," her da said, dropping his head back on his pillow with a generous sigh of relief. "Where is May?"

"I am here, Chieftain Norris," May said, and stepped closer to the bed.

"Good, I need a witness," her da said. "Listen well, Cavell, I pass the leadership of Clan Murdock onto you. You are now Chieftain Cavell of Clan Murdock. It is now yours to defend and keep safe and as was my agreement with your da, you will claim allegiance to Clan McCabe."

That remained to be seen, but Cavell kept that thought to himself.

Elsie rushed to say, "We can go free my sisters from the abbey."

"Nay they remain there," her da said with a yawn.

"Why?" Elsie asked anxiously, seeing her da drifting off to sleep.

"Brother Kendrick keeps them safe, worry not," her da said and his eyes fluttered closed in sleep.

Elsie stood and turned to her husband. "You are now chieftain with the power to free my sisters. We leave now for the abbey."

Chapter Nine

Cavell would have preferred to learn more before rushing off to Dundren Abbey, but having seen the way Sky was being kept and not knowing what was happening to Leora, he had to agree with his wife. They could not wait to free her sisters.

As soon as he and Elsie left her da's bedchamber they both rushed to gather what was necessary for them to take their leave. It was a half day's ride to reach the abbey, which meant they could reach it before nightfall and his wife's sisters would not have to spend one more wretched night in that place.

The one problem he faced was that Clan Murdock did not have a bevy of skilled warriors. Most Highlanders could wield a sword, some better than others, but battling seasoned Highland warriors was a different matter. And with mercenaries in the area, Cavell feared he would lose the ten Murdock men who he had chosen to go with him.

Melvin had volunteered to join him as well, claiming that he and Cavell alone could handle the matter better than the ten men combined. Besides, Melvin had no choice. Slayer no doubt warned him to keep an eye on Cavell to make sure he got the truth of what was going on at Clan Murdock or face his wrath. And even Slayer's men did not want to be anywhere near him when he let loose his wrath.

"On our return home we will celebrate that you are now Chieftain of Clan Murdock, and I am overjoyed my sisters will be there to celebrate with us," Elsie said, riding alongside her husband. "The clan is thrilled with the news and is grateful you will now lead them."

She only hoped he was as thrilled and would want to remain chieftain and her husband. He had not spoken a word to her about it and she worried he might refuse it and their marriage as well. She hoped by mentioning it, he might talk with her about it, but he had remained silent and watchful since leaving the clan.

"What do know about this Brother Kendrick who your da believes would keep you and your sisters safe?" he asked.

"It is the first time I heard his name, perhaps my da got the name wrong."

"Possibly, but it does tell us one thing. If this man would keep you all safe, it means you were right that your da sent you to the abbey to protect you. And with how pleased he was that I was there with you, I would think he wed you to me for the very same reason… to keep you safe."

"But from what?" Elsie asked.

"That is a good question and your da may be the only one who has the answer unless we can find Brother Kendrick and see what he knows."

"It should prove a fruitful day," she said, relieved the day was finally here that she would see her sisters freed and be reunited with them. She missed them so much but had tried not to dwell on it. She did not want to let fear rule her. It would do no good and only get in the way of what needed to be done.

106

"Until we have your sisters in hand, the day is like any other day," Cavell cautioned. "And you, wife, will remain quiet and follow my every word when we arrive at the Abbey."

Elsie bit at her lip, fearful it might be difficult for her to do that when she wanted to lash out at the monks who made them, and others, suffer to cleanse them of the madness.

"Bite your tongue if you must, to hold it, for if you let it loose with anger there is no telling what the monks might do, and I would prefer not to kill any of them."

Her eyes rounded. "You would kill them to free my sisters?"

"I am Chieftain of Clan Murdock and I have every right to stop anyone any way I choose from preventing me from removing your sisters from that place."

Elsie's heart swelled with hope hearing her husband claim himself Chieftain of Clan Murdock and doing whatever was necessary to help her sisters.

Cavell caught a sudden scent in the air and sniffed. The acrid odor was familiar. It was the smell of what was left of villages after the Gallowglass attacked and set fire to all the structures. Something had been set to burn, and the closest place would be the abbey. He cast a quick glance around and spotted it… smoke billowing in the distance, rising past the treetops.

Melvin rode toward them and looked where Cavell did. "A fire and a large one. It must be the abbey."

Elsie had caught the burning scent herself and her glance had followed her husband's. Seeing the smoke billowing high in the air had her catching her breath and her fear soaring for her sisters. When Melvin voiced her fear, she did not hesitate, she urged her horse into a run, taking off.

"Bloody hell," Cavell said and went after his wife, leaving Melvin to command the few warriors.

Smoke continued to spiral in the air and her stomach clenched, terrified of what she might see when the abbey came into view. The air grew thicker with smoke the closer she got, causing her to cough and her eyes to tear or were the tears for what she might face?

"Please. I beg of you. Please let my sisters be safe," she prayed aloud.

The sounds of crackling fire and splintering wood reached her before she saw the ancient stone walls of the monastery engulfed in flames. Her heart felt as if it shattered, fearing the monks had not gotten to the prisoners quick enough or hadn't bothered to rescue them.

Elsie threw herself off the horse when she brought it to a stop and stumbled toward the one monk she recognized, Brother Emanual. She ran at him, pounding her fists into his chest and sending him stumbling.

"Where are they? Where are my sisters?" Elsie screamed at him and went to attack him again.

An arm suddenly hooked around her waist, lifting her off the ground, and swung her away from the monk.

"Let me go! Let me go!" she yelled, shoving at the arm that felt like a shackle.

"Enough!" Cavell ordered, keeping hold of her. "We will learn nothing this way."

Elsie stopped struggling and cast a vicious glare at the monk that had him blessing himself. "If my sisters are dead, I will see that you meet their fate."

"They are not dead," a woman's weak voice said through a cough. "Water, please."

"Let me help her," Elsie said, shoving at her husband's arm.

"Leave the monks to me," he ordered and released her.

When she rushed toward the monks, Cavell went after her, but stopped when he saw her snatch the bucket of water sitting nearby them. She went to the woman, stopping briefly, her eyes suddenly filled with sorrow, and he followed her glance to see several dead bodies laid out beside each other.

Elsie crouched down in front of the woman, familiar with her. Her aged face was marred with grime and sweat, and ashes clung to her gray hair. "Drink slowly, Edith."

Edith nodded, her hand trembling as she scooped up the water to bring to her mouth and coughed after drinking it. She stopped before scooping up another handful. "Leora escaped not long after you and she promised that you or she would return and free us."

Relief twisted in her chest, and she went to ask about Sky but saw that Edith was staring at the dead bodies.

"They were forced to help put out the fire, but it was useless. There was no stopping it. It was as if the old god, Belenus, rose in anger to devour and destroy the abbey with his tongue of fire." Edith shivered as she cast an anxious glance around and kept her voice low when she said, "Please. Please don't leave me here with them. Please take me with you. I do not eat much, and I will do my share. I am a wise midwife. I have delivered many bairns. Please. Please do not leave me here, I beg you."

"You have my word, Edith. I will not leave you here," Elsie promised.

"Bless you, mistress, bless you," Edith said tearfully.

"Where is my sister Sky, Edith?"

Her eyes went wide with fear, and she let the water trickle from her hand before hugging herself tight and whispered, "He took her, then set the place ablaze."

Elsie's breath caught at the thought that rushed into her head. "Sit and drink. I will return shortly." She got to her feet and hurried to her husband and halted abruptly when she heard the monk.

"You return her to me now when I have no place to keep her?"

The monk's words reminded her of the conversation Cavell had had with the monk, not knowing it was her on market day at Pinkeny Village. Her husband had planned to return her to the monk and dissolve the marriage. Would he still find a way to get rid of her if she is not with child? Does being chieftain of the clan mean nothing to him? Does she not matter to him at all?

"I do not return her," Cavell snapped, annoyed his wife should be reminded of his intentions that were now void. "Where are my wife's sisters?"

"You have no right to inquire about them."

Cavell's anger strained his scars, giving him a demonic look that had the monk crossing himself once again. "I have every right. I am Chieftain of Clan

Murdock, and you will tell what I want to know or face the consequences."

The monk answered with haste. "The one who God graced with beautiful features escaped shortly after your wife did. The one God cursed, her face kept covered, the devil took, then set God's house to burn."

Elsie pressed her hand to her stomach. *It cannot be, please no, please,* she silently pleaded.

Brother Emanual went on to explain further when Cavell remained silent, staring at him. "He set the flame himself. Then he had his minions torch it as well. He made sure we could not stop it, though we tried and lost poor souls doing so." He glanced at the bodies. "Now we have no place to live, no place to comfort and heal those possessed of madness. We must go take refuge at the nearest monastery until we learn our fate."

"I care not about your fate," Cavell said. "I care about my wife's sisters. Did you search for Leora when you found her missing?"

"Of course, we did, and when we found no signs of her, I feared for her fate."

Cavell turned an accusing eye on the monk. "And you gave no thought to notify Chieftain Norris so he could search for his daughter?"

"I intended to," Brother Emanual said, "but I spent time in prayer hoping the good Lord would send Leora back to us."

Elsie was about to rush at the monk once again, angry that he had delayed in getting her sister help. But her husband turned to her, a warning look in his eyes as he stretched his hand out to her, and she stilled. That he warned her yet offered his hand to her made her see that he showed the monk that he stood with her.

She went to him and took his hand, and it closed around hers and kept firm hold of it.

"Where is Brother Kendrick? I want to speak with him." Cavell said.

Brother Emanual appeared a bit perplexed.

Seeing his confused look, Cavell asked, "Did he perish in the fire?"

"Nay," Brother Emanual said, and shook his head. "I was sent here when Brother Kendrick took ill many months ago to take charge and remained here upon his passing. Brother Kendrick's health had been failing for years, along with it the abbey itself. I was fortunate that my superiors believed in my ability to restore the abbey to its glory." He shook his head again. "My superiors will not be pleased that the abbey has been destroyed."

"I imagine not since they have also lost the stipend that supported this place," Cavell said.

"I have no doubt the stipends will follow wherever I go as I continue to care and treat the insane and others will show their generosity, eager to help their loved ones overcome their madness. You may consider it yourself once your wife becomes unbearable."

Elsie looked up at her husband, fearful he might contemplate the idea. He was chieftain of the clan now and it was an easy way for him to get rid of her. She almost pulled away from him, his face contorted in such anger that she barely recognized him, but he tugged her hard against him, refusing to let her go.

Brother Emanual must have thought the same, for Elsie watched him cross himself for the third time since their arrival.

"Listen well, Brother Emanual," Cavell said, fighting to keep control of his anger. "Never will my wife or her sisters ever reside in such a hell hole again. And those who you claim insane who have survived the fire will be free to go their own way today."

Brother Emanual gasped. "Only one survived and I cannot free her. She must remain in my care until her dying day as I gave my word that she would."

Cavell and Elsie turned upon hearing a frightened gasp to see Edith making her way slowly toward them.

"Please, sir, please. Your wife said I would go with her," Edith said, teary-eyed.

Elsie pushed against her husband to free herself to go help the elderly woman, but he refused to release her. She looked up at him and whispered, "Please."

The worry and caring in her soft blue eyes simply would not let him deny her and he reluctantly released her.

Elsie hurried to the woman, slipping her arm around her. "Do not worry, Edith, you will come with us, and my husband will see you kept safe."

When Edith turned her tear-filled eyes on Cavell, he knew she needed to hear it from him.

"Your home will be with Clan Murdock from this day on, Edith."

Tears began to roll down her face, leaving pathways through the grime. "Bless you, sir, bless you."

Brother Emanual stepped forward. "I forbid—"

113

Gasps filled the smokey air when suddenly Cavell was holding a dagger to the monk's throat. He had moved so fast no one had seen him draw the weapon.

"Have you not learned the consequences of angering a Gallowglass warrior?" Cavell asked, keeping the dagger's blade at his throat.

Brother Emanual trembled. "I do not mean to anger you, sir, but Edith suffers from madness and is not to be trusted and could cause harm. She was caught too late snuffing the life out of bairns after they barely took a breath."

"Lies! I did no such thing. I would never do such a horrible thing," Edith said, anger in her weak voice as she wiped at her tears.

"I beg you, sir, do not listen to her lies. She will bring harm to your clan," Brother Emanual pleaded.

"I bring harm on no one and never have, sir," Edith said. "Please give me a chance and I will prove what a good and trustworthy person I am."

Cavell was unsure who to believe or who to trust and as chieftain of the clan he had to make sure he kept the clan safe. And knowing old or young alike could cause harm, it was not an easy decision to make.

"She is old and useless to you. Let the monk have her," Melvin whispered behind him.

That would be the way a Gallowglass warrior would think, and Cavell did not hesitate to say, "The old woman belongs to Clan Murdock now."

"You've lost your courage," Melvin whispered.

"Nay, I just found it," Cavell said, his eyes on his wife hugging the old woman who had collapsed against her, weeping.

"This will not go well with the nobleman I gave my word to about Edith," Brother Emanual said, ringing his hands.

"There is an easy solution to that. Tell him she died in the fire," Cavell advised, slipping the dagger into its sheath.

Brother Emanual looked affronted, ready to argue, then stopped, his brow scrunching in thought for a moment before saying, "The other monks know."

"Another easy solution," Cavell said. "Edith will collapse in front of everyone and be declared dead. I will have my men see to her burial while you keep your monks busy with burying your dead. No one needs to know otherwise, and I will see she uses another name once it is done."

"Your men—"

"Would not dare defy my orders," Cavell finished.

"I agree, an easy and good solution," Brother Emanual said.

Cavell leaned in close to the monk. "Betray me on this pact, Brother Emanual, and I will find you and next time you will feel the blade of my dagger slice your throat."

Brother Emanual paled. "You have my word, sir, that Edith died here today."

"Good, then you will live a long life," Cavell said and left the monk's side to go to his wife and he quickly explained everything to her and Edith.

"I can do that, sir, I can pretend to die," Edith agreed eagerly. "And I will assume my mum's name, Ann. You won't be sorry for helping me, sir. You will see I am a good woman."

"Aye, Ann, you will be a good woman, or you will face the wrath of a Gallowglass warrior," Cavell said.

Edith shivered and clung to Elsie.

"See it done, wife, while I speak with others and learn more of what went on here," Cavell ordered and went to walk away, then stopped and waved at the old woman to step away. When she did, he stepped in front of his wife and gave her arm a gentle squeeze. "I know how upsetting this all must be for you, but I give you my word that we will find your sisters and bring them home."

Elsie confessed her worry. "I know Leora can well look after herself, Sky not so much, and I fear who may have taken her."

"And so you should."

Cavell turned to Melvin, the man showing up unexpectedly far too often.

Melvin kept his eyes on Cavell. "You know as well as I do that there is only one man who would not think twice of setting a monastery to burn… Lord Slayer."

Chapter Ten

Melvin's remark had continued to repeat itself in Elsie's head, but she had had no chance to discuss it with her husband. He had been intent on taking their leave from the burnt abbey so there had been no time to talk. He had avoided speaking with her about it on their journey home and even more so when they arrived at midday the next morning.

Fear poked at her, and she did her best to keep it at bay, not let it interfere and stop her from doing whatever needed to be done to bring her sisters home.

The thought continued to haunt her as she went looking for her husband after helping May tend Ann. She had repeated the fabricated story she had devised along with Cavell about Ann so many times since arriving home that she was beginning to believe it.

Ann had been found traveling alone on their return journey home. With no place to go, Elsie had offered her a home with the clan and Cavell had granted permission. It was a simple and believable enough story that no one would question, and no one had. She had worried that possibly one of the ten men from the clan might let their tongue slip one day, especially after an over-consumption of ale or wine. However, after Cavell had threatened them that if any one of them spoke about it, they would all lose their tongues, her worry faded. Cavell had made them responsible to keep check on one another, making it improbable that any of them would have a slip of the tongue.

Ann and May got along well, especially when Ann had begun detailing her experience delivering bairns, most births going well though also having her share of heartbreaking ones. Elsie was not sure where Ann would reside and was pleased to learn that Sweeney, one of the eldest members of the clan, had finally moved in with his sister, making it easier for her to look after him. It would be suitable for Ann, and Elsie had Alda see to having the cottage prepared for the older woman.

Elsie was eager to finally discuss with her husband what they would do about finding Leora and Sky and returning them home. She stopped once she entered the Great Hall, wondering where he might be, someone having told her that he had seen Cavell enter the keep. She did not think he would be in their bedchamber with so much that needed his attention now that he was chieftain.

That thought gave her a hint of where he might be... her da's solar. Though now it was the new chieftain's solar. She headed there, to a small room behind the kitchen but accessed from the keep. She stopped, seeing the door open and hearing Melvin protesting.

"I was given strict orders not to return until I had information that was worth bringing to him, and I am going to follow those orders. You have seen for yourself what he has done to men who failed to follow his orders. One blow. One blow and he broke a man's jaw. One twist of a wrist and it snapped, or he broke an arm." Melvin cringed. "I can still hear the snap of bones and the screams of pain. And his skill and speed with a dagger match your own. You don't even see him draw the weapon, just like you did yesterday with that monk. Your dagger was at his throat, and I didn't even see you draw it. I am not going to Slayer until I have information that proves helpful to him. Besides, maybe it wasn't Slayer who set the monastery on fire and abducted your wife's sister."

Elsie entered then. "If not Slayer, then who else could it possibly be?"

She halted her steps, her da's potent scent of earth with a hint of ale still permeating the air, reminding her of the vibrant man he once was. Memories hurried to remind her how he used to swing her up into his thick arms and hug her close and tell her she was the most beautiful lass and his favorite, but she was to keep that a secret from her sisters. It took many years before she and her sisters discovered he had told each of his daughters the same thing.

Melvin's snort of annoyance broke the tenuous thread of her memories, scattering them to once again fade away until once again recalled.

"I hope your sister does not stick her nose in places it has no business being if she is with Slayer since he will not tolerate such nonsense from a woman."

"My sister is a kind soul," Elsie said, fearful of what Sky might be suffering at this very moment.

"Another word for weak and Slayer cannot abide weakness. His tongue cuts sharp and there will soon be nothing left of her," Melvin said.

"If he took Sky, he did so for a reason which means she is useful to him so he will not harm her," Cavell said, seeing that Melvin's remark brought a flash of fright to his wife's blue eyes.

"True enough and if she does prove helpful, he will return her home," Melvin said.

Elsie looked to her husband to confirm it, not knowing Melvin well enough to know if his tongue was truthful.

"He's right," Cavell said. "Slayer never harms those who help him."

"How can you be sure of that?" Elsie asked, their words not as comforting as they should be.

"We wouldn't say it if we hadn't seen it with our own eyes time again and again," Melvin said, waving his hand round and round in a circle as if to make her better understand it.

That reassured Elsie… some. At least she tried to convince herself that it did.

Melvin rubbed his chin as his brow creased in thought. "Though Slayer has never been one to have patience with women."

"Leave us, Melvin," Cavell ordered, seeing worry flare in his wife's eyes and the way she hugged her arms, needing comfort against the news that continued to upset her.

When his wife approached him after Melvin left, instinct had him extending his arm in a fashion that invited her to step into an embrace, and she did, circling her arms around his waist as he hugged her close and she pressed herself against him needing the comfort of his strength. Her gentle sigh told him she was content to be there and that he was pleased to have her there made him once again wonder what it was that he was feeling for this woman. And more importantly, should he allow himself to feel anything? Somehow, though, he did not think he could stop the lingering feelings for her, no matter how hard he tried.

"Can we send a message to Slayer inquiring why he has my sister?" Elsie asked, feeling helpless to help her sister.

"We could but Slayer expects information and answers but rarely gives them. His response would no doubt be, I have need of her. I also doubt anyone here would have the courage or be foolish enough to volunteer to take a message to Slayer or that he could make it past his men safely. What about Leora? Where would she go after she escaped?"

Elsie needed no time to think about that. She knew exactly what her sister would do. "Here. Home. She would come home."

"Would she know how to make her way here?" Cavell asked, knowing most women had little navigational skills.

"Aye, she is wise in many ways and would know how to reach home and she would stay off the main pathways to avoid running into any unsavory men."

Cavell calculated her journey. "She is probably on foot and more than likely keeping to the denser part of the forest to be avoided, it would take her a few days to reach here. She should be here soon unless she ran into a problem. I will send Melvin with some men tomorrow to search the area where more than likely she would be found. He knows how to read the land well and will no doubt find something that may help us locate her."

"That will be helpful," she said and hesitated to say what else was on her mind since she should not even be thinking about it right now.

"I know what you think," he said, his two hands drifting to take hold of her waist as if making sure she could not escape him. "You fear asking me about what Brother Emanual said about me returning you to him."

It had lingered in the back of her mind waiting impatiently for a good time or not so good time to ask him about it. That time was now.

"You would have done that? Returned me to that place?"

"I can be a heartless when necessary, Elsie, and to say you angered me when you tricked me into bed does not even come close to the anger I felt. You left me no choice. You decided for me as my father did when he wed me to you and as your da did when he made me chieftain of the clan. I prefer to make my own decisions about my life, not have things decided for me." He removed his hands from her waist and turned away from her, his words reminding him that all that had happened had not been of his doing. It had all been forced upon him and what he hungered for most was freedom.

Elsie realized then how trapped he must feel, and it troubled her, especially after spending time locked away in the abbey with not an ounce of freedom and fearful of what each day would bring or not bring. She never wanted to feel trapped again or inflict such torment on another.

"I feared once you saw me you would not want me as your wife, my da believed otherwise. I gave thought of releasing you from the agreement if you found you could not tolerate me. But that was before my sisters and I were held prisoners at the abbey. I knew then that I needed you to remain my husband and I hoped you would see a benefit in having your own clan, and my clan does need a strong leader." She paused and gathered her courage, deciding she had no choice but to do this. "If it is what you want, I will release you from our marriage after you help me find my sisters and see them safe. The decision will be yours."

"The decision will be made for me if you are with child," he reminded and oddly enough he felt a wishful spark that she might be with child. How could that be when he also wished to be free?

"I can raise the child myself—"

"You think I would walk away from my own child?" he asked, a spark of anger in his voice.

That he would take the duties of a father seriously warmed her heart. "I do not want you trapped in this marriage."

"You should have given that more thought before you tricked me into bed."

"I did give it thought," she said, recalling how fearful she had been about her own deceit. It was not something that had sat well with her. "I had no choice. I was desperate for help, for my sisters, for my clan. I could see no other way."

"You gave thought to everyone but me," he accused.

"I do not offer this as an excuse, but I did not think it was necessary. Your father assured my da that you would do your duty as his son as I intended to do mine as a daughter. Your father believed we would make a good match, since your scars robbed you of your fine features and me being so ugly."

His heart suddenly beat to a mighty rhythm from the anger that soared upon hearing that. "Your da told you that my father said this?"

Elsie shook her head. "Nay, your da said it in front of me."

"He referred to you as ugly in front of you?" Cavell asked, fisting his hands at his sides, and wishing his father was standing in front of him.

Elsie saw the anger swirling in his eyes and heard it in his forceful voice and did not want to stir his temper any further. "It makes no difference now."

"It does to me. You are my wife, and you are not ugly. I have never met a more beautiful woman than you and never have I enjoyed coupling with a woman as much as I have with you."

Elsie stared dumbfounded at him.

He grabbed her by the arms, squeezing them. "You and I will settle this between us. It will be our decision, not my father's or your da's, but our decision. Our lives. Our decision. I will have it no other way."

She almost smiled, thinking he had just made a decision for them both, but she did not care. She was relieved to know that they would decide on it together, just the two of them, no one telling them what they must do. She only hoped he would find that their marriage might suit him and perhaps come to care for her after coming to know her better.

"First, we must see to helping your sisters, then we will decide about us." He released her and needing to calm his anger at his father for saying what he did about Elsie, he went to the table and filled a tankard with ale and drank half of it. He added more ale and returned to her, holding the tankard out to her.

Elsie took it, surprised he was sharing his tankard with her and took a small swallow before returning it to him.

"I believe our best course of action is to find out why your da sent the three of you to Brother Kendrick, who he obviously trusted, not knowing he was no longer there or the changes that had taken place at the abbey. He had to have feared for your safety but from whom?"

Elsie dropped down on a nearby bench perplexed. "I do not understand it. All seemed well."

Cavell joined her on the bench, sitting close enough for his arm to touch her arm, his leg to rest against her leg, their warmth to mingle and the lovely scent of her hair to drift over him. "At any time did you notice a change in your da or anything else?"

Elsie gave his question thought. "I do recall a message arriving one day and my da being agitated afterward. He refused to speak about it to anyone, getting angry at Leora when she pressed him about it. It upset her since my da never got angry at us. He might express disappointment at something we did, which was far worse than having him angry at any one of us, but he never raised his voice at us."

"You never learned what the message was about or who sent it?"

"Never and, come to think of it, it wasn't long after that that my da's illness started, and he began talking to me about an arranged marriage," Elsie said, her brow narrowing, wondering how she had missed that.

"We need to ask him about that, and I have wondered why the monks kept Sky's face covered?" he asked, his wife having avoided telling him about it.

"The monks are ignorant and fearful, that is why. Everyone says that Leora is the most beautiful out of the three of us, but Leora and I both know that Sky is beyond beautiful. She is just a bit different than most, but that small difference makes people fear her instead of seeing her true worth."

His wife turned silent and rested her head against his shoulder. He liked that when she sought comfort, she turned to him with unwavering confidence that he would be there for her, that she could depend on him, that she believed his strength would give her strength. He slipped his arm around her gently, cradling her against the curve of his shoulder and favoring the feel of her closeness. She fit him well, every bit of her and he briefly wondered if she had been crafted exclusively for him and him alone.

Cavell was content to sit as they were, not saying a word, as if all was right, and there was nothing to do but enjoy this tender moment they shared. He allowed himself to linger in the peacefulness, thinking something was bound to disturb them, pull them apart, and he waited for it, but it came from an unexpected source… himself.

126

His wife tipped her head back to look up at him and he lowered his head waiting to hear what she would say. But her lips distracted him, rosy and moist and the bottom lip thinner than her upper lip and yet they were both far more potent than any plump lips he had kissed and far more tempting. Lord, were they tempting, too tempting to ignore, and he didn't—he kissed her.

Elsie had wanted to kiss him since entering the room. She had wanted—needed—to feel that closeness, that feeling that someone cared, that unexplainable squeeze to her heart that felt so wonderful and the overpowering shift of his muscles as his arms wrapped around her. His kiss never failed to consume her and at the moment she needed him to consume her and chase away her endless worry and fear.

Cavell was unable to end the kiss, his lips being drawn back to hers each time he brushed his lips over hers, intending to end it. Their kiss was like a fine wine one lingered over, relishing and enjoying every sip, until one drank himself full. But how was it that he never felt too full to kiss his wife?

He reluctantly eased their kiss to an end, and she smiled softly, though it faded to a slight cringe, and she hurried off the bench. Annoyance jabbed at him, thinking it was his scars up close that caused her response, but he wisely and quickly dismissed the notion. She had told him often enough that his scars did not bother her, and he had seen for himself that she spoke the truth. If she did cringe, it was out of concern for him. So, he was not surprised when she returned to his side with a small crock of honey.

"I recalled my da keeping a crock of honey in his solar since I came to him often when I was young with scrapes or cuts and he would clean them and apply honey for them to heal," she said as she gently applied the sticky honey to his scars.

"You went to your da and not your mum?"

"It was to avoid a scolding from my mum for being unladylike," she said with a laugh and stuck her face closer to his. "I need to make sure to keep a good layer of honey on these scars." She tapped gently at the corner of one scar. "I can see the honey is already helping you."

He grabbed hold of her wrist, halting her touch. "Your caring touch is what helps me, wife."

His remark raised a plethora of flutters in her stomach. "I am glad to know that, husband."

Instinct or was it desire, she wasn't sure, had her brushing her lips faintly over his, then stopping seeing that he looked about to speak.

Unexpected words lingered on his tongue, but he held them back, not sure he should let them loose, let them free, for they would not free him. They would bind him forever to his wife, and yet the thought did not upset him, and he released her wrist reluctantly.

"I need to go speak with Melvin and there is much that needs my attention since I am now chieftain of the clan," he said and strangely enough felt not a bit of annoyance but rather a bit of pride.

That he once again acknowledged he was chieftain of the clan gave Elsie hope he was being more acceptant of his new leadership.

"Aye, the sooner a search is started for Leora, the better, and since I keep tally of most things in the clan, I can advise you when it comes to that."

"That would be most helpful, wife, and what will you do now?"

"May says my da sleeps after a restless night, so I will go sit with him for a time," she said since there was no longer any reason to think her da meant her harm, she did not think her husband would object.

"If he wakes, see what more he can tell you," he said and stood and walked toward the door calling out to her before reaching it. "We will talk later."

Elsie cleaned the honey off her finger then made her way to her da's bedchamber, her husband on her mind the whole way. He filled her mind most of the day, thinking of all she found pleasing and all that worried her about him, but lately her thoughts centered more on how she missed him when they were apart, a surprising revelation to her.

She entered her da's bedchamber and paused. His scent was different here than from the one in the solar. Here there was a whiff of decay rather than a potent manly scent, reminding her that her da was slowly deteriorating and there was a chance she could lose him. And that she would not let happen if she could help it, help him.

She snatched up a small bench near the hearth and placed it beside the bed and sat. Seeing him sleeping. She saw now what she didn't see before, or perhaps she hadn't wanted to see it. He had gotten thinner, his once full cheeks on the verge of turning gaunt, and gray dominated his once-brown hair. He was not improving, he was growing worse, growing closer to death, and tears pooled in her eyes.

He turned with a groan, and he struggled to open his eyes. Elsie quickly rubbed the unfallen tears from her eyes and greeted her da with a smile when he finally managed to open his eyes. She was thrilled to see him return a smile, faint as it was.

"Are you feeling any better, Da?" she asked anxiously.

"I do feel better, Elsie, and I am relieved now that Cavell is chieftain of the clan," he said. "All will be well as will your sisters."

She chose carefully what she would say to him after hearing him speak of being relieved. "Why did you send us to the abbey, Da?"

"A safe place," he said on a yawn.

"We were safe at home, Da."

He shook his head. "No longer. Brother Kendrick keeps your sisters safe."

"Safe from what, Da?"

"Not your worry, Elsie," he said, weakly waving off her concern.

Why he refused to tell her puzzled Elsie, but not so his dismissive wave. Once he did that, she knew he would discuss it no more with her. He was hiding something from her, and he was doing so because he thought it was for her own good. Somehow, she would have to get him to reveal his secret. She thought about telling him all that had happened at the abbey but dismissed it, fearing the truth might upset him badly and worsen his illness. She would go slow in delivering that news.

Instead, she said, "I learned that Warrand visited with you not long ago. Had it anything to do with clan business that Cavell should be made aware of?"

"Warrand will no doubt be in touch with Cavell as soon as he hears he is now chieftain."

"I am so sorry to tell you, Da, that Warrand was killed on his return home from visiting you and Lord Bannaty died a week later from being poisoned. Slayer now leads the clan."

Her da grabbed at his chest as his eyes turned wide, and he gasped for breath.

Chapter Eleven

"It is my fault," Elsie insisted, her steps echoing softly on the wooden floor as she paced back and forth before the crackling hearth. Her troubled expression mirrored the nervous flickering flames, and the weight of her words hung heavily on her shoulders.

"Nay, it is not," Cavell said and came up behind her to grab hold of her and wrap her in a strong hug. He disliked seeing her so upset and senselessly blaming herself and felt an overwhelming desire to shield her from unnecessary anguish.

"May said it herself after seeing my da. Any shock could worsen him, and she warned me against sharing any more news that might disturb him. So, it is my fault he has gotten worse."

"You did not know the news of Lord Bannaty and his son Warrand's deaths would shock him, and why would you? They were not friends who visited often. As you told me, you simply inquired if I needed to be made aware of anything concerning them now that I am chieftain. Your da's unexpected reaction begs the question... why was the news so upsetting to him?"

Elsie succumbed to her husband's hug, relaxing against him, and accepting the comfort he offered. "He keeps a secret, refusing to say why he felt my sisters and I needed a safe place. Why had our home suddenly become unsafe and from whom?"

Cavell rubbed her back, feeling his wife relax with each tender stroke, "A puzzle to be solved for sure."

"But how do we solve it when two of the three people involved are dead, and my da is unavailable to us for how long? We do not know."

"Someone here must have heard something, even a small snippet of what Warrand and your da discussed. A servant must have served them drinks or food. A few words are all we need to begin to piece everything together," Cavell said.

"Alda would know which servant served my da the day of Warrand's visit," Elsie said with a glimmer of hope.

"Then we will start there and find out who else in the village might know something about Warrand's visit."

Elsie eased her head back, her eyes connecting with his. "I could have killed my da."

"But you did not kill him, and he will heal soon enough with Ann offering to help look after him. May cannot give him the attention he needs with others in the clan needing her. Ann can be there for him, see that he eats and takes the proscribed brews when he should. So, you need not worry over him."

"That will not stop my worry."

"But it will ease it some and free your mind to dwell on me," he said with a teasing smile and a wink.

"My mind always dwells on you," she responded without thinking.

He grinned. "I am an impressive and unforgettable man."

His playful humor tickled her, and she chuckled softly. "No wonder you are forever on my mind."

He continued to tease playfully while finding it pleased him that he lingered on her mind. "My rightful place as your husband."

Her smile was just as playful. "Then that means I must occupy your mind just as often since I am your wife."

He took hold of her chin and gave it a squeeze. "You forever haunt my thoughts, wife."

He was about to kiss her when a knock sounded at the door.

"A moment, please, mistress Elsie," May called out.

Elsie rushed out of her husband's arms and to the door to fling it open. "My da?"

"He rests comfortably," May assured her. "I fear his worry weakens him and it would be wise to let him believe all is well until he grows strong."

"I cannot visit with him?" Elsie asked, clearly upset at the thought.

May shook her head. "Nay. I believe your visits will help heal him if you assure him that all is well and that your husband leads the clan wisely. Leave him with no burden to dwell on and I believe good health will return to him. He sleeps comfortably now. Ann rests in her cottage but is eager to help with your da's care."

Cavell waited while his wife finished speaking with May and when she left, he said what was on his mind. "I wonder what burden your da carries that caused him to become ill and continues to threaten his well-being. Or could it be a burdensome secret that threatens to be revealed after years of it being suppressed and now proves dangerous for someone."

"It could be the reason Warrand was attacked after leaving here and his father poisoned soon after," Elsie said. "If it is some sort of revenge from years ago, my da could have feared for his daughters' lives and is the very reason he sent us where he thought we would be kept safe, and the reason he wanted someone fearless enough to lead the clan."

Another rap at the door had Elsie thinking May had forgotten to tell her something but it was not the healer's voice that called out but Melvin's gruff one.

"You best come now, Cavell. Your father approaches."

Cavell turned to his wife after telling Melvin he would be right there. "My father heard that I am chieftain, that is what brings him here."

"We will welcome him," Elsie said as she left his side to open the door.

Cavell followed her, his voice stern as he ordered, "He will not be staying long and you, wife, will stand quietly by my side, throughout his visit."

"You do not get on well with your father, do you?"

"Not at all. He is a man who thinks only of himself and his legacy and since I am his second son, I do not count. My life is less important than my brother's, the heir to Clan McCabe and whose duty it is to see that the bloodline continues and to make sure the clan prospers and grows ever stronger."

Elsie held her tongue, hearing the contempt in his voice that her husband had for his father. This was not going to be a pleasant meeting and she wisely intended to remain quiet as her husband had ordered her to do. Unless, of course, she was forced to do otherwise.

"Alda," Cavell called out upon entering the Great Hall with his wife and spotting the woman about to leave the room but halting abruptly hearing her name shouted. "Bring drink but no food, our uninvited guest will not remain long."

The door burst open and a man not as tall as Cavell marched in, a confident swagger to his step from his robust body. His dark eyes were intent, shifting, taking everything in around him as he approached Cavell. Another man followed behind him and two more behind him. He was of good height and fine features.

Cavell spoke before his father could, his eyes fixed on the man who came to stand beside his father in solidarity. "It is good to see you, Harcus."

It had been some time since he had last seen his brother. They had gotten on well enough when young, but as they matured, and it wasn't until their father spent endless time preparing Harcus to one day lead the clan and completely ignoring Cavell that they drifted apart.

"Same here," his brother said.

"Enough! I will speak," Lord Philip ordered. "You need to show your guests respect and have them greeted properly. Assign someone the chore and make sure he sees it is done right. You are clan chieftain now and—"

Cavell was quick to interrupt him. "My clan, my decisions, Father."

"Your clan because of me," Lord Philip reminded with a thump of his fist to his chest.

"Still my clan. Now what do you want from me this time?" Cavell asked.

"To make sure you do what is right—"

"For you?" Cavell said, seeing his father's face scrunch in annoyance that he dared to interrupt him once again.

"For Clan McCabe," his father snapped. "So, it grows in strength and influence."

"At the helm of my brother," Cavell said with a glance to Harcus, who did not deny it.

"When the time comes Harcus will be ready to lead and as always I expect you to do whatever is necessary to see him kept safe."

"Like joining the Gallowglass and fight endless battles to keep enemies from his doorstep, or being wed and not told about it until it was done and becoming chieftain of a clan that will benefit Clan McCabe."

"Aye, and you have done your duty well and will continue to do so when you officially claim your allegiance to Clan McCabe. I have even generously brought two of my finest warriors with me." Lord Philip pointed over his shoulder to the two men behind him. "One is skilled in how to assist and counsel a chieftain and will help you carry out your duties and the other a skilled warrior who will train the men here to be fine warriors and ready to fight—"

"For Clan McCabe," Cavell said, trying to keep his annoyance at bay.

"Of course, that is what is expected of a small clan that pledges allegiance to a larger, more influential clan," his father said.

"Father is right, Cavell," Harcus said. "It benefits both our clans."

"How does Clan Murdock benefit from such an arrangement? Will you rush to defend us if attacked? Will you see we are well provided for if our crops should fail? Will you expect all the men from my clan to march off and fight for you and leave my clan vulnerable?"

Lord Philip bristled at being questioned. "You will do what I tell you so you and your clan may serve Clan McCabe well."

"My clan, my decision," Cavell repeated. "I will let you know when I decide which clan I will pledge allegiance to."

Lord Philip sputtered as he attempted to speak. "Wh-what do you mean decide which clan? It is part of the marriage agreement and what other clan would want such an insignificant clan?"

"A marriage agreement I was never made privy to, never given a choice in, so the allegiance I claim will be to a clan that I decide upon. And I have no use for either of the two men you brought with you."

"You need someone with experience and good instinct to talk with and counsel you," his father insisted.

"And someone who will keep you apprised of all that goes on here." Cavell accused.

"Something that would be in your best interest so I can make certain to avert any unwise decisions you make," his father said, shaking his fisted hand at him. "And how could you even think of pledging allegiance to a clan other than your own?"

"I am no longer part of Clan McCabe. Clan Murdock is now my clan and as a wise chieftain I would be a fool not to choose the most powerful clan."

"Which is Clan—" His father did not finish, his eyes turning wide as if realizing what his son had said. "Lord Slayer of Clan Ravinsher has asked for your allegiance."

"And promised me more than you could ever give me," Cavell said.

His father took a step forward and tried to keep the tremor out of his voice. "Slayer is insane. His father, Lord Bannaty, was relieved when his son joined the Gallowglass and not surprised when in only a short time, he was leader of a Gallowglass troop. He is a madman, and the other clans fear him, and he is even more so now with the deaths of his father and brother.

"They should fear him for he is a brilliant and fearless man, a dangerous combination, even more so that he now seeks revenge for the senseless deaths of his father and brother," Cavell said.

"You cannot do this to your clan," his father demanded. "You must honor the marriage arrangement as agreed upon. Why do you think I wed you to such an ugly woman?"

Elsie felt the rush of her husband's rapid movement rather than see him move. His hand was at his father's throat, his fingers digging into the flesh, leaving the man gasping for air while clawing at his son's hand.

Harcus rushed to help his father, but Melvin stepped forward, his long-handled battle axe gripped in

139

his hand in such a way that advised he was ready to use it, and Harcus retreated.

"Let him go, Cavell," Harcus called out with anger.

"First, you will apologize to my wife for your rude tongue and if you ever refer to her as ugly again, the scars on my face will be nothing compared to the ones I leave on yours," Cavell threatened and released his father with a forceful shove.

Lord Philip stumbled and fell to his knees, Harcus rushing to his aid. Though there was nothing his son could do as he desperately struggled for breath.

"Leave him or you will suffer the same," Cavell warned, his brother sending him a scathing look, but not touching his father.

Elsie had never seen her husband so angry, nor had she seen him so quick to inflict harm or hear him issue such a vicious threat left no doubt he would not hesitate to carry out. Fear sent a shiver through her, realizing she had just witnessed the Gallowglass warrior in her husband.

"Stay on your knees," Cavell warned when his father attempted to stand, "so you may properly apologize to my wife for your rudeness."

Lord Philip rubbed at his throat and coughed, a cloud of anger in his eyes as he glared at his son.

Cavell's hand shot to the hilt of his dagger at his waist. "Look at my wife and apologize, Father, or so help me the first strike of my blade will land across your lips."

"This is outrageous. You disrespect our father," Harcus accused.

"Hold your tongue, Harcus, or I will see that you lose it," Cavell threatened.

Fear suddenly captured Lord Philip and he hurried to look at Elsie. "Forgive my foolish tongue, my dear. You have lovely features."

Elsie did not hold her tongue this time. "I appreciate the apology even if it wasn't heartfelt and I am grateful that you offered your son in marriage to me. He is a good man, a good husband, and I care deeply for him."

She struck Lord Philip and Harcus silent, though she saw Melvin grin.

"Have some ale, Father," Cavell said, pointing to the table where Alda had left it. "It will help your throat."

Lord Philip, with the help of Harcus, went to the table eager to ease the sting in his throat.

"Melvin," Cavell called out, keeping his eyes on his wife. "See that my father and his men take their leave after they drink their fill. And, Father, you will hear from me when I am ready to speak with you." He reached out and took firm hold of his wife's arm. "You will come with me."

He was about to escort his wife out of the room, eager to find out if her words to his father were true. Did she actually believe him a good man, a good husband, but most of all was it true that she cared deeply for him?

He took only a few steps when the young lad Rory rushed into the Great Hall out of breath. He struggled to say, "You are needed, sir, right away."

Elsie stuck close to her husband's side as he hurried to the lad.

"May says you are to come immediately to her cottage," Rory said.

Cavell turned to order his wife to remain there not knowing what awaited him only to find her shaking her head, already aware of what he would say and refusing to obey the order he had yet to give to her.

"I am going with you," Elsie said and rushed to the door leading the way.

The gray skies appeared as ominous as the look on her husband's face as they hurried through the village. He was more than annoyed, and she hoped her refusal to remain behind had not added to his frustration. However, this was her clan, and she would not be pushed aside and left uninformed now that he was chieftain.

Cavell entered May's cottage without announcing his arrival. "What is so important, May, that you demand my presence?"

May stood from where she was bent over the bed tending to someone. "You must not waste time speaking with him."

Cavell went to the bed, May moving aside to stand near Elsie, who had also approached to wait near her husband.

Cavell turned a questioning look on May when he recognized the man in the bed. He was one of the monks from the abbey and she confirmed what he saw for himself.

"He does not have long," May whispered.

A weak hand landed on Cavell's arm, and he turned back to the monk, his eyes open.

The monk struggled to speak. "We barely left the smoldering ruins of the monastery when we were viciously attacked." He turned his head away and coughed, his breathing growing labored.

"Who? Who attacked you?" Cavell asked.

The monk continued to struggle for breath and his hand squeezed, with little strength, at Cavell's arm. "Gallowglass."

Chapter Twelve

The one word struck fear in Elsie. Had Slayer returned to finish what he had started and if he had been that cruel to do so, what must her sister be suffering at his hands?

The monk coughed, returning her attention to him and she listened anxiously, wanting to hear more yet hoping she did not hear her sister's name.

It took great effort for the monk to speak, keeping his words brief. "Wounded. Thought me dead. Brother Emanual begged. Mercy. Laughed at him." A tear dribbled down his cheek. "Heartless. No souls." Another tear followed as he was barely able to ask, "Why?"

Cavell had more questions than answers for him, but it didn't matter. Why, was the last word the monk would ever speak.

Cavell stood and turned to May. "Did he say how he made it here when so badly wounded?"

"Wadely, the merchant who visits here regularly came upon him and this being the closest place to get help, he brought him here. He shelters with the horses for the night, the clouds too heavy with rain for him to continue his journey," May said. "With your permission, sir, I will see the monk prepared for burial."

"Aye, May, we will see he receives a fitting burial," Cavell said and left the cottage with his wife.

As Elsie kept pace with her husband's powerful strides, she had to ask the question that lingered in her mind. "Do you think Slayer returned to finish what he started?"

Cavell shook his head. "Nay. If Slayer wanted the monks dead, we would have found them dead along with the burning abbey. He did not do this, and either did Gallowglass."

"But the monk said—"

"What he believed was true but wasn't."

"How can you be so sure?"

"Slayer rules the Gallowglass in this area and knows well that anyone who finds battle and death humorous, dare to laugh at a monk pleading for his life, will meet with Slayer's blade. It had to be the rogue mercenaries in the area."

"Why kill the monks? It makes no sense," Elsie said, troubled over the meaningless attack.

"There is only one reason they would do that… someone hired them to do so."

She shook her head, still seeing no sense in the massacre.

"Maybe the merchant can tell us something," Cavell said as they reached where the horses were sheltered to see a slim man, his gray hair hanging in a single braid down his back, sitting on a log enjoying a small meat pie.

"Mistress Elsie," Wadely said, getting to his feet. "It is good to see you again and I am pleased to hear of your marriage and to meet your husband and new chieftain of Clan Murdock." He gave a respectful bob of his head to Cavell. "It is a pleasure to meet you, Chieftain Cavell, and I am grateful for your generous hospitality."

"The generosity would be my wife's doing and will continue as long as you present no problem to the clan," Cavell cautioned.

"Never would I bring a problem to the clan—" Wadely turned silent realizing what Cavell referred to. "Clan Murdock was the closest place for me to get the monk help. I hope I did not bring any problem upon the clan by doing so."

"Tell me how you came across the monk," Cavell said.

"I did not stop often at the abbey, the monks being self-sufficient and having no need of my wares. But I smelled the remnants of a fire, and I worried it came from the direction of the abbey, so I went to see if they required help. I was shocked to find the place burnt beyond repair and some spots still smoldering. I also spotted fresh graves and tracks that led away from the place. I followed them to see if I could be of any help and—" He shook his head and paled. "I came upon an horrific scene. The monks had been brutally slaughtered. I was shocked to find one alive. He begged me to help him and so I brought him here, though I thought he would perish before we arrived. How is he doing?"

"He died," Cavell said. "Did you see any mercenaries in the area?"

Elsie heard no sympathy for the monk in her husband's voice and she could not say she had much for him as well after being held prisoner there. Her worries that Slayer had taken her sister were presently relieved. If he hadn't taken Sky, she would have faced a far worse fate if still with the monks.

"I had been warned by a farmer whose croft I stopped at to be careful that there was a rogue group in the area demanding food and drink and favors from women they came upon."

Elsie went to inquire about Leora, but her husband was already asking.

"Have you come across a woman traveling alone between here and the abbey?"

"Nay, if I had I would have offered to escort her here. No woman should be on the road alone especially with rogue mercenaries and the Gallowglass roaming the area," Wadely said.

"You came across Gallowglass warriors?" Cavell asked.

"Nay, but the monk said it was Gallowglass who attacked, which seemed odd to me since they are known for battle with foes who threaten the Highland's safety, not a group of helpless monks. Though I have heard whispers that Slayer, recently turned Lord Slayer, has gone mad seeking revenge for his father and brother's deaths. Who knows what he may do to accomplish such a task?"

Cavell did not comment on the man's remark since he was aware that Slayer would do whatever was necessary to revenge his father and brother's deaths.

"The monk said nothing else to you?" Cavell asked.

"Come to think of it, the monk repeated several times, 'I warned him. I warned him. Nothing good would come of it.' But he never said who he warned or what he warned against."

Elsie went to speak, but her husband didn't let her get a word out. He shackled her wrist with his hand, clamping it tightly.

"Food will be provided for you when you leave and coins will await you if you discover anything more about what happened at the abbey on your travels," Cavell said.

"I am grateful, sir, and will be sure to keep a keen ear for any news," Wadely said.

"Not a word," Cavell cautioned his wife in a whisper as he hurried her away, Wadely returning to sit on the log and finish his meat pie.

She went to speak again and once again he stopped her.

"I know what you intended to say."

"He knows my sister. Why not let me ask him to keep watch for her?" she asked, confused. "The more who search for her the more likely she will be found."

"What if your da is right about his daughters' safety? What if someone means one or all of you harm? Wadely inquiries would alert whatever culprit may be involved and possibly place Leora in more danger."

He made sense and it also raised a question Elsie had not given thought to. "How did you know I was at the abbey and not with my clan?"

"That is a good question and one my father can answer for us." Cavell hurried them along.

"Please slow down," Elsie said after several stumbles. "Your strides far outpace mine and you need not grip my wrist so tight. I intend to stay by your side."

That brought Cavell to a stop, and he released her wrist, annoyed at the red mark his hand had left.

"I did not mean to cause you pain," he said in the way of an apology.

"I never thought you did," she said. "I trust that you mean to protect me."

"Always," he said with a firm whisper and wished to say more to his wife, but first he had to speak with his father and see that he and Harcus took their leave. "We need to talk with my father."

"Aye," she said, though would have preferred they talk alone, sensing he had more to say to her. She would make sure they talked later, for now… she took hold of his hand and they hurried to the keep.

Cavell walked over to the table where his father and two men sat drinking and without preamble asked, "First you told me I was to go to Clan Murdock to meet my wife, then I was told she wasn't there, then you said you weren't sure where she was until finally you sent me to the Dundren Abbey. Why the confusion?"

"You would need to ask your father-in-law," his father said. "I wondered if he had had second thoughts about our agreement when he failed to present his daughter, but he assured me he hadn't." He squinted his eyes in thought. "I do recall him saying something about your wife being required to help him with something concerning her sisters and I reminded him that Elsie's duty was now to her husband. It wasn't long afterward that Norris told me Elsie was at the abbey awaiting your arrival."

"Did he tell you why his daughter waited at the abbey?" Cavell asked.

His father shrugged. "I assumed that he sent her there to spend time in prayer so that she would make you a good wife and see to her duties without complaint. Now tell me what problem took you from having a drink with your father."

That his father had not found his questions curious reminded him how self-absorbed the man was, and he had no intentions of telling his father what went on here. He would, however, alert him to what happened at the abbey.

"I received word the abbey burned, and the monks were attacked and killed when they left to seek shelter at another abbey."

His father's eyes shot open wide in shock, and he stumbled over several words before he was finally able to speak. "They are all dead?"

"All," Cavell confirmed.

"Who? When?" his father asked at a loss to say more.

"A group of rogue mercenaries from what I hear and within the last day."

His father rushed to his feet. "We need to go. Our trade with the north could be affected by this murderous bunch. We will talk again, and I expect you to honor the agreement I made with Norris."

"My clan. My decision," Cavell repeated what he had already told his father several times.

"You might want to remember that it is your clan because of my decision," his father said and stormed out of the room along with Harcus, and his two men took quick steps to follow behind them.

***

"I wonder if it is possible, though reason puzzles me, that Leora did not head home after her escape," Elsie said, after entering her bedchamber with her husband later that evening.

"Where would she go if not home?" Cavell asked, stretching his shoulders back to ease the aches that plagued him.

Elsie stared at him as she gave his question thought, though it was more the way his chest and arm muscles grew taut as he stretched. She could not help recalling their one night together and how he so easily lifted and shifted her when they coupled.

The distinct memory almost had her forgetting what he had asked her and thankfully she was quick to recall it. "I do not know where she would go if not home or the reason for her not returning home. Leora is not fearful like me—"

Cavell interrupted her with a chuckle. "You… fearful?" He chuckled again. "You do not know yourself, wife, if you believe that."

He thought her fearless? That was far from the truth. "I do what I must but that doesn't mean I am not fearful."

"You underestimate yourself. Besides, fear resides in everyone. It is whether you have the coverage to rule over fear or let it rule you. You definitely have courage, wife."

"You are so sure?" she asked, thinking otherwise.

"I am proof of it."

"How so?"

"It takes courage to wed a Gallowglass warrior and even more courage to hunt him down and slip into his bed without him realizing who you truly were." He walked over to her, resting his hands on her waist and lowering his head enough to look questioningly into her eyes. "Now, wife, do you have the courage to tell me if you were truthful with my father when you told him that you cared for your husband deeply?"

"I need no courage to speak the truth. I do care deeply for you. You have not been unkind to me. You have kept me safe since meeting you, and you did not hesitate to return to the abbey to help my sisters once you learned the truth. And I find I enjoy your company. You are mostly easy to talk with and I favor your kisses."

His smile teased as he playfully praised himself. "I am a good kisser."

Elsie liked his playfulness. It always brought a smile to her face and no man had ever teased a smile from her as her husband did now. No man had ever wanted to make her smile like her husband did now.

"Since you are the only man who I have ever kissed, I will trust your word on that," she said.

"That you will, wife, since I am the only man whose lips will touch yours." He sealed his edict with a powerful kiss as if to leave a mark that let all know that she belonged to him.

Elsie had savored every kiss with her husband, fearful it might be the last since he might decide to walk away from their marriage. However, hearing him declare that his lips would be the only ones that ever touched hers made her think that he had decided to remain in the marriage.

He finished the kiss with a brush of his lips over hers, then whispered, "Only me, only ever me."

"Aye," Elsie whispered, "only ever you."

His words combined with hers rang like a declaration in his head. If they pledged themselves only to each other, what did that mean?"

He stepped away from her and went to fill a goblet with wine that had been left for them.

His words as well as her own had her asking, "Do you care for me, husband?"

She asked the very question he was asking of himself. "A good question, wife, and one with which I struggle."

"Why?" she asked and went to take the goblet of wine he held out to her, then he poured another for himself. "It is simple enough to answer. You either care for me or you do not."

"It is not that simple, wife."

"It is not that difficult," she countered.

"How do you know you care for me?" he asked accusingly as if intending to prove her wrong.

She responded promptly. "I feel it."

"What do you feel?" he challenged, needing to hear and know if what he was feeling was similar to what she felt.

Her response came easily, letting her words flow without restraint, finally able to release what had been building inside her. She waved one hand out wide. "Everything. It seems like life itself is more alive when I am with you. I think my heart smiles when you are near, I feel content, and when you embrace me, I feel—cared for. A blessing for sure since I had been warned that it might take time for me to feel anything at all for you. So, I do understand if you have yet to have any feelings for me, though I hope with time you may come to at least care for me, if we choose to remain in the marriage."

Her words hit him like a punch to his gut to think their marriage would end and he would see her no more, make her heart smile no more, never embrace her again, never…

He grabbed the goblet from her hand and placed it and his goblet on the table and turned with such force toward her that instinct had her jumping back. But his hand caught her by the back of her neck and yanked her toward him.

"Listen well, wife, you churn my insides, twist at my heart, never leave my thoughts, and arouse my manhood with a simple look. I try to make sense of it, but I can't, and I can't stop what I feel. We have not known each other for long, but I feel I have known you forever. So, aye, I care for you more than I should, more than makes sense, more than I thought myself possible of caring. But there is the warrior within me that tells me to fight it, to stay free, to not bind myself forever to a woman, to a clan."

"And who is winning?" Elsie asked softly.

154

"Bloody hell," he said frustrated. "You are."

He held her neck firm as his lips came down on hers in a possessive kiss.

Chapter Thirteen

Elsie had wondered, along with her sisters, what a kiss would feel like. They would giggle when debating over it, sometimes cringe at the thought and other times sigh with how wonderful it might be. Never had their debates come close to imagining just how amazing a kiss could be or that kisses got even better along the way, or the way kisses stirred the senses. Or how much better they were when you discovered just how much your husband cares about you.

She had enjoyed every kiss she had shared with her husband, but this kiss—this kiss—was special. It was filled with how much he cared for her more than he should, and she swore she could feel the difference.

His lips demanded but then so did hers and it was a demand both answered, lingering in it and sparking their passion that had been restrained since their first time together. Now, though, it was ready to be set free, to explore and enjoy as they did that one night.

"Bloody hell!" Cavell said in a labored breath when he abruptly ended the kiss.

He stepped away from her, leaving her puzzled and a bit dazed.

He stepped close to her once again and grabbed her hand to shove beneath his plaid. "This is what you do to me with a kiss, just a kiss, not even an intimate touch. You turn me rock hard with a kiss."

Elsie gasped, her hand brushing his swollen shaft and she did not hesitate to wrap her hand around it or say what she felt. "I love the feel of you."

"Damn," he muttered, bringing his brow to rest on hers while warning himself not to do anything foolish until he was sure of… what? What was it he was looking for from his wife or was he looking for something from himself? He did know one thing he was sure of… he wanted his wife's hand to continue stroking his shaft.

"I love the feel of your shaft, but I love it even more when you slip inside me and make me feel the most marvelous sensations."

"Is that an invitation, wife?"

"You do not need an invitation, husband, I am here whenever you want me."

He raised his head to look into her soft blue eyes. "That hungry for me, are you?"

Elsie heard the lilt of teasing in his voice, but the simmering look in his eyes told a different tale and as her hand continued to stroke him, she whispered, "Always."

Do not do this. Not yet, a voice in his head warned.

He could almost hear his throbbing shaft protest. *Nay! Nay! Nay! Do not walk away!*

Elsie saw not only hesitation in his eyes but doubt as well and something sparked in her though it wasn't passion. She released his shaft and walked away from him. "Your shaft says one thing and your eyes tell me another. You hesitate and there is doubt in your eyes. You are unsure. The next time we couple, if we should ever again, it will be because we both are sure how we feel and we care enough to be intimate, care enough to remain in this marriage."

Cavell went to her, keeping his hands at his sides, though he itched to touch her. "Are you forbidding me from touching you intimately?"

"From touching me at all," she corrected. "It will do no good for us to become too familiar with each other. As I told you, I have already come to care deeply for you, and I worry about the pain your leaving might cause me if I grow to care even more for you. I suffer enough with the temporary loss of my sisters. I do not want to endure the pain of a permanent loss of someone I hold dear."

"You, wife, do not dictate what I can and cannot do. If I wish to hold your hand, touch your arm, kiss you, then I will."

"Aye, I cannot stop you, but I cannot be forced to reach for your hand or rest my hand on your arm or return your kiss."

How was it just moments ago they were professing how they felt about each other and now she was saying she would no longer reach out and take his hand? If anything, her reaction made it easier for him to convince himself that he had been wise not to rush and couple with her.

"Have it your way, wife. For now," he said and walked out of the room, closing the door behind him.

Elsie, on the verge of tears, walked slowly over to the bed and sat. She did not know where she had found the strength to speak to her husband as she did, she only knew that in this she would not be ignored or dismissed. After sharing a night of coupling with him and the way he had made her feel, truly feel, even though he had believed she was nothing more than a paid woman for the night, she wanted to know how it would feel to couple with him if he truly cared for her and for no other reason.

He did say she was winning, but she would not continue to win if she simply surrendered to him and waited to see how he felt. He would either truly miss her touch or it would not matter to him and that would make all the difference. That would let her know how her marriage might go or how it would end.

***

"I do not recall what we spoke of yesterday when you visited with me," her da said, sitting up in bed, a bit of color to his cheeks.

It had been two days since she had last spoken to her da and informed him about the deaths of Slayer's father and brother and two days since the argument with her husband that had had him leaving their bedchamber and not returning there since.

Elsie pushed thoughts of her husband aside so she could give her da all her attention, but it was difficult.

She feared she had made a foolish mistake and had ruined any chance of remaining married to him.

"Elsie, are you all right?" her da asked.

Seeing the familiar concern in his aged face when he worried that something troubled her brought a smile to her face. She could always count on her da's love and advice. Only this was a subject she could not discuss with her da, and she didn't want him to worry about her. She would have to figure this out on her own.

"I was just trying to recall myself, Da," she said, and he smiled, relieved. "I believe I was telling you how well Cavell is doing as the new chieftain."

"I never had a doubt he would," her da said. "That is why when his father, Lord Philip, asked for an arranged marriage between Cavell and Leora I refused."

The shock of his remark turned Elsie silent. Her da had never mentioned that to her.

"I knew what Lord Philip was up to. He figured his son would not refuse the marriage if wed to a beautiful woman, but Cavell and Leora would have never gotten along. They would have been at odds constantly." He shook his head. "Nay, I knew you were perfect for him. You would not demand, rather you would reason and sacrifice to make things work. Of course, if you had told me the scars on his face were too much for you to bear, I would not have agreed to the marriage. But I knew you wouldn't do that. You are the dutiful daughter I can count on."

A dutiful daughter forever doing what she must, no matter the cost to her.

"Cavell should be grateful he has such a good wife."

"I am."

Elsie turned, almost falling off the bench, to see her husband entering the room.

"You were wise, Norris, in refusing to match Leora with me," Cavell said, coming to stand behind his wife and placing his hands on her shoulders to give them a squeeze. "Elsie is a perfect fit for me… dutiful and reasonable."

"That's my Elsie, unlike Leora who is headstrong and too wise sometimes for her own good. How do I ever find a husband for such a daughter?" He sighed. "Then there is my Sky, a beautiful soul from the day she was born but with an unjust curse to bear. I asked myself what man would want either of them, but miracles do happen."

"What miracles, Da?" Elsie asked, thinking her da sounded as if a miracle had been found and he had plans to see Leora and Sky wed.

Her da ignored her question, his glance going to Cavell. "I should tell you that your marriage to Elsie includes a pledge of fealty to your Clan McCabe, if I haven't already mentioned it, though I am sure it will not be long before your da makes you aware of that."

"He already has," Cavell said.

Elsie was relieved that her husband made no mention that he had not decided who Clan Murdock would pledge their fealty to, though she doubted it would be to Clan McCabe with how Cavell felt about his father.

Elsie went to repeat her question about miracles when Ann entered the room.

"Sorry to disturb, mistress, but your da needs his brew and a nap."

Her da's smile beamed brightly. "And a tale. Ann always entertains me with a fine tale while I enjoy my brew. She has a way with storytelling."

"Go on with you now, sir, for praising me like that," she said with a chuckle. "It must be that magic potion I am putting in your brew that makes you speak so kindly of me."

Elsie's da laughed, a hardy laugh that she hadn't heard in some time. Ann's tender and frequent care was doing wonders for him, and Elsie was relieved. She had hope now that her da would grow ever stronger and be with them for a long time to come. And soon, she would be able to question him without worry.

"Come, wife," Cavell said, his hand clamping on the sides of her shoulders and lifting her off the bench. "We will leave your da to Ann's excellent care."

Elsie made no protest when her husband took her hand to lead her out of the room, though she kept a light hold, not the tender squeeze she would give his hand when he would take hold of it, which had been her way.

Once outside the bedchamber, the door closed, he released her hand. "Melvin has finally returned from scouting the woods. I thought you would like to hear what he has to say."

Instinct had her hand touching his arm, thrilled with the news. "Aye, I would."

His glance fell on her hand where it lay on his arm, and she quickly pulled it away.

161

"A dutiful daughter makes a dutiful wife, so you do everything out of duty?" he accused more than asked.

"I have done everything expected of me since I was young. Caring deeply for you was something I did for myself." She turned and hurried down the curving staircase.

"Damn," he muttered, her response twisting at his heart, and he hurried after her, glad he did, seeing her slip and about to take a tumble down the stairs.

He rushed forward, hooking his arm around her waist and yanking her to her feet before she hit the stone steps. He had no need to yank her against him, she fell against him of her own accord, resting her head on his chest and taking a heavy breath. Good Lord, but he missed having her in his arms, smelling the sweet scent of her hair, and holding her close.

"You are safe," he said, feeling a slight shiver race through her.

"I know," she said, her words muffled against his hard chest. "You always keep me safe."

"And I always will," he said.

She raised her head to look into his eyes. "Will you?"

He knew what she suggested. If he did not honor the marriage agreement, he would not always be there to keep her safe. The last couple of days had been miserable for him, his wife keeping her word that she would not touch him. He had not realized how much he had grown used to the small intimate acts they shared. How was it that he missed the way she would grab his hand and cling firmly to it as if she had no intentions of letting him go? And bloody hell if he didn't miss sleeping next to her, even if he had to rise before her and leave their bedchamber or risk giving her a good poke since his shaft was eager to do just that each morning.

Why was he keeping himself detached from his wife when he wanted nothing more than to be as close as possible to her?

Elsie saw it in his eyes then, surprised by it. "You're afraid?"

"I fear nothing," he snapped.

Things suddenly made more sense to Elsie, and she spoke from her heart. "Know that I will always be here for you, beside you, and loving you no matter what."

Cavell had no words. They were stuck somewhere in his throat or had his heart turned him silent from the shock of hearing her say 'loving you'? Could she truly, possibly, actually… love him?

She took hold of his hand firmly. "Come, I am eager to hear what Melvin has found."

He led her down the stairs, his thoughts on her remark. He was a Gallowglass warrior. He had fought endless battles fearlessly. He had faced death many times without an ounce of fear. There was not a man alive he did not fear raising a sword against even if it might be foolish. Yet, his wife had realized what he had not. He feared loving her, and why? Because he feared losing her and he did not know if he could stand such horrible and endless pain. But if he did not allow himself to love her at all, he would be something he never thought he ever could be… a coward.

"It is only a scratch," Melvin said, yanking his arm away from May so he could take a large swallow of ale.

"The wound is red and warm, and something looks to be embedded in there," May said, grabbing hold of his wrist to shove his arm down to rest on the table once he put the tankard down.

"What happened, Melvin," Cavell asked when he and Elsie reached the table.

"A few men surprised us," Melvin said, yanking his wrist free of May's hand. "Had to handle most of them myself, the men with me not much good at fighting."

"Murdock men are good fighters, it is that you are an exceptional fighter that you feel they lack fighting skills," May said in defense of the men.

Melvin shrugged. "That's a good point."

May grabbed his wrist again and slammed his arm down on the table, Melvin wincing. "Now you will let me look at the wound or I will think you a coward."

Melvin's eyes shot wide. "Watch your tongue, woman. I am no coward."

May stuck her face close to his. "Then prove it."

"Do what you will, woman, then leave me be," Melvin said and grabbed the tankard with his other hand and drank.

"Men," May said, shaking her head.

"Women!" Melvin shot back, wrinkling his nose.

May laughed. "Try living without our favors."

Melvin looked ready to shoot back a remark, then clamped his mouth shut.

Feeling sorry for Melvin, May the winner in that round, Cavell asked, "What happened?"

"A small bunch of stray mercenaries came upon us wanting whatever food or drink we had. I told them we would share some with them, but they wanted it all. I told them that was not about to happen. Punches started flying, I will say the Murdock clansmen did not back down from the fight, but it ended quickly when I managed to finally grab my battle-axe. One look at its long handle and they bolted, realizing they were about to be slaughtered by a Gallowglass warrior. I got the wound in the fight, though what caught my arm I don't know."

"Whatever it was, it was wood," May said. "There is a splinter in the wound which if left in could turn putrid and you would lose your arm or your life."

"I would rather lose my life than my arm," Melvin said. "So, don't think you'll be hacking off my arm."

"Then it is a good thing I spotted your wound and tend to it so you don't lose either," May scolded.

"Then be done with it, woman, so I don't have to suffer your mouth anymore," Melvin ordered.

"You will suffer my mouth as long need be for your wound to heal properly," May said.

"Enough squabbling," Cavell ordered, eager to hear what Melvin may have discovered. "Tell me what you found, Melvin."

"Nothing that pointed to a lone woman traveler," Melvin said disappointed. "Though I was surprised to learn from a crofter that Noble had been in the area days ago."

"What would Noble be doing around here? His family's isle is at least two days from here."

"I thought the same myself, but he could have been doing some scouting for Slayer. He tracks like no other.

He is more successful at tracking people than Slayer's hounds," Melvin said.

"Slayer has hounds?" Elsie asked.

"A vicious bunch," Melvin said.

"Sky befriends animals easily," Elsie said, thinking if her sister could befriend the hounds, they might offer her some protection.

"Not Slayer's hounds. They obey only him," Melvin said.

"He's right," Cavell confirmed. "The hounds are a vicious lot. No one goes near them, but Slayer and they dare not obey anyone but him."

Maybe so, Elsie thought, but there had not been a wild animal in the forest that Sky had not been able to befriend. She had a special bond with animals. Their mum had said it was because the animals sensed that Sky had a kind soul and would never harm them. Perhaps Slayer's hounds would realize that and offer her some protection. The thought gave her hope for her sister's safety.

"It's a puzzle," Melvin said, looking at Cavell. "How does a lone woman, as beautiful one as many claim she is, survive on her own?"

Melvin was not puzzled. He was stating the obvious to Cavell that the woman could not have survived, and she had either been captured by the rogue band of mercenaries or she was dead. Something Melvin spared Elsie from hearing directly.

"Perhaps this man, Noble, a fellow Gallowglass warrior, might know something about Leora. Can you send a message to him?" Elsie asked, ever hopeful.

"Not sure where to send it," Melvin said. "If Noble is helping Slayer, he could be anywhere. OW!" Melvin turned a scowl on May.

"Got it!" May said proudly, displaying a long sliver of wood. "And you are lucky I did."

"Good now you can leave me alone," Melvin said ready to yank his arm away.

May stopped him. "The wound needs wrapping, and I will be keeping an eye on it. Do not go anywhere," she ordered. "I need to get salve and cloths, so stay put."

"She dictates too much," Melvin complained as he watched her leave the room.

"May is an excellent healer, you should pay mind to what she advises," Elsie said.

"Tell me, will Slayer collect the information you gather for him the usual way?" Cavell asked.

"Aye, he will send someone," Melvin nodded and said no more.

"We can get word to Slayer then about my sister," Elsie said eagerly. "And maybe he will know where Noble can be reached."

May returned, her face pale. "Word has just arrived. The body of a woman has been found by a crofter at the far end of the clan border. She drowned and she has reddish blonde hair like Leora."

Chapter Fourteen

"How many times must I tell you that you are not coming with me?" Cavell asked, shaking his head in frustration. "I have twelve clansmen going with me who can say with certainty whether it is Leora or not."

"Bodies pulled from the water after substantial time are often bloated behind recognition. I would know at first glance, while the others will not," Elsie said, annoyed she would be left behind.

"I will not risk your safety with an unruly bunch of renegades roaming the forest, and I can travel faster without you along, which means I can return by this evening." He gestured with his hand to stop her from speaking. "If necessary, I will bring the woman here so that you can see for yourself if she is your sister." He raised his hand for a second time to stop her once again from speaking. "I do what is best and you will adhere to my command, wife."

"Your word on that?"

Cavell scowled, annoyed. "I would not say it if I did not mean it." He saw the worry in her eyes and cupped her chin. "You have my word, Elsie. I will bring the woman here, if necessary."

"I am grateful," she said and turned her face to brush a light kiss on his palm.

The brief, intimate gesture shot a wave of passion through him, and he silently cursed the unexpected reaction. Not that he didn't enjoy it, but he would rather have had time to do something about it since his wife no longer avoided his touch. It was time for them to talk and settle what would come of their marriage.

"If all proves well, we talk when I return home, wife," he said, hoping the drowned woman was not Leora, for he knew the pain she would suffer and that did not set well with him.

"I will be waiting—with hope."

Cavell gave her a quick kiss and mounted his horse.

"One more thing, husband," Elsie said, looking up at her husband. "Leora can swim."

***

Elsie kept busy, seeing what needed her attention since her absence. Kara joined her at one point, and she taught the little lass more about numbers as they looked over the planting fields and Elsie took stock in her head of how much would need to be planted for a sufficient harvest that would easily feed the clan.

She was not surprised when people offered encouragement that it could not be Leora who had been found. Someone had commented on Leora being a good swimmer, but Elsie knew that didn't matter. A good swimmer could still drown. She knew the clan worried along with her since Leora was beloved by many.

However, she was surprised that people continued to tell her how grateful they were that she had agreed to wed the Gallowglass warrior. They felt much safer with him now being chieftain. No one made a remark about his scars, not even the little lass Kara. They all appreciated him as did Elsie and she hoped he realized how much he was valued and how no one would want to see him leave. She certainly did not want him to. Where once duty had taken priority when it came to marriage, that was no longer so. She found her husband a good fit and believed they would work well together. Given a choice, now that she knew him, she would agree to wed her husband most willingly.

"Mistress Elsie."

Elsie shook off her thoughts and turned a smile on Ann walking toward her. "Is everything all right with my da, Ann?"

"Your da improves little by little each day which is good. His new son-in-law protects the clan, and he believes all his daughters are safe." Sorrow showed in her aging eyes. "I pray along with the clan that Leora is not the woman found drowned."

"She is a good swimmer," Elsie said, knowing it did not matter but it gave her hope saying it.

"I have heard from many that she can talk any man into anything, and I saw it with my own eyes," Ann said with a chuckle. "She had the one young monk so besotted that he forgot to lock her cell one night. That was how she managed to escape." Her voice lost its humorous lilt. "My heart broke hearing her tell Sky to stay strong that either she or you or you both would return for her. It had to have taken all her strength to leave poor Sky there alone."

Elsie turned to see why Ann suddenly smiled then waved. It was May.

"I promised to join May on her visits today with a few of the clan women who will give birth over the next few months. I look forward in helping May deliver yours and Chieftain Cavell's bairn one day, first of many to come, God willing."

Elsie waved to May as Ann went to join her, then she turned and continued to catch up on her many chores that had been neglected while she was gone. Unfortunately, her mind lingered on Ann's comment about delivering Elsie's first bairn. It was too soon to tell if she was with a child, but the possibility filled her with joy. She had always wanted a sizeable family to fill the keep with endless talk and laughter and nieces and nephews that Sky could spoil since she and Leora intended to see their sister kept safe and that meant remaining with the clan. Neither she nor Leora would ever trust any man to wed Sky, and luckily their da had agreed.

She stopped, pressing her hand to her chest. Her heart hurt thinking that Leora, in her stubbornness to seek help, could be dead, and the innocent Sky could be suffering horrendously at the hands of the leader of a group of Gallowglass warriors.

With her heart aching and her mind much too occupied with worrisome thoughts she went about her chores and time passed much too slowly for her, but as dusk finally settled over the land, she gazed off into the distance wondering how long her husband would be and what news he would bring.

She reluctantly returned to the keep after night had fallen and with her anxiety growing, she paced in front of the hearth in the Great Hall. Every creak and rustle of the castle had her heart skipping a beat, hoping it was the sound of her husband's arrival. He should have returned by now and while she worried over the news of her sister's fate, she also worried something may have happened to him.

"You worry needlessly," Melvin scolded. "Cavell is Gallowglass. No rogue mercenary has a chance against him or a few for that matter. He fights like a heathen just as all Gallowglass do. I have seen him take five men down within the blink of an eye, he is that fast and precise with his weapon."

Elsie stopped pacing and smiled sparingly. "You try to save me worry by telling me this and for that I am grateful."

"I speak the truth," Melvin said gruffly and parked himself on a bench at one of the tables and filled a tankard with ale.

"You have been a longtime friend of my husband?" Elsie asked and joined him.

"Not long to most but for those who fight in battles together it has been a lifetime. The Gallowglass share a brotherhood, and I am proud to call Cavell my brother."

"Were you in the battle that scarred his face?" she asked since her husband never mentioned it, she hoped

Melvin might shed some light on it since she could not help but be curious.

"Aye, and it was a vicious fight, unexpected invaders from the north, more crazy than fierce warriors. Cavell was fighting a horde of them when one was able to slash him in the face. Blood poured from the wound, but he kept fighting, and even when he was slashed again, he kept fighting. By the time it was done, a dozen invaders lay at his feet, and he was unrecognizable, blood covering his face, running down his neck and soaking his garments." Melvin grew silent for a moment. "The scars changed him. He once had a charming, teasing nature, and women flocked around him, not so afterward. He withdrew as men avoided him, his scars a stark reminder of the exceptional warrior he is and fearful they had no chance of surviving should he raise a weapon against them. And the women?" He shook his head. "They favored him no more, his alluring smile and charming tongue gone."

"His charming tongue returns," Elsie said, her smile brightening as she recalled the few times she heard and favored it.

Melvin smiled broadly as he pointed at her. "Aye, that is the smile I saw Cavell draw so easily from women."

Elsie's smile grew seeing Melvin smile, never having seen him do so before now. He appeared much less threatening when he smiled. A thought tugged at her, one she tried not to think about too often. What if her husband's scars healed and he regained his fine features? Would he once again be tempted to charm women? The honey was working well on his scars and if she did not apply it to his face, May chased after him insisting she be allowed to apply it. The scars were beginning to look less angry as well as appearing as if they were finally healing. He might soon be as handsome as he once was while her plain features had not changed at all and never would.

"Cavell is lucky to have wed you and have his own clan. I enjoyed going into battle, often looked forward to it, having felt lost without it until… I came here. Your clan has treated me well as if I am one of them, and though May can be annoying it grows easier to talk with her. I now see the benefits of belonging to a clan."

"Don't you belong to Slayer's clan?"

"Nay. Slayer sends the Gallowglass warriors wherever needed."

Elsie wrinkled her brow. "So, you spend most of your time in battle?"

"Mostly."

"There are that many battles to fight?" she asked.

"Small ones, large ones, in between ones, we fight them all if asked. Fighting is my only skill. I know nothing but fighting."

"You probably know more than you think, and you would be a benefit to any clan."

"Even yours?" Melvin challenged rather than asked.

"You most definitely would be beneficial to Clan Murdock."

"How so?" he asked, perplexed.

"You could train our clansmen for battle, teach them about battles, but most importantly, you could serve my husband well by being his trusted counsel."

"You mean that, don't you?" Melvin asked stunned by her suggestion.

"I do. You and my husband work well together and you respect and trust him as does he trust and respects you. It is important for a chieftain to have a counsel he can speak freely with, trusting his word would never be repeated unless given permission."

"I would never divulge anything Cavell told me in confidence."

"I will mention it to my husband," Elsie said, glad Melvin lingered in talk. It kept her mind a bit occupied, though not entirely. Thoughts of her husband continued to dominate her mind and her worry for him grew as they continued to talk, and the night grew late.

"Can I get you anything, mistress?" Alda asked.

"You are still here, Alda?" Elsie asked. "You need not wait for me. Go and seek your bed. It has been a long day."

"It is difficult to rest knowing news of Mistress Leora may arrive at any moment," Alda said, her eyes shining with tears.

"Leora is a strong one. She will survive no matter what it takes to do so," Elsie said, trying to believe it herself.

Elsie jumped, as did Alda when the door to the Great Hall swung open and their breaths caught waiting to see who it was.

Elsie was off her seat in a flash when she saw it was her husband and she took swift steps to him, flinging herself into his arms when she got close enough, relieved when he caught her in a tight hug. She buried her face against his chest, the scent of the forest thick upon him and she heard the beat of his heart pounding hard and strong from a demanding ride, a sign of his eagerness to return to her.

Relieved he was home safe, she finally looked up at him. "What took you so long? I was so worried something had happened to you?"

That his wife inquired about him first rather than her sister spoke loudly of her love for him, and it was at that moment he knew that his wife was not insane, he, however—without a doubt—was insanely in love with her.

He brushed a strand of her silky hair off her cheek with the stroke of his thumb. The simple touch sent a myriad of feelings rushing through him, relieved to have her in his arms. "I had to make certain of the drowned woman's identity so that when I told you she was not Leora, you would know I spoke the truth."

Elsie let out a huge sigh of relief that she was certain had been stuck in her since hearing the news and asked, "You brought her here for me to see?"

"It wasn't necessary. The news had gone out to other clans besides ours and a woman from a neighboring clan knew at first glance it was her sister."

"How could she be so sure?" Elsie asked, fearful a mistake could have been made.

"The dead woman was missing a finger not recently severed and the sister confirmed that her sister had lost the exact finger when she was a wee lass. But I waited for the man about to wed the woman to arrive, and one look at her and he broke down in tears."

"My heart aches for them both," Elsie said, knowing how the woman must feel, for she would have been devastated had it been Leora.

"It is good news for Clan Murdock," Melvin said when Cavell and Elsie joined him at the table, Cavell eagerly accepting the tankard of ale he held out to him.

"God bless the dead woman," Alda said solemnly then smiled. "But wonderful news that it wasn't Mistress Leora. I will get you food, sir."

"Not necessary, Alda, ale will do. It is late and all is done here for the night. You are free to take your leave."

Alda bobbed her head and left, a smile lingering on her face.

"Is it known what happened to the woman?" Melvin asked.

"From what I could learn from the woman's intended, the dead woman, Esta, was to meet him in the woods at a spot where they usually went when they wanted to be alone. He was late in getting there and was surprised when she was not there and worried when she never arrived. A search was done but she wasn't found."

"Or she got there first and so did someone else," Melvin suggested.

"You stay quiet, wife, but your thoughts are churning," Cavell said, seeing the pinch of her brow.

"Did she have reddish blonde hair?" Elsie asked.

"She did," Cavell confirmed.

"It is only a thought and danger can lurk in the woods—" Elsie stopped, thinking she might be foolish to mention it.

177

"Say what you think, wife," Cavell said, for he wondered if her thoughts mirrored his own.

"The dead woman, Esta, had the same color hair as Leora. What if whoever took her was looking for Leora?"

"And when they discovered their mistake, they killed her," Melvin suggested.

A sudden thought hit Elsie that left her almost speechless, and she took a moment to calm herself before she spoke. "Or their mission was to kill Leora in the first place."

Chapter Fifteen

Cavell took hold of his wife's arm worried she might faint, she paled so badly.

Her muscles tightened at his touch, a silent response to the burgeoning emotions that her own words had stirred with her suggestion and the possible consequences it could bring.

"Could my da be right?" Elsie asked, thinking her da had spoken the truth all along about keeping his daughters safe. "Could someone wish my sisters and me harm?" She continued not waiting for a response. "What does this mean for my sisters?"

"Something we need to consider and discuss, but not tonight. It is late and we need rest before we tackle such a serious task," Cavell said and turned to Melvin. "We will talk in the morning."

Melvin nodded and downed what was left in his tankard as Cavell escorted his wife out of the room and to their bedchamber.

There was much he had wanted to say to his wife, had planned to say to her about their marriage, but now was not the time, not with the worry of her sisters so heavily on her mind.

They were barely through the door of the bedchamber when Elsie flung herself into her husband's arms. It wasn't desire he felt emanating from her but rather vulnerability, creating an atmosphere charged with uncertainty. She was seeking from him what her da had depended on him for, his ability to keep her and her sisters safe. She need not worry, he intended to see that no harm would befall her, and he would do whatever it took to keep her sisters from harm as well.

"This is a nightmare," Elsie said, keeping herself pressed tight against her husband, the strength of his shifting muscles as he hugged her close easing some of her fear. "My da knows something he is not telling us."

"No more tonight, Elsie. We will discuss this anew tomorrow and determine how to pursue it. Now we sleep."

While he often thought of coupling with his wife, his only thought now was to hold her close and keep her safe.

"I cannot sleep knowing my sisters' lives may be in danger."

"There is nothing we can do right now. Sleep is best so we can wake with fresh thoughts and possibilities," he advised.

She pulled away from him. "You sleep. I cannot."

"It does you no good to lose sleep. You will need your strength to deal with this."

"Strength?" She shook her head as she paced by the bed. "Nay. It is fear that drives me to do what I must just as always."

"You have nothing to fear. I am here now and as your husband I will handle this."

She stopped pacing, her face scrunching in question. "My husband? In name but not in heart. You do not care for my sisters as I do. You do not worry that they may be suffering endlessly. You do not love them and would do anything for them," she argued vehemently.

"You're right. I do not care for your sisters like you do or worry intensely as you do for them or love them as you do."

Elsie gasped, shocked when his arm swiftly hooked her around the waist and yanked her against him, barely having seen him move.

"But I love you, wife, more then I should, more than I thought I could. While I have come to care for you, I have only recently realized that I love you, though I believe I have loved you since first meeting you. It was seeing the terrible pain on that young man's face when he had looked upon the body of the woman he was to wed, the woman he loved, the woman who he planned to build a life with, and I watched him break down in tears that the realization struck me. When he had finally been able to talk, I could not only see the devastating pain in the young man's eyes but an emptiness as if he had lost part of himself, he had loved Esta that much.

"His pain was palpable, for it mirrored my own if I was to ever lose you. I told you the decision would be ours about whether we remain in this marriage or not, but I rescind my word since I do not want to live without you, wife, my heart would break, and I would be but a shell of a man without you. So, you are stuck with me as your husband, but I can give you my word on one thing and that is that I will never rescind the overpowering love I have for you. My love for you will grow strong and deeper every day and remain with me beyond my dying day."

Elsie's eyes flooded with tears, and she swiped at them as they began to roll down her flushed cheeks one by one. His declaration of love left her so stunned that she could think of only one response. "I love you too."

Cavell chuckled as he smiled. "Something I knew and was waiting for you to have the courage to tell me."

"You did?" she asked surprised then saw a playful glint in his eyes and she smiled. "It is what you hoped, husband."

"More like prayed," he said with a chuckle and hugged her gently. "I do love you, wife, and always will," he said, needing to say it again, needing her to know, needing to hear it himself.

"And I will love you more, more and more every day," she said finally finding her voice.

Cavell wiped a tear off her delicate cheek and, subtle as it was, he could feel a stir of passion course through her body. And the air seemed to crackle with an invisible current that drew her ever closer to him, though neither of them moved. He wiped at another tear that lingered on her cheek and his light caress seemed to heighten the intensity in the air, as if a delicate balance teetered on the edge of their declared love.

"I am going to make love to you, wife," he said.

"Aye, please," she said eagerly.

"Shed your garments," he ordered gently.

Seeing her husband shed his own garments made the task much easier for her, though her hands trembled as she did. She wanted this, had wanted him to couple with her of his own free will to truly seal their marriage. And now they would, not out of duty, but because they loved each other.

Another rush of fresh tears spilled from her eyes as she shed the last of her garments and she turned her face away from him to hide them.

His naked body was suddenly pressed against hers, flesh against flesh, warmth against warmth, love united, and he turned her around slowly in his arms.

He wiped at her wet cheeks. "If you prefer not to—"

"Happy tears," she said quickly.

He chuckled and swung her up in his arms, her arms rushing around his neck as he carried her to the bed. "Then I fear you will be weeping all night."

She smiled. "I look forward to it."

She did until he placed her on the bed, and he stood beside it to look down at her, his glance roaming over her naked body. She was far too exposed, far too vulnerable, and she quickly reached for the blanket.

He grabbed her wrist, stopping her. "Nay. The last time we coupled in the dark. I want to see all of you this time." He released her arm.

Fear turned her eyes wide. She had not considered this… being naked in front of him. He would surely

183

find her lacking. Her arms hurried to cover her small breasts.

Cavell sat on the bed beside her and gently pried her arms off her breasts. "You are beautiful, wife."

He kissed her lips gently before leaning down and lavishing each nipple with kisses and nips, enjoying the feel of how hard they grew against his tongue while he ran his hand down along her waist to give her slender hip a squeeze.

He lifted his head. "You have the softest and most beautiful body."

The passion in his eyes, the tenderness of his loving touch, the truth in his strong voice had Elsie saying, "You make me feel beautiful."

"Fear hides your beauty, wife. Let it go and know I love you," he urged gently as his lips descended on hers in a kiss.

His words touched her heart and she felt something melt in the uncharted depths of her innermost being, something she had carried for far too long, something she was finally giving herself permission to let go... that she believed herself plain, unattractive, therefore, no man would love her and yet here was a man who loved her deeply.

She eased her lips off his, needing to say, "I am beautiful, and you are handsome."

He smiled. It had been a while since he heard a woman say that and he could see in his wife's gorgeous, soft blue eyes how very much she meant it. And he loved her even more.

"We make a perfect pair," he said and stretched out on his side next to her in bed.

"Aye," she said and sighed softly. "And we will have the most beautiful children."

"Many, many children," he teased, nipping playfully at her neck, and causing her to giggle.

She loved his playful side, it kept her worries at bay and kept her smiling, something she had not done often.

His mouth returned to her lips, his hand to her breast to cup and squeeze gently, and—

"I am sorry to disturb," came the voice along with the sharp rap at the door.

"May?" Elsie asked, thinking it was the healer but not sure.

"Aye. I am sorry, mistress, but your da is agitated and insisting on seeing you. I fear he may undo all the good he has gained if he does not calm down."

"I will be right there, May."

"I will be in his bedchamber," May said.

Elsie went to look at her husband, but he was already getting out of bed, and she worried he was upset with her. "I am sorry—"

"There is no reason to be," he said, offering her his hand to help her out of bed. "I cannot say I am not disappointed, but the night would not have gone well if we ignored the summons. We do what we must. Our time together will come soon enough."

"I am lucky to have you as my husband," Elsie said as she took his hand, and he tugged her out of the bed.

"Aye, you are wife," he said with a playful wink and gave her a quick kiss.

Elsie ached to return to bed with him and make love, but as he said, they do what they must, what duty calls for. She was just glad she had her husband by her side now, so she no longer saw to her duty alone.

Once they donned their garments, they hurried to her da's bedchamber. He was waving his hands, insisting Elsie be summoned.

"I am here, Da," she said and hurried to the side of his bed to sit.

"Elsie," he said, his eyes wide with worry as he reached his hand out to her, and she quickly took hold of it. "I cannot recall if it was a dream or you actually spoke to me about it. Did you say that Brother Kendrick was no longer at the abbey?"

May shook her head at Elsie, warning her not to further upset her da.

Elsie hesitated. They needed information from her da to be able to help her sisters, but his well-being was at risk as well.

Cavell stepped around his wife to stand at her side. "Brother Kendrick has passed, Norris, but another brother took his place, and I am sure Brother Kendrick passed on any information you shared with him."

Her da's face lost some of its worry. "True. True. Brother Kendrick was a kind soul and would make sure he informed his successor of things that might come to pass. And I did secure my daughters' safety. They would be collected from the abbey and protected." He shook his head and waved his hands once again. "No one must know, not ever. Not ever." He chuckled. "A tale that is all it is… a tale." His chuckle died and his glance fell on Elsie. "I promised your mum and I never ever broke a promise to your mum." Tears pooled in his eyes. "I miss her so much. I wish I could be with her again." He rubbed his eyes to chase away the unshed tears. "We need to talk, Cavell," her da said seriously. "There is much you need to know. Go, Elsie, this is between your husband and me."

Cavell nodded at his wife. "Go and get some sleep, Elsie. We will talk."

Elsie was reluctant to leave but understood this might be an opportunity for them to learn something that could help her sisters.

"Aye, husband," she said, standing.

Cavell gave her hand a squeeze and ordered softly, "Get some sleep."

"I will wait for you," she whispered, and he shook his head but smiled.

***

Elsie woke the next morning, not sure how long she had slept and disappointed to find herself alone in bed. She hurried to dress, freshen her face with a splash of water, and her mouth with dried mint, then rushed from the room to find her husband and see what he learned from her da if anything.

She stopped at her da's bedchamber to see if he could still be there, but her da was fast asleep and alone.

Elsie entered the Great Hall to see servants huddled in hush conversations. She headed toward Alda as soon as she spotted her. She did not have to ask what was wrong, Alda hurried to offer the news.

"A body has been found in the woods, not far from the village. Chieftain Cavell and Melvin went there.

The dead man is unfamiliar to the men who found him. The clan worries what it might mean with rogue mercenaries in the area."

"All will be well. Chieftain Cavell will see to it," Elsie said, speaking confidently about her husband's ability to protect them.

"Our clan does not have a strong fighting force," Alda reminded.

"Worry not, Alda, Chieftain Cavell will know what to do to keep our clan safe," Elsie assured her. "Now, can you tell me where in the woods the dead man was found?"

The question terrified Alda, her eyes rounding wide. "You cannot think of going there, mistress. It is not safe. Chieftain Cavell would not want you to venture there on your own."

"Did he leave word that I was not to join him there?"

"Nay, but—"

Elsie quickly interrupted her. "He left no word, so I am free to see for myself what is going on. So, Alda, where was this dead man found?"

Chapter Sixteen

Elsie ventured into the woods, knowing exactly where to go once Alda described it. The crisp spring air was filled with the invigorating scent of blooming flowers and the subtle rustling of leaves in the gentle breeze reminded her of the many enjoyable times she had spent in the woods with her sisters. She smiled at the sunlight that filtered through the budding canopy above, casting a warm glow on the forest floor, hoping the sun would linger for the day. She and her sisters loved it when the forest awakened from its winter slumber, bursting with vibrant green hues, and bluebells could be found growing almost everywhere.

The memories were pleasant, but they also reminded her of her sisters' plight and her smile faded as she walked deeper into the woods, drawing closer to her destination. She wasn't sure what she suddenly felt, something out of the ordinary, a sudden shift in the atmosphere—an unsettling feeling that rushed

189

gooseflesh over her. She stopped and a shudder ran through her as she listened. A strange hush had settled over the area as if the very forest held its breath.

Her footfalls were the only sound she heard in the forest. She should have given more thought to coming here alone. What if the killer still lingered about?

She was relieved, after taking a few more steps, to hear voices. She was close. She would reach her husband soon.

The voices suddenly stopped, and Elsie halted her steps. Was it her husband ahead or was it someone who heard her footsteps and stopped speaking to listen to her approach?

Fear flared in her, causing her to hesitate, but she could not linger in hesitancy, it would do her no good. She took a cautious step forward, keeping as close to the large tree trunks as possible so she could slip behind one if necessary.

The voices hadn't resumed but she was pretty sure they had come from just up ahead around the small bend, close to where the body was found. She proceeded slowly, cautiously, fearfully.

Elsie took barely a few steps when a powerful arm hooked around her, locking her arms to her sides, and lifting her clear off the ground, and she let out a scream as she squirmed and kicked her legs and tried to break free. It was impossible. She was completely shackled to the man.

"Be still and tell me what you are doing here, wife," Cavell ordered.

Elsie breathed a heavy sigh of relief. "You frightened me."

"As you did me when I spotted you creeping around here," he said and planted her on her feet.

She hurried to turn and face him. "You found a dead man. I wanted to see him."

"Why?" he demanded.

"I heard he was not familiar to the men who found him, and I thought I might know who he is."

"You don't and what were you thinking of coming here alone?" he asked, annoyed, though fearful as well, something he was not used to feeling.

"How do you know that I would not know the man? And you are right I should have given more thought to my decision to come here alone," she admitted, her fear just beginning to fade.

"Bloody hell, you should have," he admonished, his heart thumping wildly thinking of the danger that could have befallen her when he discovered the footfalls he had heard and thought were the culprit's, belonged to his wife.

"I did not mean to upset you," she said. "I will be more cautious next time."

He shook his head and snatched hold of her arm. "There won't be a next time, wife. Unless I give you permission to follow me, you are to stay put until I return."

"I cannot do that," she said firmly.

He could not keep the shock from his face, his eyes turning wide. "You refuse to obey me?"

"At times I might, though not intentionally, more out of necessity," she said as if it made perfect sense. "You never answered me. How do you know I wouldn't recognize the dead man."

191

"Because I know him. He is Gallowglass," Cavell said and tugged her along as he walked. "We will discuss your disobedience later."

"There are more important things for us to discuss."

He stopped abruptly. "There is nothing more important than your safety and you being unwise when it comes to it." He resumed walking, once again tugging her along with him.

Elsie held her tongue since she had no defense. She had made an unwise decision, but she learned from it and would not be so foolish to repeat it… unless necessary.

They rounded the bend and her eyes fell on a chilling sight. She had seen dead bodies before, helped prepare several for burial, but never had she seen a man with so many stab wounds or his throat sliced.

Melvin stood looking down at the dead man while the few clansmen who had accompanied her husband stood aside, whispering to each other, all clearly worried.

Melvin's head shot up. "Slayer will be furious when he learns what was done to Clyde. He will demand revenge for the brutal killing. I will go and inform him."

"And risk the same happening to you?" Cavell asked, shaking his head.

"Slayer needs to know, and I am not afraid," Melvin said with a defiant lift of his chin.

"We both know that Slayer will send someone when Clyde does not return in a timely manner," Cavell said.

"But what do we risk by waiting?" Melvin asked. "What if forces gather that we do not know about? Slayer needs to be prepared."

"Don't you think he doesn't already know that?" Cavell asked. "Have you ever known Slayer not to be prepared or that he never fails to be one step ahead of his foe?"

"He was not prepared for his brother and father's deaths," Melvin reminded.

"That says something in itself," Cavell said.

"I don't understand," Melvin said.

"With all the tentacles Slayer has spread over the Highlands and beyond, he would have at least heard stirrings about his brother and father being in possible danger, but he hadn't. So, were both men the targets, or were they simply in the way of the true targets?"

Elsie understood what her husband meant, and it sent a chill racing through her as well as complete confusion. She returned to the question that haunted her. What reason could anyone have for wanting her and her sisters dead?

"I would not be surprised if Slayer has more men on the way to us," Cavell said. "We will give it a few days and if we hear nothing from him, then you can go and inform him of what happened here."

"Aye, Slayer does have a vast network of friends and foes," Melvin said. "No doubt he is aware of some things already. But I will be ready to go if we do not hear from him in a few days' time."

Cavell let his hand slip off his wife's arm so his arm could circle her waist and once he did, her body sunk against his. She tried not to show it, but the sight of the dead man disturbed her. It would disturb anyone not used to seeing a sight common on a battlefield.

He turned just enough so his body blocked the view of the dead man.

Keeping his voice low, Melvin said, "The clan is vulnerable without experienced warriors."

"Something I intend to make sure Slayer knows," Cavell said. "In the meantime, we start preparing the men here to be better trained to fight when necessary. We form a plan to follow if attacked, so everyone knows what to do and panic does not ensue."

"Slayer was right about you knowing how to weigh options to any given situation. Something he lacks at times," Melvin said.

"Which is why he will send men when Clyde fails to return," Cavell said. "Now let's get Clyde to the village and prepared for burial."

It was a relieved and silent procession that entered the village, not a word having been spoken on the return trek. Cavell had ordered silence when they traveled, so any unfamiliar sound to the woods could be detected.

Elsie had been relieved to hear only the usual sounds of animals scurrying in play or birds calling out, not a single footfall had been heard. However, chatter started as soon as it was learned that the dead man was a Gallowglass warrior. All worried what it might mean for the clan.

"You need to be more cautious, wife," Cavell said as he continued to keep his hand wrapped around hers as they walked to the keep. He had not let go of her hand since they had begun their trek back. He worried if he did let go, she might somehow be snatched away from him.

"Aye, you are right," she agreed. "I was so eager to join you and see what you might have found that I did not consider the possible consequences."

That she realized her error lightened his concern and with a playful smile he boasted, "I am always right, and you would do well to remember that."

She loved when he turned playful, and she chuckled and feeling playful herself said, "I suppose that is true since you are the perfect husband."

He laughed, then raised her hand that he held and kissed it. "Perfection, wife. I am pure perfection."

She chuckled again. "And so very humble."

Elsie let out a small gasp when her husband suddenly stopped and turned, keeping her shielded with his body.

"Forgive me, sir, I do not mean to intrude I but wanted a word with you," Wadely said, a slight tremble to his voice.

"Have your say, but never approach me without calling out," Cavell admonished.

"Aye, sir, aye," Wadely said, bobbing his head. "With the news about the dead man and with the rogue mercenaries roaming the woods, I fear traveling the roads now. I would like your permission to remain here until worries can be put to rest. I have seen you wear a leather breast covering at times. I am skilled with leather work and can make whatever you need for yourself or the clan to do my share while here."

"A fair offer, Wadely. You are welcome to remain here and take your leave when you choose," Cavell said.

"Much appreciated, sir, and when you are ready let me know what leather work you need, and I will get started on it right away."

"I will speak with you soon about that," Cavell said, and with several more bobs of his head, Wadely took his leave.

"Mistress Elsie! A moment, please?"

Cavell turned with his wife, recognizing Edith's— Ann—he had to remember Edith was now Ann, voice.

Elsie understood Ann's steps were slow not so much from age but from her time spent in the small cell, since her own bones ached at times. So, she hurried her own steps to the woman, her husband following behind her.

"Is something wrong with my da, Ann?" Elsie asked anxiously.

"Nay," Ann was quick to confirm. "His naps grow shorter, which is what he is doing now, napping. A good sign that tells us he does not require as much rest as he once did. May and I agree that it is time for him to get out of bed, a short time daily, so he can regain strength in his legs."

"That is wonderful news, Ann," Elsie said, relieved her da was finally improving. "He has benefitted greatly from your help."

"I am grateful to be part of the clan and do my part like any member, mistress, but that is not all I wanted to tell you," Ann said. "Your da spoke in his sleep, something about a promise he made to Terena."

196

Elsie smiled softly. "Terena is my mom, and he made a promise to her to keep me and my sisters safe."

"Hmmm," Ann said, shaking her head slightly. "That wasn't the promise he spoke of. He said, 'I keep the promise, Terena. I keep the promise. Our daughters will never know.'"

Elsie was at a loss of what to think or say.

"Secrets," Ann said, shaking her head again. "All families have them, small and large ones and some are easily discovered while others are buried forever. Your da heals and will one day be able to tell you the secret. I must be off, mistress, I have expectant mums to visit."

"Elsie," Cavell said, his wife remaining silent after Ann disappeared from sight. His wife turned her head to look at him, but he could see from her blank expression that she was at a loss to speak.

"We will solve this mystery," Cavell said with a firmness that left no doubt he would not have it any other way.

The strong tenor and determination in his voice pulled Elsie from her foggy thoughts. "What possible secret could my mum and da have shared about their daughters? And is it that secret that causes us harm?"

"You heard Ann. Your da grows stronger. Soon he will be able to answer all our questions. Until then we will see what we can find out ourselves."

"From whom?" She hastily responded to her own question. "The elders in the clan. There may be something one of them says that would begin to unravel the mystery."

Melvin came running toward them. "A young lad begging for help. His family's croft is being attacked."

"How many?" Cavell demanded.

"Five, from what the lad saw. I can go—"

"Nay, I am chieftain, and I must go. You will remain here since it could be a trap to draw us away so the clan can be more easily attacked. I will take three good-fighting men with me. You make sure the men here have their weapons ready to fight if necessary."

"They will be ready. I will make sure of it," Melvin assured him. "You best hurry. There isn't a moment to spare."

"Go," Elsie urged when her husband turned to her. "It must be Jeremy, eight years now—"

"Aye, that's the lad's name," Melvin confirmed.

"He has two older brothers, as brave as he is, and a younger sister no more than five years. Hurry and help them," Elsie urged, even though she feared for his safety.

Cavell grabbed her around the waist and lifted her to plant a firm, quick kiss on her lips, then ordered, "Stay safe and wise, wife."

"You as well," she said as he placed her back on her feet, then watched him hurry off.

Elsie was grateful to be kept busy, her mind constantly on her husband and his safety. Melvin reassured her each time their paths crossed that she need not worry that her husband was skilled enough to fight five mercenaries on his own without so much as a minor wound.

Elsie wanted to believe Melvin, but fear kept her doubtful, though not about leaving Melvin in charge while her husband was gone. He had the men and women organized with weapons within a short time and he even devised a plan if an attack should happen. The pregnant women were instructed to take the children to the keep and barricade themselves there until the fighting was done. When a woman asked what would happen if the clan was defeated, Melvin had turned a serious snarl on her and said, "Clan Murdock will never lose a battle!" A cheer followed and confidence of victory soared.

It wasn't until near evening that she had a chance to stop at May's cottage and speak with her.

"Your da does well," May said and pushed herself up off the bench to stand as Elsie approached her cottage."

"Sit. Sit," Elsie urged. "I will join you."

May dropped down on the bench and rested her head back against the cottage.

"I know my da does well. I spoke with Ann earlier. I am not here to discuss him, and you look absolutely exhausted."

She lifted her head. "It is the dead man. I have never seen anything as brutal as that. Either the stab wounds or the sliced throat would have killed him, yet he suffered both where only one was necessary. That speaks of rage or revenge."

May's words followed her to the keep long after they had discussed other things. She wondered if someone wanted revenge against Clyde personally. The Gallowglass? Slayer?

Little sleep last night and worry for her husband exhausted her even more and had her skipping supper and going straight to her bedchamber. She had hoped her husband would return tonight but the length of battle could not be predicted nor could casualties and the injured. It could be days before he returned.

She made use of the fresh bucket of water left by the hearth and washed herself, and as she did so, a brief conversation she had had with Alda popped into her head. She had asked Alda if she had heard anything discussed with Warrand or Lord Bannaty when they visited with her da. Alda told her that she found it strange that no servant was allowed in Norris's solar when he talked with the men and that not a peep was heard from either man on their separate visits when they took their leave. Usually, visitors talked freely in front of the servants as they exited the keep, thinking all servants were deaf. Not so with either visit, both men spoke not a word. It made Elsie think that whatever was discussed was not meant for anyone to hear or know about. But why?

She slipped into a clean sleeveless shift and freed her hair of the braid to run the comb through it several times, praying for the safety of her husband and the men who were with him as she did.

She was about to get into bed when she heard footfalls rushing up the stone stairs and she feared she was about to receive terrible news. She approached the door slowly and it was flung open before she reached it.

Her husband stood in the doorway shirtless, his arms and chest damp and his hair wet, as if he had washed but had not fully dried himself. His eyes settled on her, staring with an intensity she had never seen before now, and she shuddered.

He stepped into the room, swinging the door shut behind him and his hand went to his belt to untie it. "Take that shift off, wife, and come here to me… now!"

Chapter Seventeen

Elsie shed her shift, a slight tremor to her hands as she did, eager to make love with her husband but anxious, seeing the fiery passion flaming in his eyes. And when his plaid fell to his feet, she saw just how passion-filled his need was for her.

She stood frozen, the room bathed in a soft, ethereal glow that allowed her to admire every inch of him, the width of his shoulders, the scope of his muscled chest, his thick muscled arms, his slender waist, and the power of his protruding manhood. Her own passion quickly responded to her unhasty perusal, further firing her desire.

"Come here, wife, now," he ordered.

Her eyes met his and their gazes locked in a magnetic embrace. She stood there, aware of the pulsating passion between them, drawing ever more powerful with each passing second. The air crackled with anticipation, heavy with the weight of unspoken desire.

Elsie did not realize she took a step, then another until she was standing in front of him, the potency of his gaze holding her there, unable to move.

He reached out, his fingertips gently brushing against her soft skin. She leaned into his touch, her eyes fluttering shut, reveling in the tender caress and a current surged through him, further igniting his fiery passion.

Everything around Elsie faded away. Only this moment mattered. Only this moment existed.

With aching tenderness, Cavell traced the contours of her face, mapping the path from her temple to the curve of her jawline. His touch left a trail of delicious shivers in its wake, and he was reminded of the perfection of their first time together, thinking he had been a fool to wait so long to share such pleasure with her again.

He lowered his lips to hers and they met in a soft collision, a union of souls. It began as a delicate exploration, a gentle dance of vulnerability and trust. Their mouths moved in perfect synchrony, exchanging stolen breaths. The taste of each other consumed them, the sweetness mingling with a hunger that threatened to devour their senses.

He coiled his arm around her waist and yanked her to him, needing to feel her naked against him and he held her there, as if she were the missing piece of his existence.

The heat radiating from their entwined bodies was both a comfort and a provocation, stirring a primal fire that consumed Elsie's thoughts and inhibitions. Never had she known she could ever ache for a man as she did now for her husband and never had she known she could love a man as deeply as she loved her husband.

With tender kisses trailing along her jawline, Cavell savored the softness of her skin, committing every sensation to memory. Her body arched, seeking the pleasure that only he could provide. His free hand roamed the slight curve of her waist, traveling down over her backside to give her soft cheek a squeeze, leaving a trail of intense need in his wake.

With a suddenness that startled her, her husband scooped her up in his arms and carried her to their bed.

He pressed his brow to hers and whispered, "I have an ache for you, wife, that I fear I will never satisfy."

She brushed her lips over his. "Good, then I won't wear you out since I feel the same."

He placed her on the bed and stood a moment looking down at her. She thought she would feel exposed, vulnerable as she once did, but not this time. Seeing the raw passion for her in his eyes, she felt nothing but the unadulterated passion that she had for him and eagerness for it to soon consume them both.

He dropped down over her, the muscles in his arms taut as he kept himself hovering a breath above her. "My lips have missed the taste of you."

She let out a gasp when his mouth began to leave a trail of tender and demanding kisses and nips along her body, starting at her breasts and working his way down. A collision of desire and ecstasy sent shockwaves through her, and her hands reached out to grip the blanket beneath her tightly.

He raised his head, a low, rumbling growl emanating from him. "I cannot wait. I need you now."

She stretched her arms out to him. "I am yours. I will always be yours."

203

His mouth captured hers in a rough kiss as if sealing her words as his knee slipped between her legs to spread them farther apart and she opened eagerly for him.

He leaned to the side a moment as his hand slipped between her legs and he slipped a finger inside her.

She moaned, eager for more than his finger.

"You drip with readiness," he said, wanting to make sure he would cause her no discomfort.

"The very reason why you should not wait another moment," she said, arching her body invitingly.

Cavell's response was to slip over her, though he stilled once he settled his shaft between her legs. "Hold on to me, wife, I intend to make this memorable for us both."

She gripped his arms, his remark firing her passion, eager for the memory.

He entered her gently at first, building in a rhythm she matched, that turned more demanding until his thrusts rocked her body, and she could not contain her moans of pleasure. They echoed through the room, and she feared they echoed through the keep. Still, she could not contain them, the intense pleasure would not allow it.

Time stood still as they surrendered to the intoxication of their love, losing themselves in a realm where only they existed. Pleasure surged through their veins, building and crashing like waves against the shore. They moved as one, their bodies entangled, their desires merging into a singular force that defied the constraints of the mortal world.

"Now, Elsie, now!" Cavell commanded and she screamed, joining him in an explosion of pleasure that gripped them and would not let go.

Elsie hugged her husband with what little strength she had when he dropped down on her, the last waves of passion finally subsiding, and she still enjoying each one. She did not want to let him go when he went to roll off her, but her strength had yet to return to her. She was pleased when he took her with him, and their bodies instinctively entwined like vines.

Cavell found pleasure in the symphony of her contented sighs and their shared labored breaths. He held her tightly as she did him and he thought he heard their hearts beating in unison and that somehow their souls had forever been linked by the intense love that neither had expected yet both were grateful to have discovered.

Passion having exhausted them both, they fell asleep to wake later and make love quickly but no less intensely and they slept once again. Morning found them spent but smiling.

"I love you, Elsie," he said, tenderly pushing a strand of her soft hair off her cheek.

"I love that morning greeting," she said, his words warming her heart.

"Then I shall greet you that way every morning since I do not believe there will be enough time in this life to tell you how much I love you." He almost pulled away when she rested her hand on his cheek, his scar, but he stopped himself. Her touch was one of love and he relished the feel of it.

"Then we both will remind each other often and not only in words," she said, her smile growing.

"Aye, wife, often," he said softly and was about to kiss her lips when her stomach rumbled loudly. His brow narrowed. "When did you last eat?"

She went to turn on her back, but he quickly hooked her waist and stopped her.

"When?" he demanded.

"Yesterday with you."

"We go eat now." Knowing she would protest, he added, "I will tell you about the attack on the croft."

Elsie got out of bed in a flash and hurried into her garments. "Are they all well? Was anyone harmed?"

"I will tell you while we eat, since I am just as hungry."

Cavell grabbed his wife's arm when she went to rush down the stairs after leaving their bedchamber. "You will follow behind me since you seem to have a propensity for falling down the stairs."

"That was one time," she argued but followed behind him.

"That is not what your da told me when I talked with him alone."

"That was when I was young and always in a hurry," she said and poked him in the back. "Did you ask my da about me or did he volunteer the information?"

"I asked and he was more than willing to share. He is very proud of you, Elsie, and of your sisters. He says you have all grown to be fine women."

Elsie felt tears well in her eyes, but she kept them locked away since they were steps away from the Great

Hall and she would have no one see her teary-eyed. She stopped when she saw the room was crowded, clansmen and women lingering about.

Alda approached and bobbed her head when she stopped in front of them. "They have come to pay their respects, sir, and to thank you for saving Pell and his family. They know now that you will fight for them without hesitation."

Elsie thought her husband might protest, having engaged with the clan to learn about it but not having come to truly know the people. She understood that he had become used to avoiding people because of his scars. The clan did not see his scars as others did. To them, his scars were a sign of courage and honor to be respected and he had proved it by saving several of their own.

She watched as her husband graciously accepted the appreciation and praise the people offered him. But Blaine, Jeremy's five-year-old sister, stole everyone's attention when she ran to Cavell and grabbed his leg in a hug as she looked up at him with tears in her eyes and said, "I love you."

The whole room quieted to see what their chieftain would do as did Elsie, curious as to his response.

Cavell scooped up the little lass and said for all to hear, "I will rescue you, Blaine, whenever needed, as well as all in the clan."

Cheers rang out for their chieftain's loyalty to the clan and Elsie felt her heart swell with pride for her husband.

"Food and drink to all who want it," Cavell called out and when Blaine's mum came to get her from

Cavell, the little lass smiled and kissed him on the cheek before going into her mum's arms.

Cavell slipped his arm around his wife.

"Looks like I have some competition for your heart," Elsie said teasingly.

"She is a pretty, little thing, and she doesn't mind my scars," Cavell said and cast a quick glance at the lass. "I wouldn't mind us having a daughter. Though, I would not let a man get near her and I would make sure she married a good man."

That he spoke of future children with her touched her heart.

They went to the dais Cavell had ordered made for them with a table large enough to seat four and looked out on the small room. It was a matter of respect, he had explained, for the chieftain and his wife to have a place of honor to sit. He had then whispered it was also because he wanted her to himself, the two other chairs for those he would invite to join them, when necessary.

"Maybe two or three sons first, so they can help me protect a daughter or two," Cavell said, after thinking about it and assisted her to sit before sitting himself.

Five bairns. She smiled, having often thought of having several children. Her heart swelled with happiness. She would have what she once thought only a dream, a loving husband and family.

Cavell reached for a quail egg from the bowl on the table that held several and began to peel it as he spoke. "Blaine was nowhere in sight when I got to the croft and I had no time to search for her, the situation needing my immediate attention. I was relieved to see her mum fetch her from a hiding spot once the fighting was done. Her da and mum had wisely taught her what to do if the croft came under attack." He handed her the peeled quail egg and reached for one for himself. "Her brothers, though young, fought to protect their home. They have minor wounds and their da fought bravely, even with a more serious wound to his arm. May assures me that he will heal nicely."

Elsie finished the last bite of the egg before asking, "Did you learn why the men attacked the croft?"

"They were fierce fighters with no intentions of surrendering or being taken prisoner."

"What are you saying?" she asked, thinking she understood but also thinking it made no sense.

"Your husband killed every one of them from the tale that's being told," Melvin said, with pride as he came to a stop in front of the dais. "They were ready to kill Pell and his family when Cavell arrived. He disposed of them fast enough."

Elsie's eyes turned wide on her husband. "Is that true?"

"The men I brought with me from Clan Murdock helped," Cavell said.

Melvin snorted. "Barely." He raised his tankard. "Now that rogue bunch of mercenaries know who they are up against… the Gallowglass."

"I am no longer Gallowglass," Cavell said.

Elsie was glad to hear that, worried that he might somehow be pulled back into the group.

"Once a Gallowglass warrior always a Gallowglass warrior," Melvin said and raised his tankard when Alda walked by. "More ale, Alda."

"It is morning and you have already had your share of drink for the day," May said, coming up behind him.

Melvin rolled his eyes before turning to face her. "You are not my wife and—"

"Thank the good Lord for that," May said.

"Amen to that," Melvin agreed, "so off with you."

"You told me you were a man of your word," May said.

"I am an honorable man, and an honorable man always keeps his word."

May snatched the tankard from his hand so fast Melvin had no time to stop her. "Good. You gave me your word that you would help me settle Pell and his family in one of the cottages so he can heal. We do that now."

"Bloody hell, I did give you my word," Melvin said, glancing longingly at his tankard May placed on the dais's table. "But I get to drink once we're done. We always celebrate a victory with ale and food."

"Melvin's right about that," Cavell said amused that May took charge of Melvin so easily.

"Celebrate later, work now," May said and hooked her arm around his, not letting him get away and hurried him out of the room.

"I think they favor each other," Elsie said.

Cavell laughed. "I doubt that, wife. They are always at odds with each other and look ready to battle after a few words."

"Similar in some ways to how we were when we first met," she reminded with a smile.

He shook his head. "Vastly different. We were wed, connected whether we liked it or not. Melvin has claimed repeatedly that he has no wont to settle down and raise a brood of children. His life consists of battle as will his death or so he claims."

"Melvin told me that he feels differently since being here. Clan life is more to his liking than he thought, and I believe he would make you a fine, trustworthy advisor. You should speak with him about it. And I believe you claimed most adamantly that you did not want to be wed, yet here you are, our marriage sealed firmly," she said, reminding him of last night with a gleeful twinkle in her eyes.

"Aye, a decision of our own choosing," he reminded.

"Not really," Elsie said, eagerly spearing a small piece of cheese with a knife.

"I did not force you to remain wed to me," he said, annoyed that she would think that the decision was his alone that they remained wed. "Though I was a bit demanding, you came to me willingly."

Elsie leaned close, resting her arm against his. "I had no choice but to remain wed to you—"

Cavell bristled ready to dispute her nonsensical claim.

She pressed her finger to his lips to halt his words. "I had no choice because I love you. You have my heart, and I cannot live without it, which means I cannot live without you. I don't want to. I love you, husband."

Cavell brushed a kiss across her lips. "I am a lucky man to have your love." He smiled. "And you are a lucky woman to have such a handsome husband."

Elsie knew he teased, yet he didn't tease. His scars continued to trouble him and her as well since his scars were healing and, once again, she worried what would happen when he was as handsome as he once had been and she remained the same.

Cavell caught the slight pucker of her eyes. "I but tease, wife."

She kept her voice low. "Your scars heal nicely. You will be as handsome as you were soon enough, but I will still be—"

"Beautiful," he said, finishing before she could. "Do you forget I told you how beautiful you were last night? I will remind you again and again, if necessary, though I do enjoy telling you so it will be no chore. You are the most beautiful woman I have ever known or will ever know, and I will battle anyone who says otherwise."

"You will not," she scolded. "Knowing you would do such a chivalrous thing is enough for me. Besides, that you believe me beautiful is all that matters to me."

"To Chieftain Cavell and his wife, Mistress Elsie!" a man called out, his tankard raised high, and cheers rang out and tankards were raised.

It went on like that for a while, talk interspersed with praise and cheers as the unexpected celebration continued.

Melvin returned, rushing to the dais, Cavell ready to hand him the tankard he had left half full, but there was something about his hasty steps that told a different tale.

"You need to come talk with Pell," Melvin said, bending toward Cavell. "There is more to the attack than first thought."

Chapter Eighteen

The day was overcast with a slight chill in the spring air, but one would think the sun shined with the smiles and greetings bestowed on Cavell and Elsie as they followed Melvin through the village.

"Pell was in no shape to talk once the battle ended," Cavell said, explaining to his wife as they walked and while responding with waves and nods to the endless greetings. "Between his wound and his worry about getting his family to safety, there was little time to enter into a discussion."

"Aye, Pell said much the same," Melvin said, continuing to lead the way. "Now, however, feeling better and relieved his family is safe, he wants to talk, feels it is important to do so."

Elsie was eager to hear what the man had to say and hurried into the cottage when her husband held the door open for her to enter first, something she had to get used to since no man had ever done that for her, though she stepped aside once inside for him to take the lead, and Melvin remained by the door.

"Sir," Pell said with a bob of his head and tried to get out of bed.

"Stay as you are," Cavell ordered. "I am glad to see you look much better, and how are your sons doing?"

"They are well, sir, thanks to your bravery. I sent them to join their mum in the celebration." Pell tilted his head to look at Elsie, Cavell partially blocking her from view. "The clan is indebted to you, Mistress Elsie. It is because of your loyalty to us that you wed the man of your da's choice and secured the clan an exceptional chieftain."

Elsie remembered Pell as a big man with a pleasant nature. She saw him and his family mostly on market days. He was not overly tall, but he had a large girth to him with hair he kept cut close to his scalp.

She responded with a smile. "My da chose wisely for me, Pell, but if the decision had been left to me, it would have been an easy one to make. I would willing wed my husband for he is a good and honorable man."

His wife's words pleased Cavell, but he was more pleased that she intentionally voiced how she felt about him to Pell. The farmer would be sure to share Elsie's words with his wife and she with other women and the news would spread, as Elsie intended, so all knew that she cared about her husband. Would it make a difference to anyone? He did not know, but he knew it made a difference to him that she wanted it made known.

214

"What did you wish to tell me about the attack, Pell?" Cavell asked, a busy day ahead of him as well as the time he intended to spend alone with his wife.

"Not so much the attack as the men who attacked. I have seen all five men in the area on several occasions, though not together… separately. Though one time I did see two of the men together. Not that I spoke a word to any of them at any time, I just recall seeing them."

"Where did you see the two together?" Cavell asked.

"At market day at Clan McCabe and I saw one of the other men alone at market day here at Clan Murdock. I think what made me notice them was the way they appeared to watch everyone and everything that was going on while other people were busy haggling with the merchants."

"When was this?" Elsie asked, taking a step to stand beside her husband.

"I think around two moon cycles ago or more since it was a chilly day at market when I saw the two."

"Did you not think of mentioning the oddity of the men's action to someone?" Cavell asked.

"I did, sir," Pell said with a nod. "When I spotted the one man alone here at Clan Murdock on market day, I went straight to Chieftain Norris and told him about it. He was concerned and asked if the man had focused his attention on anyone in particular in the clan. I hadn't given it thought since it is common to see men unable to take their eyes off Mistress Leora. But the fellow had not taken his eyes off her. His glance followed her everywhere. That news truly upset

Chieftain Norris and understandably so. He told me if I saw the man around here again to let him know."

"This man did not approach Leora at any time?" Cavell asked.

"Nay, sir, his glance remained on her just as other men's eyes often did, though unlike other men, he never smiled as he watched her. Could this have something to do with why they attacked my croft? I cannot make sense of the attack. If you had not shown up when you did—" Pell fought the tears rushing to cloud his eyes. "I fear the croft is no longer safe for my family and yet the animals and land must be tended to, and it takes the whole family to see it done. We have no choice but to return home today."

"You and your family will remain here until I can secure your safety at the croft. Your animals will be brought here until then and the land can see to itself for now. Rest and grow strong," Cavell ordered. "We will speak again."

Melvin spoke once outside. "Someone was scouting the area, which means it was no rogue bunch of mercenaries who attacked the croft. But why attack a small croft?"

"And what interest do they have in Leora?" Elsie asked, her worry for her sisters growing.

Cavell took his wife's hand, closing it firmly around hers and she quickly grabbed hold letting him know she welcomed his strength as he walked away from the cottage, Melvin following along.

"I know what you are thinking, Melvin," Cavell said after they walked a bit in silence. "And I agree. We need warriors here who cannot only fight, but whose

216

presence alone will warn against attacking. There is much more that goes on here than rogue mercenaries causing problems."

"I knew you would see reason. We need Slayer's help. Pledge allegiance to him and he will send more than enough warriors. I can leave today with a message from you."

"Not today, Melvin. There is more I need to learn, more Slayer needs to know before you go. Until then, take a few men with you to Pell's croft and bring the animals here."

"Laurel should be asked if there is anything she needs from the croft," Elsie said.

"I will get May to speak with her," Melvin said.

"Go and see it done and we will talk more later," Cavell said.

Silence walked with them after Melvin went to do as Cavell commanded, until Elsie finally spoke. "Like you knew what Melvin was thinking, I know your thoughts. You do not want to wait any longer to talk to my da. You want to know now why he fears for his daughters' safety."

"We cannot wait any longer. We need to know," Cavell said, having already decided.

"We should talk with May first—"

Cavell stopped at the foot of the keep's steps and turned to his wife. "A chieftain often must make difficult decisions, and this is one of them. Do I worry more about your da or your sisters? Given that choice, wife, which would you choose?"

217

Elsie gasped lightly. "How foolish of me. I had not given thought that while I was trying to save my da, I could lose my sisters."

"You were trying to do the best for all of them when sometimes it is not possible. I would give my life to save what daughters we may have one day, and I believe your da would do the same. But he has improved and perhaps learning his daughters are not as safe as he planned, might give him the strength to do what he could to help save them."

Elsie gripped her husband's hand tightly. "Let's do what we must."

She was relieved to find May leaving her da's bedchamber, but it was her husband who spoke to the healer.

"I need to talk with him and while it may upset him. It cannot wait."

"Go easy if you can, sir," May said with a nod of understanding, then looked to Elsie. "Your da improves, then slips back again. I fear he may never regain his full strength and I sometimes wonder if he wants to. He often talks of missing your mum. I think he would prefer to be with her."

Elsie understood what her da was feeling. "They were close and seemed to grow closer as they aged and they never tired of spending time with each other, never stopped smiling at each other, and they always held hands when walking through the village. They got their strength from each other and my da lost not only his strength but part of himself when my mum died. He has never been the same."

"Go gently, for his strength wanes today," May advised.

"Melvin needs your help," Cavell said. "He needs you to speak with Laurel. Find him and he will explain."

"Aye, sir, and so you know, Ann sits with him now."

Cavell held his wife back from entering the room as May took her leave and when her footfalls could be heard no more on the stairs, he said, "This may not be easy for you. You are not alone. I am with you always."

"I sometimes felt alone even when my sisters were here, though I could never understand why. But I have not felt alone, not for a moment, since being with you." She went to kiss his cheek, but he captured her lips in a loving kiss.

"You chased away my loneliness the moment I met you," he said after ending their kiss with a gentle brush of his lips across hers, then turned a playful scowl on her. "Then you proceeded to frustrate me."

She smiled. "Thank you, husband, for easing my heart before facing this task."

He squeezed her hand and opened the door.

"Cavell. Chieftain Cavell, I should say, and Elsie, it is good to see you both," Norris said with a weak smile.

Ann vacated the chair by the bed.

Cavell turned to the woman after his wife sat, her hand quickly reaching for her da's frail one. "Give us time."

Ann bobbed her head and left the room.

"Da, we need to talk," Elsie said.

219

"Your brow puckers. Something upsets you," her da said, his own brow scrunching in concern.

"I need to ask you something," Elsie said hesitating, worried how her questions might affect her da and possibly damage any progress he had made.

"You can talk with me about anything, dear Elsie. That will never change no matter how old either of us gets. Now tell me what troubles you."

"I worry about the threat of danger to me and my sisters. What danger is it, and who causes it?"

"What nonsense do you speak?" her da asked, appearing befuddled. "None of you are in danger."

Her da had forgotten he had mentioned it to her. She wasn't sure if that would be helpful or a deterrent. "You mentioned we were in danger, and you had to keep us safe when we spoke. Keep us safe from what or from who?

He pulled his hand from hers waving it. "You are all safe, I saw to it. I promised your mum."

"Safe from what, Da?" she asked gently, not wanting to agitate him.

Her da stared at her, though she didn't think he was seeing her. It was as if he was caught in a memory, and she hoped it would turn out to be a helpful memory.

"You were so tiny when I first held you. Your mum and I feared you wouldn't make it, but she took good care of you, fought the devil himself to keep you alive." He smiled and chuckled. "Unlike Leora, who made herself known from the start." His smile faded. "Poor Sky worried us the most. We knew the problems she would face and were unsure how to help her. But your mum and I loved each one of you with…" He

220

shook his head. "I knew the time would come. I knew it. I told your mum that…" He shook his head. "No more talk. I am tired."

Cavell stepped forward. "I need to know what I am up against, Norris."

Her da stared at him as if lost for a moment before he spoke. "Your da wanted Leora for you, but I knew that was wrong. Elsie was the one for you."

"Why did Warrand visit with you?" Cavell asked, hoping a different question might get some results and lead to some answers.

"Warrand was here? I missed his visit?" Norris asked, appearing confused. "Did he send me a message, or did I send him one? I don't recall. You see to what Warrand wants, Cavell. You are chieftain now and I am too tired to talk anymore. We will talk another time." He rolled on his side and pulled the blanket up over his shoulder and closed his eyes."

Cavell went to reach out to Norris, intending to get answers from the man, but his wife grabbed his hand, stopping him. She shook her head at him, got up, and walked to the door. Cavell followed, annoyed.

"We have to—"

"Shhh," she scolded as she closed the door. "It will do no good to batter him for answers. It is obvious he is confused and whatever he tells us may be worthless. We must catch him when he is more himself, only then we will get the truth from him. We talked about speaking to elders in the clan. I will see what I can learn from them."

"You are right," Cavell said reluctantly. He was used to getting what he wanted from people by force.

But they had been the enemy. Norris was not his enemy. He was his wife's da who she loved, and he needed to be treated with respect.

"We will speak with him again soon," Elsie said, and again Cavell reluctantly agreed.

The Great Hall was nearly empty when Cavell and Elsie entered it. Most had gone off to see to their daily chores. Laurel and her children had left, Alda telling Elsie that the woman was relieved to learn they were not returning to the croft just yet, and she went with May to talk with her husband about anything they might need brought to the village.

Cavell caught his wife in an embrace when they stepped outside and kissed her lightly, enjoying the feel of her in his arms where he knew without a doubt she belonged. "I would prefer to spend the day in our bedchamber making up for the intimate time we missed, but I must see to gathering some men that are skilled enough with a weapon to post as guards."

"We can rendezvous there later," she said in a conspiratorial whisper.

"I look forward to it," he whispered close to her lips, then kissed her again, though not lightly this time.

She rested her brow on his chest. "You leave me breathless and wanting."

He slipped his finger beneath her chin to lift it and seeing the passion swirling in her soft blue eyes, he almost deserted his duties to carry her off to their bedchamber. He wisely reminded himself that the clan needed protection.

"Anticipation will make our impending liaison even more pleasurable."

"You best watch out. I may come find you not too long from now and drag you to our bedchamber," she cautioned playfully.

He kissed her quickly and warned teasingly. "Not if I find you first."

He stepped away from her and hurried off, afraid he would surrender to the desire that surged through him for his wife.

Elsie stood with her eyes on her husband, hoping it would not be long before he came in search of her. She shook her head. She could not remain lost in thoughts of rendezvousing with him if she was to get anything done. And the first thing she intended to do was to speak with some of the elders in the clan.

Her da was an honorable man, a man of his word. When he made a promise, he kept it. He had mentioned repeatedly how he had promised his wife he would keep their daughters safe, but had he also promised to keep a secret? Was he purposely avoiding answering their queries to do just that—keep a secret?

She was determined to find out the truth behind the need to keep her sisters and her safe. Then she could confront her da with it and he could confirm it without breaking a promise to his wife.

Elsie knew who she would speak to first and she smiled when she found the elderly woman sitting on a bench outside her cottage, stitching a small garment.

"Do you have news, Mab, that you are not telling us about?" Elsie asked with a chuckle as she pointed to the garment fit for a bairn.

"You are pretty when you smile, and you laugh more recently and so does your husband. You are good for each other," Mab said and held up the garment. "After taking one look at your virile husband, I know it won't be long before you are with child, so I got started right away on a garment for him or her, whichever you are blessed with."

Elsie sat beside Mab on the bench, surprised to hear the woman call her pretty.

"I am glad you smile more often now and that you take the time to talk with others. You have always been far too serious, too busy to talk, too busy taking on chores that your da should have seen to. You were more chieftain of this clan than he was, if you don't mind me saying so, mistress."

Elsie chuckled again. "Have you ever held your tongue, Mab?"

The old woman grinned. "I had my moments, few, but I had them."

Elsie laughed and gave thought to Mab's remark. Had she avoided people while thinking people avoided her? Had she hid away in plain sight? Had she allowed her plain features to rule her choices?

Mab continued stitching while she talked. "My first husband, Norman, let me know fast enough he would not tolerate my opinions—obey or else. I felt the back of his hand far too many times before I got wise and held my tongue in front of him. I can't say I was sorry when he died of a fever caused by a wound he would not let me or the healer tend. We were barely wed two years and I miscarried two bairns within that time. I was more careful in finding my second husband." She smiled. "I found out what it meant to be truly loved when I met and wed William. We had a good life together and I still miss him. But he gave me three great sons and they gave me a bunch of grandchildren and I even have great-grandchildren now."

Elsie listened, amazed she never knew that about Mab. She would acknowledge the woman with a nod now and again, but she had never taken the time to talk with her. Not so, Leora. She had spoken to everyone, and she probably knew all about Mab's two husbands and great-grandchildren.

What was it Leora used to say to her? "Stop hiding, Elsie, and be you."

Mab went on talking and Elsie went on listening, enthralled with talk of Mab's life, laughing at some and shedding a tear with her at other times. It was when she mentioned the wonderful midwife who delivered all three of her sons that Elsie recalled her reason for wanting to talk with Mab.

"Did that same midwife deliver me and my sisters?"

Mab shook her head. "Nay. Your mum didn't deliver any of you lasses here at home." She smiled softly. "The women always warned your mum not to travel after she learned she was with child since she always managed to get stuck where she was and delivered the bairn away from home."

That news caught Elsie by surprise.

"Though she did suffer those two miscarriages here at home."

"My mum had two miscarriages?" Elsie asked, not having known that.

"Aye, before you were born."

225

"So, none of us, not me, Leora, or Sky were born here at home?" Elsie asked, finding it odd not one of them had been born here.

"Not one of you and truthfully, you could barely tell when your mum was with child. All of us were envious that she carried small, not like most of us who were huge when with child."

"Do you know where I was born or either of my sisters?"

Mab stopped stitching and gave it thought. "I'm sorry but I don't recall. Your mum never made mention of it to you?"

"She talked of the deliveries but never mentioned where they took place. I assumed it was here."

Mab smiled. "Not important where, more important she had good care, and you lasses arrived here in great shape. That is what every woman prays for, a safe delivery for mum and bairn."

"I will visit with you again," Elsie said when ready to take her leave.

"I would very much like that, Mistress Elsie," Mab said, tears catching in her aged eyes. "You are a good daughter for wedding a Gallowglass warrior. We all feared he would not treat you well and we did not want that for you. I am glad Chieftain Cavell is an honorable man."

Elsie beamed with pride. "He is an honorable man and I love him with all my heart."

Mab grinned. "That is obvious with the way you look at him and I am glad he looks the same way at you."

Elsie felt guilty as she continued through the village. She should not feel so joyful with Leora missing and Sky in the clutches of Slayer and everything else that was going on, but she overflowed with joy whether it was right of her to do so or not.

It was odd but she felt as if she had just fully opened her eyes to the world, allowed herself to see it differently and it was all because she didn't let her doubts and fears stop her. Even when they crept up to poke at her, she had stayed strong. Perhaps Leora was right. Perhaps she had been hiding—hiding from herself.

Elsie let out a gasp when she was swept off her feet and into a tight embrace.

"You are all mine now, wife."

Elsie grinned in anticipation.

Chapter Nineteen

They rushed to the keep hand in hand, Cavell scooping her up in his arms once in the Great Hall. Some servants smiled and others giggled watching their chieftain and his wife head for the stairs and whispers of Mistress Elsie getting with child soon circled the room.

Cavell gave no thought to anything but his wife and he hurried up the stairs with her tucked in his arms. He hadn't been able to get her out of his mind since they had spoken of a rendezvous. His thoughts grew to a craving that had been difficult to ignore until he finally surrendered to the gnawing hunger for his wife.

"I want you naked," he whispered in her ear, then nipped along it with his teeth.

Elsie shivered, his playful nips sending gooseflesh rushing over her and igniting her passion that had simmered since they had parted.

"I love seeing every inch of you naked," he said, pushing the door to their bedchamber open with his shoulder.

She chuckled and hugged his neck, admitting something she never expected to enjoy. "I like seeing you naked as well."

Cavell kicked the door shut with his foot, then nuzzled near her car. "I have a premonition that we will be naked often."

He set her on her feet, and they hurried out of their garments, and she barely discarded the last of her garments when his hands landed on her waist, and he lifted her. Instinct had her wrapping her legs around his waist and her arms going around his neck, and when she did, his hands moved to cup her backside and his mouth settled on her lips in a hungry kiss.

Her husband had kissed her many times but there was something different about this kiss, a deeper connection of sorts, as if they became one, and an intoxicating mix of emotions ran through her sending her desire spiraling.

The kiss heated, turning more demanding, and suddenly she was shoved against the wall as her husband tore his mouth away from hers, leaving her breathless.

"I am far too hungry for you, wife," he said through labored breaths.

"Not as hungry as I am for you," she said and cupped his face in her hands. "Take me now, husband, or I will be spent before you slip into me."

Cavell dropped his brow to rest against hers and warned with a growl deep in his throat. "I will ride you hard."

"Stop teasing me and do it," she urged.

He swung around away from the wall and carried her to the bed and dropped her down on it. "On your knees," he ordered and flipped her over to slip his arm under her waist and pull her onto her knees.

He positioned himself behind her, grabbing hold of her backside as he slipped easily into her wet, tight sheath, and her groan of pleasure joined his own. He moved slow at first, but not for long, his need and her own too great to linger. He plunged into her hard and fast and he saw her grip the bedding to keep herself as steady as possible as her moans grew with his every thrust.

He held his pleasure at bay wanting them both to linger in it, let the depths of their pleasure sink deeper so that their climax would be that more powerful.

Elsie squeezed her eyes shut tight and gripped even tighter to the bedding as she groaned from the pleasure of his hard plunges. Good Lord, but it felt good, far too good for it to end too soon.

The feel and sound of flesh slapping against flesh intensified the senses as did his fingers digging into her backside as he held her firmly. His strength alone was intoxicating but it was the power of his thrusts driving her closer and closer—she cried out his name, letting him know she was close, so close.

He increased his rhythm just enough to send her over the edge and explode with pure passion and she enjoyed it even more when she heard him roar in satisfaction. She loved that he continued to thrust into her to get every last ounce of pleasure he could for them both since it caused her to climax again, not as hard but just as pleasurable.

Cavell dropped his head back with one last forceful groan and eased his grip on his wife's backside. Then he slipped gently out of her, and she collapsed down on the bed. He stretched out beside her, tugging her on her side to rest against him.

"You are all right, aren't you? I didn't hurt you, did I?" he asked softly near her ear.

"You tortured me with immense pleasure," she said with a chuckle. "And I loved every moment of it."

"Then I shall torture you more often," he said relieved, and kissed her warm cheek.

"I will have your word on that, husband," she demanded with a soft laugh.

"You have it, wife," he said, feeling a happiness he never thought possible but was so grateful to have found with her. And to think he had not wanted to remain wed to her. "I will be forever grateful that you pursued me and trapped me in this marriage or else I would have lost the best, most loving wife a man could ever hope for."

Elsie turned to face him with a slight frown in her brow. "You don't feel trapped anymore, do you?"

"We both stayed wed of our own choosing, neither of us are trapped, but," —he grinned playfully— "if I had to be trapped I would want it to be with you."

"Likewise," she said and shivered.

"Your chilled," he said and hurried a blanket over them.

231

"We should return to our duties," she said, though she did not want to leave her husband's strong arms.

"The only duty you have right now is here with your husband," he said as if it was a command.

She smiled. "Aye, husband."

"A good, obedient wife, I like that."

"That reminds me," she said excitedly, snuggling against her husband, and proceeded to tell him about her talk with Mab.

He tapped her nose gently. "You, wife, will not be traveling anywhere when you are with child," Cavell ordered, his thought only of her and their bairn's safety. "And how could your da let her travel when she was with child? And how odd that not one out of the three of you and your sisters were born here at home."

"That was my thought," she agreed. "I mean, I could see one possible delivery away from home, but all three doesn't seem likely."

"And it has you wondering," he said, seeing curiosity swirl in her soft blue eyes. "What are you thinking, wife?"

"I don't know, but something is amiss."

He caressed the spot between her eyes when it narrowed in concentration. "Maybe your da could explain it to you."

"Can he?' she questioned. "Or is it part of the secret he keeps from us? And I wonder if he wants us to discover the secret so that he does not break his promise to my mum."

"I can understand that, for I would not break a promise I made to you."

"I would want you to if it meant it would help someone," she said.

"But not if it was meant to harm and with your da worried for you and your sisters' safety then to break this promise could bring harm to those he loves."

"I am going to talk to a few more elders and see what they know of my mum's travels while with child and see if I can piece this puzzle together. If I at least get close to solving it, my da will have no choice but to confirm what I know, allowing him to keep his promise."

"A wise choice," Cavell agreed, wondering how anyone could have thought his wife insane. She was an intelligent woman possessing the skill of numbers and dedicating herself to overseeing the clan, which left her little time for anything else. She did more for others than she did for herself.

"You will not wait long to send word to Slayer, will you?" she asked anxiously.

"You want word on your sister, don't you?"

"I worry about Sky every day. I need to know she is safe and not in harm's way."

"I will have Melvin take a message to Slayer soon and request word on Sky," he assured her.

Her brow shot up. "Request?"

"No one ever, not ever, demands anything from Slayer, or you will learn a difficult lesson," Cavell warned. "I will make sure Melvin tells Slayer how worried you are about your sister. I am sure he will allow her to send a message to you."

***

It wasn't until the next day that Elsie got to speak with another elder in the clan and she laughed at Clara's tales of when she was young, finding them amusing and interesting.

"Stubborn is what my da called me. Persistent was my mum's name for me. I was forever getting into something, my da would say, whereas I believed them to be adventures. My da worried I would never meet a man who could tame me." Clara laughed. "Luckily, I met a man I could tame." She lowered her voice. "Every time he went to admonish me, I kissed him which, of course, led to other things. Never had a problem with him." She laughed again, her full cheeks dusting a gentle red. "It wasn't until years later when age withered us both that my Walter confessed that it hadn't taken him long to realize that I was distracting him on purpose. Instead of telling me, he used it to his advantage. It is no wonder we had nine children."

Elsie laughed again, had hardly stopped laughing since sitting to talk with Clara.

"I owe my good marriage to your mum," Clara said with a soft smile, "God bless her. It is because of her I realized how a husband needed to be treated if I wasn't prone to obedience."

"How so?" Elsie asked curiously.

"I came upon your mum and da and heard them arguing. Actually, they weren't arguing, it was your da who was angry. No one ever saw or heard your da angry with your mum… until me. They didn't see me, and I was young and curious, so I listened. Your mum handled your da in a similar manner. She remained so clam and spoke gently to him, then she kissed him and took his hand and with a smile led him to the keep. Your da went willingly and with a smile. Your mum was a good and kind soul, bless her."

Elsie was careful how she worded her question. "Do you recall what they argued about? I am curious since I never heard them argue."

Clara's brow puckered, giving it thought, then she smiled so wide you could see she was missing a tooth. "Your da said not again, Terena. Something like… I worry what will happen and your mum said he need not worry all would be well, but your da insisted it was dangerous and that it was the last time she would do this. Later I realized he must have been talking about her traveling when she was with child, for sure enough, she returned home with Sky and never had another bairn again."

"Traveling after giving birth could not be easy for either mum or bairn," Elsie said, hoping Clara might say more that would help.

"The women all talked and worried when she arrived home with Sky. Your mum was pale and your da so concerned, and Sky only hours old. Your mum had to have delivered on the road home. But when we finally saw Sky, we understood why they were upset, God bless the sweet bairn. Such a curse for a child to carry. But you and Leora protect her just as your mum did, good sisters that you are. You are a good woman, Mistress Elsie," Clara said. "And we are all proud of you."

Elsie's mind was churning when she left Clara and she could not believe what she was thinking, did not

235

want to have such unbelievable thoughts, but after hearing what Clara said, it could be possible and it certainly would be a secret her da and mum would keep for the safety of their daughters. She had to find her husband and speak with him about this.

When she spotted May, she hurried to her and asked, "Have you seen Cavell?"

"I haven't seen him," May said. "Is something wrong? You look upset or are you not feeling well?"

This was something she would not share with anyone but her husband, so it was easier to allow May to believe she was feeling ill rather than upset.

She pressed her hand to her stomach. "A roiling stomach and I wondered if Cavell felt the same since we both ate the quail eggs this morning."

May's eyes brightened. "Or perhaps it could be something else. Have you missed your monthly bleed?"

Elsie went to shake her head and stopped.

"You are not sure, are you?" May asked when Elsie remained silent.

"It is at least a week away," Elsie said, having gotten accustomed to keeping track of it since she first got her monthly bleed.

Leora had warned her that if she did not bleed monthly, then it meant she carried a bairn. It was not until she learned how a bairn got inside of a woman that she stopped worrying that she would round with child. She had gotten so used to keeping track of it that she continued to do so. She thought Leora had purposely made her worry but when she mentioned how a woman got with a child to Leora, her sister had cringed and insisted she would never have children since she would never do something so disgusting as allowing a man to stick his shaft inside her.

"You could be showing early signs of being with child," May said low so no one could hear. "Do you know if your mum showed early signs? Sometimes daughters follow as their mums did."

"I don't recall her ever mentioning it," Elsie said and with what Clara had said, her thought took on new concerns.

"I can give you a brew to calm it," May offered.

Elsie shook her head. "It does not bother me that much."

May smiled. "It would be wonderful news to hear. Let me know if you continue to feel unwell and I will see you get that brew to help you."

Elsie walked away, her mind in more turmoil. She wasn't in a rush to speak with her husband any longer. She preferred a bit of time alone to think and perhaps make more sense of what Clara had told her. She went to her favorite spot behind the keep to sit under a large spruce, its bottom branches spreading wide creating a lovely canopy.

How did she make sense of what she was thinking? Could it even be possible? And if it was, why had her parents done such a thing? Question after question swirled in her head and it wasn't until she felt a raindrop hit her that she looked to see it was raining and had been for a while, the ground beyond the spreading spruce branches quite wet. She had been sitting there longer than she intended and she hurried to her feet and to rush into the keep and to the Great Hall to find her husband.

"WHERE HAVE YOU BEEN?"

Elsie jumped, startled at her husband's bellowing voice when she entered the Great Hall.

He was in front of her before she could speak. His hand latched onto her arm, and he rushed her straight to his solar.

He swung her around to face him after he slammed the door shut. "Do not EVER—EVER—disappear like that again. I was mad with worry about you, especially after speaking with May.

"I am not sure yet that I am with child," she assured him.

"What?" he asked, his eyes spreading wide in shock.

She bit her tongue, though she should have bitten it before the words slipped out. And she should have known May would not have said anything since it was for Elsie to tell her husband when the time came.

"Are you with child?" he asked, shaking his head. "May said you had an uneasy stomach and was concerned that I might have one too since we both ate the quail—" He shook his head again and repeated the question. "Are you with child?"

"May suggested I might be, but my stomach is not uneasy. She asked if I was upset or feeling ill when she saw me, and it was easier to admit feeling ill than to tell her why I was upset."

Cavell moved his hand off her arm to rest it at her waist. "You will tell me why you are upset, but first—"

"I do not know yet if I am with child and I won't know for at least a few weeks. You can rest assured that you will know before anyone else does, husband."

238

He lowered his brow to rest against hers. "It would be most welcoming news, wife, but I warn you, nay, I beg you NEVER again put me through the heart-wrenching fear I suffered when I could not find you after speaking with May. I imagined a litany of horrible scenarios of what might have happened to you, and I was ready to battle the devil himself to find you."

"I am so sorry to have caused you such torment," she said, for she would have felt the same if she had been unable to find him. "I got lost in my thoughts and when I do I go to a spot I have gone to since I was young to think." Seeing his eyes turn more attentive, she told him what she knew he wanted to know. "I go and sit under the large spruce behind the keep."

She felt his whole body lose its rigidness as he stepped closer to her and eased her to rest against him.

"Thank you for sharing your secret thinking spot with me. I will know to look there but I will not disturb you."

"I do not mind if you disturb me. I had gone there before coming to talk with you about something I learned that upset me and it might be nothing and yet I think it is something."

"You will sit, and we will talk," he said, hearing how upset she had gotten.

Elsie grabbed his arm, fright filling her eyes. "I don't know if I am who I think I am."

Chapter Twenty

After walking with his wife to a chair and seeing her seated comfortably, Cavell filled a goblet with wine and handed it to her. "Drink."

Elsie took a few sips, her mind churning, and placed the goblet on the table beside the chair, then reached out and took hold of her husband's hand, glad he had moved a bench in front of her to sit and repeated what Clara had told her about her parents.

She sighed heavily and shook her head not believing what she was about to say. "I think the secret my da promised to keep might be that my sisters and I are not my da and mum's true daughters. It makes me think that my mum traveled to who knows where to take newborn bairns who were not wanted or whose birth could cause someone a problem. Hence, the reason my sisters and I could be in danger after all these years or at least one of us."

While he did not want to believe it, his wife's assumption of what the elderly woman had told her made sense. It also made for a far worse situation. If someone of any power or influence discovered the birth of a child that could put his power in jeopardy, or she could be used to his benefit, the person would stop at nothing to find her.

"What do you think?" she asked when her husband remained silent.

"I agree what you think makes sense and that it could possibly make for an extremely dangerous situation."

"Do you think it could be why Slayer took Sky?"

Cavell thought a moment. "I don't think so. Knowing we wed, he would have never kept such revealing information from me. He would have told me that you were possibly in danger. It is something he must be made aware of since he has Sky."

"Oh God, what of Leora? We have no idea where she is. Someone may have taken her," Elsie said, fear causing her hands to tremble.

Cavell reached out and took his wife's hands in his. "We will find Leora. First, we need to speak with your da and confirm what we suspect. Then I will send Melvin with a message to Slayer and ask for help from the Gallowglass in finding Leora."

Elsie leaned forward to kiss her husband gently. "I don't know what I would do if you were not here to help me."

Cavell smiled. "You hunted me down by yourself. I do not think anything would stop you from finding your sisters. You are a courageous, determined woman, Elsie."

"I am only finding my courage, finding myself, and you have helped me with that."

"You have helped me more, wife," he said. "You stopped me from drowning in my own self-pity and loved me in spite of the arse I was when we met."

She laughed. "But it all worked out well since I love you arse and all."

He laughed as he took her in his arms and hugged her tightly. "And I love you and I particularly love your arse."

They lingered in the moment of levity, both aware of what was to come, though Cavell wished it could be different. His wife and her sisters had suffered enough, but he feared their suffering was about to get worse.

"We cannot wait to talk with your da," Cavell said, releasing his wife reluctantly.

"I know and this time he will have no choice but to speak the truth."

***

Elsie stood beside her da's bed, her husband standing next to her and her hand clinging tightly to his as she repeated what Clara had told her. Once done, she said, "I have a thought, Da, that since you made a promise to Mum never to reveal the truth it would not stop you from confirming the truth if found out. So, Da, I believe the promise you made to Mum was to never reveal that Leora, Sky, and I are not your true daughters. That Mum conveniently made all believe that she gave birth on planned trips you made to rescue unwanted bairns."

242

Norris sighed as if a huge burden had been lifted off him and he pushed himself up to sit straighter in bed as if he had suddenly regained his strength.

"You and your sis—the other two lasses were not unwanted. Your mum and I loved and continue to love the three of you as if you were our own and to us, you are our own. Your mum was heartbroken when she miscarried twice and then never got with child again. The old healer we had at the time told your mum about unwanted bairns and the horror some of them suffered. Your mum insisted we do something and so the healer informed us when a bairn in need was to be born. Your mum stitched a pouch to wear so she would appear she was with child, and we planned to travel when she was close to delivery.

"What Clara heard was me telling your mum that the third bairn, Sky, would be the last one. Our healer warned us that the midwife who delivered the bairns would no longer continue to do so and that another midwife had been discovered doing the same and she had been hanged. Sky was the last delivery the woman made. Besides, we could not continue to pretend to travel while your mum was with child." He stretched his hand out to Elsie. "Forgive me, Elsie, but I could not break the promise I made to your mum, and I feared if the three of you learned the truth, you would hate me for it and the thought my daughters would no longer love me tore at my heart. So, I kept my promise and kept my tongue silent."

Elsie left her husband's side to take her da's hand and sit beside him on the bed. "I could never stop loving you, Da, and I love you and Mum even more for saving me and I know Leora and Sky would feel the same. We will always love you, Da, no matter what." She hugged him and was glad to feel his arms close with some strength around her.

"Do you know by chance who the parents are or anyone who may know?" Cavell asked.

"Nay. My wife and I were given no information about the bairns other than they were not wanted and to be truthful, neither my wife nor I wanted to know. We thought it better that way. Though I wondered often if the midwife knew."

"Did you ever ask her?" Elsie asked.

Norris shook his head. "I never met her. The bairns were handed to me and your mum by a stranger who barely spoke to us."

"What happened that made you fear for your daughters' safety?" Cavell asked, eager to learn more and was taken by surprise by Norris's response.

"Your father, Lord Philip," Norris said, wiping a few tears from his eyes after his daughter left his arms. "Not that he knew what he was revealing. I wasn't even sure of it myself. He came here wanting to arrange a marriage between you and Leora. He believed it was wise to see our clans joined since our lands border each other. He referred to hearing about a group of mercenaries scouring the Highlands in search of a female child born around twenty years ago. He knew nothing of the person looking for this woman or why the person wanted her found. He only knew the mercenaries were determined to find her and they were letting no one stand in their way. I did not believe it was anything more than coincidence and whether I believed it or not, I could not take a chance. Clan Murdock is no match for a group of mercenaries. I needed to keep my daughters safe, and my only choice was to wed them to strong warriors who could protect them."

"You planned to find husbands for Leora and Sky and never mentioned it to them or to me?" Elsie asked, clearly upset that her da did not discuss it with her or her sisters. Though he probably knew they would all object, at least to a marriage for Sky.

"I had no time to think it over, much less plan. When Cavell's father talked with me about an arranged marriage, he pointed out to me that Cavell was Gallowglass and people feared the amazing strength and remarkable skill of the Gallowglass. That was what I needed to keep my daughters and my clan safe. It was not an easy decision to make but a necessary one."

Elsie tilted her head, her brow narrowing as she looked at her da. "Are you saying that my marriage to Cavell was not the only marriage arranged? That you agreed to marriages for Leora and Sky as well?"

Her da glanced away for a moment as if not able to look at his daughter.

"Da, look at me!" Elsie demanded, fear taking hold of her for what her da may have done. "Are my sisters wed?"

Norris turned to look at his daughter, nodding his head. "I had no choice. They are safe now. When I contacted Lord Bannaty about a marriage for Leora and one for Sky to a Gallowglass warrior, he was more than agreeable. Warrand arrived here with documents, and I signed them."

"You wed Leora to Warrand?" Cavell asked.

"Heaven forbid, he is too kind of a soul to straddle him with Leora," Norris said, startled by the suggestion. "Warrand wanted Sky, but he assured me the Gallowglass warrior he had chosen, Ingeuus, would make Leora a good husband."

Elsie's hand went to rest on her chest in a senseless effort to calm her racing heart. "Da, don't you recall me telling you that Lord Bannaty and Warrand are dead?"

"I thought I dreamt you told me that? It is true? Where is Sky?" Norris looked anxiously at Cavell. "You must go and get Sky from the abbey. Today!"

"Slayer took Sky from the abbey, Da," Elsie said, her worry for her sisters raging.

Norris sighed in relief. "That is good. He protects his brother's widow."

"Slayer would definitely make sure his brother's widow was protected. He will let nothing happen to her," Cavell said, and braced his hand on his wife's shoulder, offering her comfort and reminding her that he was there beside her. "Sky is safe with Slayer."

Elsie calmed knowing now why Slayer had taken Sky and that she was safe with him. But eventually, when all was settled, she would see Sky brought home.

"Has Leora been united with her husband yet?" Norris asked. "I half expect her to arrive home refusing to honor the marriage arrangement."

"You told her nothing about the marriage, Da?" Elsie asked.

"What do you think her response would have been?"

Knowing Leora, Elsie laughed.

"Precisely what she would have done right to my face… laughed." Norris shook his head slowly. "I had to get her wed. I had no choice. I had to protect her. Warrand assured me there was no better Gallowglass warrior than Ingeuus for Leora. Your sister has no choice but to find her way with her husband. So, did he retrieve her from the abbey yet?"

Elsie was left no choice but to tell her da the truth. "Leora is missing, Da."

Norris bolted forward. "What? What do you mean she's missing? What happened to her?"

"It is time he knows everything, Elsie," Cavell encouraged.

Elsie started with her sisters and their arrival at the abbey, ending with the burning of the abbey and the deaths of all there. She did not mention Edith, now Ann, being the only one to survive.

Her da glared at her in disbelief. "Good God, what have I done to my daughters? I would have never sent you there if I—"

"We never thought that, Da, not me, Leora, or Sky," Elsie assured him, the hurt in his eyes undeniable.

"Oh God, what they must have done to Sky," he said, tears rapidly welling in his eyes.

When Elsie remained silent, Cavell spoke up. "They kept her chained to a wall and a hood over her head. If I had been made aware of the situation, which I should have been, I would have gotten her out of there."

"Why didn't Elsie tell you when you fetched her from the abbey?" Norris asked confused.

Cavell left his wife to answer her father.

"I wasn't there. Thinking no one would come to help us, I escaped and went looking for Cavell to help me free Leora and Sky," Elsie said, a sense of guilt striking her. "If I had only stayed there, we would all be safe by now."

Surprisingly, it was her da who came to her defense. "Nonsense, Elsie. You believed you had no other choice. You did what you had to do."

Elsie realized then that her da must have felt the same when learning she and her sisters could be in danger.

"And more importantly," her da said, "you succeeded. You found your husband and brought him home and he will help bring your sisters home, for whether you share the same blood or not you are sisters of the heart and always will be."

"You are right about that, Da," Elsie said, tears she had been fighting close to spilling. "Leora and Sky will always be my sisters and you will always be our da."

"That I will be," Norris said shedding more tears.

Elsie was quick to hug him, and he was quick to return the hug. His hug lacked the strength it had only a short time ago and she realized how much their talk had cost him.

"You need to rest, Da. We can talk more another time," Elsie said.

"But Leora, we need to find her," her da said, his voice trembling with worry.

"I will see to it, Norris. You have my word," Cavell said.

Elsie was as relieved as her da when he dropped back against his pillows, his head sinking into them.

"I will keep you apprised of all we learn, Da," Elsie assured him.

"I know you will, Elsie. You are the strongest of your sisters and the wisest, though I wonder if Sky is wiser than she lets people know. I am glad Slayer looks after her until we can bring her home. And I am glad that I chose wisely for a husband for you."

"As am I, Da, for I love Cavell with all my heart," she confessed with a soft smile.

"And I love her," Cavell said, his strong voice booming in the room.

"I am relieved I did well for you, Elsie," her da said, fighting to keep his eyes open. "I only pray I did the same for your sisters."

"Sleep, rest, and worry not, Da, Cavell and I will see to Leora's and Sky's safety."

Cavell took hold of his wife's shoulders to bring her to her feet. "He will sleep well knowing he is no longer alone in this."

Elsie leaned into her husband, and she let herself rest against him, relieved when his arm went around her and kept her snug against him as they left the room. He settled her in his solar, having a hot brew brought for them both and sat in the chair next to her after adding more logs to the fire to chase the chill from the room.

Cavell did not wait. He delivered the news he was sure his wife wanted to hear quickly. "I know who your sister was wed to."

Chapter Twenty-one

Elsie thought repeatedly of the conversation concerning her sister's husband that she had had with Cavell several days ago.

"Ingeuus is Latin for Noble. Leora is wed to the fiercest of Slayer's Gallowglass warriors and his best tracker. He follows Slayer's commands without question and Noble expects obedience from all he commands, and no one dares do otherwise. He will find Leora… of that I have no doubt."

Her response to her husband upon hearing that had been, "You do not know my sister."

His response had continued to worry her. "Noble is an honorable man but also a rigid one. It is why his troop of men is an elite troop within the Gallowglass. His warriors obey him, and he will expect the same from his wife. And I can tell you now that Noble is a decisive man. He will not take his commitment to the marriage lightly. He entered it with all intentions of keeping Leora as his wife."

Elsie worried Leora would not accept the fierce Highlander as her husband, let alone get along with him. Leora did not do well being dictated to. She had a mind of her own, a strong one, and had often done as she pleased, to the worry of her da and mum, since she had been young.

Right now, Elsie only cared that her sister was found safe. What would become of the marriage she had no idea, and it was not for her to decide. Though presently, with her and her sisters' lives being in possible danger, she hoped Leora would think wisely about the marriage.

She pushed the recurring thoughts from her head and continued keeping a fast pace through the village. Melvin was leaving today to go and speak with Slayer, and she wanted to make sure he remembered the message correctly she had told him to deliver to Sky.

Elsie smiled when she spotted her husband standing beside Melvin not far from the keep where the lad Rory waited with Melvin's horse. That her husband was growing more handsome by the day was undeniable. The honey had worked well on his scars. In a few weeks many would fade away to be seen no more and the deeper ones would no longer look as angry, though some scars would remain but none that would rob him of his fine features.

Her smile grew when he spotted her and he stretched his arm out to her, and she hurried to him to be caught in a snug embrace.

She turned to Melvin, and he raised his hand. "You do not have to repeat the message to me for the hundredth time. I will make sure I deliver every word of it to your sister Sky and return with one from her."

"Bless you, Melvin. I so appreciate it," Elsie said.

"Have you the healing pouch I prepared for you if you should need it?" May asked as she hurried toward Melvin.

Melvin turned. "I do and you need not worry that I will need it."

"Do not be stubborn," she chided. "You never know what may happen."

"I am a skilled warrior, I know what I do," Melvin argued.

"It is better to be cautious than stubborn," May snapped.

"At least I will not have to listen to your endless harping while I am gone."

"And I will no longer waste time harping at you for being foolish," May shot back and walked away.

Melvin turned, shaking his head as he gazed at the ground. "She is impossible so why am I going to miss her?"

"I am going to miss you too, you impossible fool," May shouted.

Melvin's head shot up. "How did she hear that?"

"You speak louder than you think, and I have exceptional hearing," May called out as she kept walking.

"She drives me crazy," Melvin said, looking to Cavell.

"Did you ever consider that you care for May, Melvin?"

"I am not sure what I feel for her," Melvin said confused. "She frustrates me and yet I enjoy being with her, even arguing with her."

252

"You said you will miss her. That tells you something," Cavell said. "Go speak with her, for you leave shortly and your chance will be gone, and you may regret it."

Melvin turned and rushed off. "May! Wait! I want to talk with you."

Elsie was grinning when her husband's glance fell on her, and he quickly pressed his finger to her lips.

"I do not want to hear you were right about them," he ordered with a tap to her lips.

She chuckled. "There is no need for me to tell you what you already know."

He squished her tightly against him and laughed. "That I have a brilliant wife."

Shouts suddenly filled the air, people began grabbing weapons, and someone shouted, "A troop rides on the village."

"Get in the keep!" Cavell ordered, pushing his wife toward it, and letting several oaths fly when he reached for his sword at his waist, and it wasn't there.

"I will fetch your sword," Elsie called out, knowing exactly where it was, and ran into the keep, her husband's warning to once again remain in the keep barely reaching her ears.

She ran up the stairs, blaming herself for his lack of a weapon since she had kept him in bed extra long this morning with a need that required extra time, not that he complained about it. He was only too happy to satisfy her and himself. But then they hurried to dress, having taken too much time, and his sword had been forgotten. She grabbed the sword, struggling with its weight and hurried as best she could down the stairs.

253

Elsie's heart pounded a furious beat when she saw women and children rushing into the Great Hall as she entered.

The young lass, Kara, was clinging to her mum crying and other bairns clung to their mums sobbing as well.

"Is the kitchen secure, Alda?" she called out, seeing the woman and several servants trying to calm the bairns.

"Aye, mistress. No one can enter there," Alda assured her.

Elsie went straight for the door.

"Don't go out there, mistress," Kara's mum warned, and other women joined in the warning.

Elsie paid them no heed. She needed to get her husband's weapon to him. He was defenseless without it. That's not what she saw when she ran out of the keep. She froze as she watched a warrior on a horse swing an axe at Cavell. Her husband was a blur, he stepped out of the way so quickly and just as quickly yanked the warrior off the horse. He wrestled the axe out of the warrior's hand and with one swing felled him.

"GET IN THE KEEP!" Cavell shouted at her and felled another warrior who descended on him.

Elsie felt helpless. She wanted to help but she was wise enough to realize her presence distracted her husband. She was about to go into the keep when she saw May struggling to get an injured clansman to the keep. She set the sword aside on the steps and hurried to help May. She got him up the stairs and left May to get him inside and rushed down the stairs to retrieve the sword and spotted Mab trying to make it through the fighting to the keep.

Again, she did not hesitate. She went to help the elderly woman. Seeing the fighting was centered in one area, Elsie turned Mab around and took a longer but safer path to the keep. As they approached the keep, her eyes went wide with fright. Her da stood on the bottom step, Cavell's sword gripped in his hand. At one time, her da could easily wield a sword, but seeing how he struggled to hold the weapon it was obvious he did not have the strength to fight.

May appeared at the top step and she waved her forward. May hurried to her to help Mab while Elsie ran to her da. She wasn't fast enough. A warrior descended on him easily knocking the sword from his hand and then his meaty fist grabbed him by his shirt and shook him.

Rage, hot and furious, had Elsie running straight for the warrior and as she got near, she heard him shout at her da.

"Which one is it? Which one? Tell me!"

Elsie launched herself at him when she was close enough. She landed on his back, her arms going around his neck, her fingers raking at his face then poking at his eyes to deliver whatever torment she could so he would release her da, and he did.

Unfortunately, she was no match for him. He reached back and grabbed her by the back of the neck and flung her off him, as if she was nothing more than an annoying gnat, to land hard on the ground. Her breath whooshed out of her, and she lay there trying to regain it.

The warrior's large hand came down on her to grab her by her tunic and launch her to her feet with such force that she felt the slam through her entire body.

"Tell me which one belongs to him, or I will collect all three," the warrior said, his eyes on her da. "And see the other two dead."

"I don't know. Please, I don't know, or I would tell you," her da pleaded frantically.

"Then I will collect all three," the warrior said. "And since you are useless to me…"

He was about to raise his axe when Elsie was suddenly ripped out of his grasp and tossed to the side as her husband plowed into the warrior.

When she regained her wits, she wobbled to her da, still dazed from the two falls, and they huddled together as they watched Cavell fight the warrior. It did not take long. Once the two men got to their feet, it took little time for Cavell to snap the man's neck and have him fall at his feet.

Cavell descended on his wife with a fury that had her da trying to step in front of her.

"Don't make me push you out of the way, Norris," he threatened with a growl and her da wisely stepped aside.

Cavell's fury turned worse when he saw his wife's tunic had been ripped down the center and along with it part of her shift, leaving one of her breasts partially exposed.

He yanked the pieces together in one hand and fought to contain his temper as he commanded. "Get in the keep and so help me God stay there! No matter what, stay there!"

"Aye, husband," she said, placing her hand over his and feeling his grip ease.

"I cannot lose you, Elsie," he said as if explaining himself.

"Or I you," she said. "Stay safe and alive."

"Behind you!" her da called out.

Cavell was already turning, having heard someone approach rapidly, his body shielding his wife from the warrior running wildly toward him. Elsie had barely enough time to retrieve her husband's sword off the ground and Cavell grabbed it from her and greeted the stunned warrior with a sword through his gut.

Elsie rushed to wrap her arm around her da and hurry him up the stairs as fast as she could and once there, she turned to see her husband about to enter the fray once again and fear gripped her so tightly that her breath caught.

Her da said what she feared. "There are too many of them."

Tears welled in her eyes, fearing for her husband and fearing that her clan would fall today.

Suddenly vicious roars filled the air as another troop of warriors entered the village and her fear soared until… *Gallowglass*. The warriors were Gallowglass.

"Gallowglass!" her da cheered.

Elsie cheered with him and let her tears fall in relief.

"Listen to your husband, get inside," her da ordered.

"You as well, Da," she ordered, and they entered the Great Hall together.

257

Seeing Elsie's tears and gripping her torn garments, the other women looked at her with fright. She quickly reassured them, wiping the tears away and smiling. "Tears of joy. Gallowglass warriors have arrived to help us."

Shouts and cheers filled the room and bairns began to smile as their mums explained that all was well.

Elsie prayed that she or any of the women would not become a widow today as she raced up the stairs to change her garments, leaving her da in Ann's care. She changed her garments quickly and returned to the Great Hall.

She waited with the women, cringing along with them when the clash of swords turned louder and time seemed to go on forever. She feared as they did that things might have worsened for the clan, but she fought against the fear and kept reassuring them that all was well.

A sudden pounding on the door, had women clutching their bairns while others took up arms ready to defend.

"It's over! You are safe! Open up!" Melvin demanded and everyone cried out in relief.

Melvin glanced around quickly but May spotted him first and hurried to him.

"You're hurt," she said, seeing the blood on his face.

Melvin grabbed her wrist before she could touch his face. "We need help with the injured. Besides, the blood is not mine," Melvin said.

"And the dead?" one woman called out fearfully.

"None of ours only theirs, though there are wounded. Our clan fought well," Melvin announced proudly.

Cheers sounded and the women hurried from the keep with their children to find their husbands.

Elsie wanted to do the same but spoke with Alda first. "Food and drink, and sweets for the little ones, as much as you can prepare. All will need it, but first, let those with loved ones go see that they are well."

The servants who rushed from the room thanked her profusely as they hurried past her.

"Go and see your husband, Elsie," her da said.

"You should not have even given thought to entering the fight, Da," Elsie scolded, seeing he did not have the strength to protect himself.

"I will not die a coward in my bed. I will take up arms against anyone who dares to harm Clan Murdock whether I have the strength for it or not," her da argued. "Now go. Ann will look after me."

"Aye, that I will, worry not, Mistress Elsie," Ann assured her.

Elsie left the keep, relieved that her da would be well cared for and reached the village to see dead warriors being dragged away and the less seriously injured warriors being tended to by their loved ones and May tending to more serious wounds. Her search for her husband was delayed since she stopped to help those in need and when she saw Mab and Clara doing their best to herd the young ones together so their mums could help with the wounded, she hurried to them.

"Alda has sweets waiting," Elsie called out with a smile and nodded to the two older women.

"I'm going to get there first," Clara shouted and made ready to run.

The children squealed and took off running except Kara, she stood looking at Elsie a bit dazed.

Elsie went to her and bent down in front of her. "Are you all right, Kara?"

"I counted them," Kara said, nodding. "Twenty in the clan were wounded, twenty-five lay dead, many more ran away from what I heard said, and fifty warriors arrived and only five were injured."

Elsie could see the task Kara had set for herself had left her upset and the only way to help her was to set her to do a pleasant task.

Elsie stood and took the little lass's hand. "You did excellent, Kara, but I need you to do more counting for me. Can you do that?"

The little lass appeared hesitant, and Elsie understood she feared what the chore might be.

Elsie hurried to tell her. "I need you to count how many sweets the children, Clara, and Mab eat so that Alda will know how many more might be needed."

"I can do that," Kara said eagerly.

"Go with Clara," Elsie said with a nod to the older woman who had lingered behind, waiting for the lass. "And watch out for Clara, she likes her sweets and can be sneaky." Elsie chuckled and nodded to Clara.

Clara grinned, understanding Kara needed comfort and smiles.

"I will be watching you," Kara said, taking the older woman's hand to walk with her to the kitchen.

"But I am a sneaky one, you may not catch me," Clara teased playfully and the two walked off, Kara assuring Clara that she would know just how many sweets she ate.

Elsie turned and found her husband standing behind her, his sword still gripped in his hand, blood dripping from it and spatters of blood on his garments and a few on his face.

She stepped close to him, ready to wipe the blood off his face, but he grabbed her wrist to stop her.

"I don't want you marred by battle. I will see to it myself."

There was a softness in his eyes she hadn't expected after the battle but when he spoke, she understood why.

"You do well with bairns, speaking to them gently, understanding their needs," he said, releasing her wrist. "You will make a good mum to our children."

Elsie went to step closer again and he stepped away. "Nay, I will allow no remnants of battle to touch you."

"I need to touch you, feel you alive against me," she said, not understanding the overpowering need she felt for him.

"It is the threat of death that makes you need to feel alive, to know you survived, to know it is real," he said, having felt it himself many times but none so strongly as now that he had his wife. "Later I will show you how very much alive we both are."

"CAVELL!" came a powerful shout.

"I must speak with Eldon, the leader of the troop who came to our rescue," Cavell said. "See that drink and food is made ready for him and his warriors."

"It is already done," Elsie said, wanting desperately to at least hug her husband.

"I will see you in the keep," he said and turned to go and stopped to glance back at her. "Your da?"

"He suffered no harm."

Cavell nodded and turned away from her and she had to stop herself from running after him and hugging him tight. He was chieftain of the clan and he had responsibilities to see to, and as his wife, so did she.

She hurried to assist May in seeing to the injured. She sectioned off a portion of the Great Hall where the less seriously injured could be treated and could be free to partake in ale and food once done. Serious injuries were treated in the person's home where family could look after them.

Elsie did not see her husband again until what felt like endless hours later when he entered the Great Hall with a large man of a sizeable girth, the man who had shouted to Cavell when she had been talking with him.

Her husband had washed his face and the blood spatter had been washed off his garments as best as possible and his sword showed not a drop of blood. Curious to what the man had to say to her husband, she gravitated toward the two as they walked to the dais.

"You have an honorable clan, Cavell," Eldon said as they rounded the dais.

"That I do, Eldon," Cavell said and heard the chair creak as the large warrior dropped down on it in exhaustion.

A servant was quick to fill the tankard in front of Eldon and he drank it down by the time she finished filling Cavell's vessel. He held it out to her to fill again.

"Your visit could not be timelier or more appreciated, Eldon, but what brought you here to begin with?" Cavell asked.

"Clan Murdock was not my destination. Slayer sent me to find a rogue troop of warriors that may have been connected to his father and brother's deaths. I was to return the leader to him. They were the ones who brought me here." He chugged down more ale before he continued. "We found their tracks and followed them here. The idiots led us to their own demise. Unfortunately, the leader is among the dead, and Slayer is not going to be happy about that."

"No doubt your tracker is on the trail of a few that ran off when they realized victory would not be theirs today."

Eldon nodded. "Aye, he'll leave signs for us to follow. Slayer would not want me to leave you and your clan vulnerable. You are chieftain now, pledge fealty to him and he will send a troop of warriors to make their home here to help grow and strengthen your clan. It will also allow me to leave a few warriors here until others arrive. At least then you will not be so vulnerable to attack. Unless you intend to pledge fealty to your father's clan."

"Did Slayer assume that, or did he receive word of it?" Cavell asked.

"There is not much Slayer doesn't hear. You know as well as I do that he has eyes and ears all over the Highlands. I believe I know you well enough to know you would make the wisest decision for your clan and pledge your allegiance to the clan that would prove more beneficial to you."

"Or the clan that I trust more," Cavell said.

Eldon grinned. "Then it's Lord Slayer you pledge your fealty to."

"Aye, Clan Murdock pledges its allegiance to Lord Slayer of Clan Ravinsher," Cavell confirmed, not caring what his father would think.

Eldon stood, raising his tankard. "Clan Murdock pledges its allegiance to Lord Slayer and, of course, the Gallowglass!"

Cheers rang out and Elsie saw the relief on the faces of those in her clan. They now felt protected, something they had worried about ever since her da had taken ill.

Once the cheers settled and Eldon sat, Cavell said, "You will report back to Slayer once you have caught one or two of the mercenaries?"

"Aye, I will take them to Slayer and let him deal with them," Eldon confirmed. "It should take no more than a day, so we should be home in about three days' time."

"Melvin was about to leave for Clan Ravinsher with a message I have for Slayer. I would prefer he travel with you than alone and he can return with the troop Slayer sends me."

"Melvin is always welcome to travel with my troop. He is a skilled and fearless warrior."

"And better than you are with an axe," Melvin said, having neared the dais.

Eldon's bulk shook with laughter. "You never fail to praise yourself, Melvin."

Melvin grinned. "You mean I never fail to tell the truth."

"There is truth to that," Eldon said with respect. "Be ready to leave tomorrow at dawn."

The men got lost in talk of past battles and deeds and Elsie drifted off to leave them to talk, and having done what she could for the injured in the room, she left and went to see if May needed help.

It was several hours later when Elsie stepped out of the cottage with May. "It is night already?" She gave a hasty glance to the night sky, clouds hiding any signs of the stars.

"Time gets lost when tending serious injuries. Your only thought is on fighting to save the person, May said. "You have done enough. Go to the keep and rest."

"Heath will be all right, won't he? Brit is due to deliver their first bairn any day now," Elsie asked, worried for the young man and his wife.

"Heath is young and strong and with rest and care his wound will heal and he will do well," May said. "Now go and rest yourself. It will be a busy day tomorrow seeing to how the wounded are doing."

Elsie nodded and wished May a good evening and walked to the keep.

"You should not be walking alone at night."

Elsie jumped after having taken several steps, her hand hitting her chest in shock, the sudden voice from the darkness frightening her… until she realized who it was.

"You frightened me," she said, scolding her husband when he stepped out of the darkness in front of her.

"You were gone far too long from the keep and I am in far too much need to have you naked in my arms not to come look for you," he said, and his arm went around her waist to grip it firmly. "Time to retire for the night."

His lips found hers and his kiss spoke of his need and fired her own.

It took little time for them to reach their bedchamber and once inside, the door closed, locking everyone and thing away from them, Cavell ordered, "I will have you naked... now!"

Chapter Twenty-two

Elsie was about to toss the last of her garments aside when her husband's arm coiled around her waist and drew her back against his warm, naked body. His hand grabbed the garment from her and flung it away, then his mouth descended on the curve of her neck to nip and kiss and send gooseflesh rushing over her.

"Perfect. You are perfect in every way," he whispered between nips.

She gasped softly when his teeth nipped at her neck, sending more gooseflesh racing over her. But it was her husband telling her that she was perfect while standing naked in front of him that soared her love for him and fueled her passion. Though it also may have been the way his hand roamed over her, caressing her breasts and teasing her nipples with playful pinches before moving his intimate strokes along her stomach on his way to settle his fingers between her legs while continuing to feast teasingly on her neck.

"I have thought about touching you like this since the battle ended," he whispered and nipped at a sensitive spot on her neck that sent a sensuous shiver through her.

Another gasp of pleasure escaped her lips and when he slipped a finger inside her, she gasped louder.

She groaned, her passion building far too fast. "I will not last if you continue to pleasure me like that."

"Good. I want you to come like this and then I am going to toss you down on the bed and make you come again."

His words fired her desire along with his fingers as they teased, delved, and worked magic on her until, unable to stop it, her passion suddenly burst, and she cried out in release.

Still reeling from her climax, Cavell did as he said. He tossed her down on the bed, knelt between her legs, placing them over his shoulders, grabbed her by her bottom to lift her just enough to sink his rock-hard shaft deep into her wet sheath and had her crying out in pleasure.

He needed this, had needed it since the battle had ended. He needed to sink deep into her, feel her come alive to his touch, feel her love, and blend as one, always together as one.

He loved how she instinctively responded to the rhythm he set for them and at times demanded more from him like now. She could not get enough of him, nor could he get enough of her. She had woken something buried in him and he never felt as alive as he did with her when they made love.

He enjoyed watching his shaft penetrate her repeatedly, loved hearing her moan with pleasure, seeing the way her hands madly gripped the bedding, but most of all he loved looking into her soft blue eyes and seeing them hot with passion for him.

"Cavell!" she called out, desperately.

He kept firm hold of her backside as he quickened his pace, and it wasn't long before their passion exploded simultaneously as did their roars of pleasure that filled their bedchamber longer than usual.

Cavell reached for her hand when they finally lay side by side and wasn't surprised to find she was reaching for his. Marriage may have brought them together, but love was what joined them as one forever and the way their hands constantly sought each other's proved they never wanted to be parted.

"I love you, Elsie," he said, turning on his side to face her.

Elsie turned, her hand going to his face to stroke it gently. "Not as much as I love you."

"That is debatable," he argued playfully.

"What isn't debatable is that we love each other and that is all that matters."

"On that we agree," he said and kissed the palm of her hand.

He tucked her against him after pulling a blanket over them. No talk was needed, nor did Cavell want to talk, and he was glad his wife did not want to talk either. Right now, all both wanted was the comfort of each other's arms, and, to no surprise to Cavell, the exhausting day soon claimed them both in sleep.

***

Elsie sat beside her da's bed worried. Ever since the attack two days ago that her da had tried to participate in, he had lost strength and continued to do so.

"I am sorry, Elsie," her da said tearfully.

269

She took his hand. It barely had any strength to it. "Nonsense, Da, you have no reason to be sorry."

"I should have been stronger, protected you lasses better and now it's too late." A tear ran down his cheek.

"You did protect us," Elsie argued. "You wed me and Leora to strong warriors and Sky is safe being the widow of Slayer's brother. Worry not, Da, all will be well."

Her da tried to grip her hand but he was barely able to close his hand around hers. "Leave the past in the past. Don't open what should remain closed… forever." He closed his eyes. "I am tired, Elsie."

"Sleep, rest, and grow strong, Da," she said, placing his hand on his chest and pulling the blanket over it.

His eyes opened suddenly. "I love you and your sisters, Elsie, always remember that."

"And we love you, Da, and always will," Elsie said, feeling as if he needed to remind her one last time. She felt a hand on her shoulder and looked up to see Ann.

"I will sit with him, Mistress Elsie."

A terrible fear that she would lose her da descended over her as she left the room reluctantly. She didn't want anyone to see her upset, so she hurried through the keep and outside. A chilled breeze rushed to embrace her but felt more like cold arms wrapping around her and she shivered. The somber, gray clouds overhead didn't help any. It was as though nature itself predicted doom.

"What's wrong?"

Elsie hadn't noticed she had stopped just before entering the village and was hugging herself, and she hadn't realized it was her husband who had spoken to her and when she did see it was him, she ran to him.

Cavell caught his wife in a tight embrace, worried something was terribly wrong with the way she buried her face against his chest and how her arms wrapped snug around him.

"What's wrong, Elsie?" he asked again.

Elsie did not want to voice her thoughts for fear she would bring them to life. She preferred to remain locked safely in her husband's strong, warm arms.

This time he questioned her simply by saying her name. "Elsie?"

He was worried, she could hear it in his voice, as she would be if he did not respond to her if in a similar situation.

"My da," she said, looking up at him. "I fear he is going to die. I don't want to lose him, not yet."

Cavell said the only thing he could think to say. "Then tell him how much you need him. Your sisters need him. His future grandchildren need him. Maybe then he will fight to live as he did when his clan was under attack. I know he misses your mum, but I don't think your mum would be happy if he left you and your sisters at a time you all need him the most."

Elsie felt as if her husband had lifted a burdensome weight off her shoulders. "You are right. I must remind him of how much he is needed here and how my mum would expect him to help us through this difficult time." She kissed him. "You are a wise chieftain who gives wise advice."

271

"I am more a husband who loves his wife and does not like seeing her upset." He grinned. "Though you are right about me giving wise advice and you should remember that when next you disagree with me."

She chuckled and before she could respond, a Gallowglass warrior approached them.

"Your father and a troop of his warriors approach."

"Escort him to the keep. His troop waits on the outskirts of the village, and when he leaves see that he is followed unseen to our border," Cavell ordered and took his wife's hand to walk to the keep. "This is one of those times you should accept your chieftain's wisdom and—"

"I am not leaving you alone with your father," Elsie said, clutching tightly to his hand to demonstrate her intentions.

Cavell should have been annoyed that his wife argued the point with him, but instead he was pleased. She stood by his side no matter what and would let no one, not even him, make her do otherwise.

"It is working well with the Gallowglass warriors Eldon left here," Elsie said, letting him know there would be no more discussion of her leaving his side. "They guard the village well."

"And they soon will be showing the men how to improve their fighting skills so they will feel more confident if faced with battle. That is just the beginning of my plans for Clan Murdock. I am going to talk with Slayer about a trade route we can establish since he trades with the Northmen."

"We have nothing to trade."

"There is always something to trade," Cavell said. "We will talk more about it another time."

"Maybe you should talk with my da about it," she suggested, thinking it might help for her husband to include her da in such a plan and give him more of a reason to grow strong.

"I will do that," he agreed, thinking that perhaps it might give him an opportunity to somehow learn more about where Norris and his wife got the unwanted bairns. It was imperative they find out all they could so they could determine who meant them harm.

"Why is it that my men are made to wait outside the village?" Cavell's father bellowed before he even brought his horse to a halt in front of the keep. "And how dare you pledge allegiance to Slayer when it was part of the marriage agreement that you pledge the Clan Murdock's fealty to Clan McCabe."

Cavell's eyes pinned his father with a heated glare when he dismounted. "That is the chieftain's decision to make and now that I am chieftain of Clan Murdock, I decide on who the clan's allegiance will go to and it is not Clan McCabe."

Anger spewed with his father's every word. "If it were not for me, you would not be chieftain of this clan."

"One good thing you did for me in my life, and I am grateful for it. But I rule here now, Father, and I decide what is best for my clan, not you."

"You will regret this decision," his father said, shaking his fist at him.

Cavell released his wife's hand before taking a sudden step toward his father. "Are you threatening me, Father?"

"I should have known better than to entrust you to accept the agreed upon marriage conditions. You were never an obedient son," his father accused.

"And you were never a good father," Cavell shot back. "I would say that evens things out between us."

"You are no son of mine," his father spat in disgust.

"That would be good news. Tell me it is so," Cavell fired back.

His father mounted his horse. "Mark my words well, Cavell. You will regret this day."

Cavell watched as his father made his way through the village, calling for people to get out of his way. He had always been a demanding man and sometimes cruel as Harcus could be at times and truthfully so could he.

You are not my son.

His da had said those words so often to him through the years that they meant nothing to him, though they had upset his mum when she heard it. She always reassured him that he was his father's son. He would have preferred he wasn't.

He felt his wife's hand slip gently into his and he gave it a squeeze, grateful she was there beside him.

"My father never gives up that easily," Cavell said. "This is not over between us."

The thought hung heavy on Cavell as he walked through the village with his wife concerned what his father might do in retaliation. He always struck back when he believed he'd been wronged even when it was obvious, he hadn't been wronged. His mum had tried to calm his father when his temper erupted but she would feel the back of his hand when she did and after a while she stopped trying and he had been glad she did, worried his father would hurt her badly. He had been away when she passed, and he was sorry he never got to see her one last time.

Elsie hated to see her husband in such a dour mood. More and more lately she was getting a glimpse of the charmer he once had been, and she found she favored him. The only way she knew to change his mood for the better was to…

"We should return to the keep and spend time alone," she suggested, and her heart melted when he turned a generous smile on her. Scars or no scars, the man's smile could devastate the heart.

"What are you suggesting, wife?" he asked teasingly.

"That we do something we both find extremely enjoyable."

"And what is that?" he asked, scrunching his brow as if perplexed.

He knew full well what she meant but he wanted to hear her tell him she wanted to make love with him, see the passion that would spark in her lovely eyes, hear the desire drip from her words and feel the urgent tug of her hand.

His groin tightened, seeing a spark light in her eyes. He stopped and with a gentle twist to her arm to bring it behind her back, he eased her tight against him. "Tell me what you want, Elsie."

275

"You," she whispered, and a shout stopped their lips from joining.

"SIR!"

The sudden, sharp shout had Cavell turning.

One of the Gallowglass warriors stood not far from them. "A troop of Lowland warriors approach."

Chapter Twenty-three

Cavell stood with his wife at his side on the keep's steps watching the leader of the Lowland troop and one of his men make their way toward them. He saw how the man wrinkled his nose in disgust as he glanced around. The Lowlanders believed the Highlanders were barbarians, ignorant, and living a tribal existence compared to the Lowlanders wealthier, more knowledgeable, less clannish, and far more engaged with the English who the Highlanders did not trust.

He had seen it for himself when he and Noble had been sent to deliver a message to a man in the Lowlands. He and Noble could not leave the area and its people fast enough. And neither he nor Noble ever wanted to return to a place that lacked honor.

Cavell didn't wait for the leader, a young and not at all seasoned warrior from the look of him, to bring his horse to a stop. He called out in a commanding tone, "What are you doing here, Lowlander?"

Anger creased the man's brow at the rude greeting. "I am Frewen, and I have come in search of a woman."

"You don't have enough women in the Lowlands?" Cavell asked and the Gallowglass warriors who surrounded the two men laughed.

277

The young leader realized only then that he was encircled and, to him, not by warriors but savages, and sweat broke out on his brow, a sure sign of fear.

"Have your say, Lowlander, and be on your way home," Cavell warned.

"Frewen," he reminded of the name. "The woman I search for was brought to the Highlands against her will and—"

Cavell didn't let him finish. "Highlanders don't take women against their will, especially Lowland women. They are not strong enough to survive the Highlands."

The man ignored Cavell's disparaging remark and continued speaking. "To find this woman I was to speak with a woman being held at Dundren Abbey who knows the whereabouts of the young woman I search for, but with the fire there and the attack on the monks, we cannot confirm for certain whether she survived or died."

That revelation brought a worry to Cavell and no doubt to his wife as well. He didn't waste time to see what he could find out what the leader knew, if anything, about Elsie and her sisters.

He hurried to ask, "Who searches for her?"

"That is not your concern," Frewen said with an arrogant tilt of his head.

Cavell stared at him as if in contemplation, then moved with such speed, that it sent a rush of air at Elsie causing her to gasp, though it caught in her throat, when she saw her husband reach up, grab the young man by his shirt, rip him off his horse, and shake him senseless.

"You will speak to me with respect, or I will cut out your tongue," Cavell threatened.

Frewen looked terrified, and his situation worsened when the Gallowglass warriors began laughing and Elsie saw why. The young leader had peed himself.

Cavell shoved the man away from him, sending him tumbling against his horse. "Now you will tell me what I asked, for I will not ask it again."

"I do not know, sir," Frewen said and quickly continued. "I was given orders by my commander to go to Dundren Abbey, the last known place of the woman and begin my search there and return with the young woman once I found her."

"Do you have a name or description of this woman at the abbey?" Cavell asked, his concern growing with his wife standing right behind him.

"I doubt she is referred to by her given name, Eudora, and by now she probably has gray hair and an aged face. Would you know if anyone fitting her description survived the fire or the massacre of those at the abbey?"

Edith.

Why would they be searching for Edith, now Ann?

Cavell knew what he had to do. "A woman you described perished in the fire."

"Do you know where she is buried? My commander would want it confirmed."

"I thought Lowlanders considered themselves intelligent," Cavell said.

Frewen drew his shoulders back, taking a defensive stance that did little good since the front of his garment was stained wet. "We are, sir."

279

"Then what did you not understand when I told you she perished in the fire?"

The Lowlander looked confused, then his eyes widened. "The fire left little of her."

"Bones were all that were left," Cavell confirmed.

"Then how can you be sure it was the woman I look for?" Frewen asked as if his query somehow proved Cavell ignorant.

"Her bones were found in the cell where she was kept," Cavell said and watched the Lowlander's spark of confidence deflate.

He regained it for a moment when he asked, "Were you told this or did you see it for yourself?"

Cavell stepped toward the Lowlander. "Are you calling me a liar?"

Frewen pressed himself against his horse, anxious to keep distance between him and Cavell. "Nay. Nay, sir. I ask a question of you that I know will be asked of me."

Cavell began to admire the young Lowlander. As frightened as he was, he still attempted to accomplish the task he was sent to do.

"I was there and saw for myself, and I also spoke with Brother Emanual, the monk in charge of the abbey. Will that be enough for your commander, or do we have to suffer another visit from Lowlanders?"

"I do hope it will be enough, sir, for I have no desire to return here."

"I am glad to hear that, though you are welcome to spend the night on the outskirts of the village and take your leave tomorrow at first light," Cavell offered.

"I am grateful for the offer, but we will be on our way."

"Be careful, Lowlander. There is a rogue group of warriors lurking in the woods and attacking whoever they wish and leaving few alive."

The Lowlander paled. "Is it Gallowglass?"

The warriors around him laughed.

"Do you know anything of the Gallowglass?" Cavell asked.

"I was told they are cruel and soulless warriors who would die rather than surrender and that they carry long-handled axes and use them with exceptional skill and—" Frewen stopped talking suddenly, realizing several of the warriors surrounding him held such a weapon.

Frewen barely got the words out. "You're Gallowglass."

"That we are," Cavell confirmed and with pride he had not felt in a while.

Frewen quickly offered an apology. "I meant no offense to your kind."

"Our kind? Cruel and soulless warriors?"

"It was what I was told," Frewen said.

"You are better off seeing and deciding for yourself before you judge someone," Cavell advised.

"I will consider that, sir, and now I will take my leave."

Cavell nodded to one of the Gallowglass warriors as he watched the Lowlander and the man with him ride off.

"Take a few men and follow him and his troop to the clan's border. I do not know how they have managed to survive the Highlands since arriving here."

The warrior nodded and went to carry out his task.

"What do you think, wife?" Cavell asked, his eyes still on the Lowlander.

When he got no answer, he turned and was not surprised to see his wife gone. He knew where she went, though he would have preferred that she waited for him. He shook his head and entered the keep.

***

"Mistress Elsie said to join her in your solar, sir," Alda said when Cavell entered the Great Hall.

Cavell stopped upon hearing Ann's voice, the door to his solar ajar.

"I knew this day would come. Secrets never remain secret forever."

He entered, shutting the door behind him so that no one could hear what was being discussed and went to stand in front of Ann, turning a stern expression on her. "I will tolerate no more secrets. Edith, Ann, Eudora, whoever you are, you will tell us everything, for if I find out you lied, the consequences will be harsh."

The older woman looked ready to collapse and Elsie was quick to guide her to a chair and help her sit.

Elsie kept her tone gentle, seeing how the woman's hands trembled and how she had paled after Cavell issued his warning. "Why didn't you speak up about this?"

"Fear, Mistress Elsie. Fear that has plagued me these many years."

"You have no choice now, Ann. Or is it Edith or Eudora?" Elsie asked.

Cavell remained silent, not interfering, knowing the older woman would respond more easily and readily to his wife than to him. But, if necessary, he would take charge.

"I am Edith, though I must remain Ann now, and it is not me those men search for. It is my sister Eudora."

Elsie sat in the chair beside Ann and reached out to rest a comforting hand on her arm, purposely directing her attention to her, knowing that her husband easily intimidated Ann with the way he stood so tall and menacing in front of her.

"My sister Eudora fell in love with a man I tried to warn her against, but she refused to listen. She went with him to live on the border of the Lowlands and Highlands. I hadn't heard from her in years when she suddenly appeared at my door one day and asked for help. Her marriage had proven disastrous, and he left her for another woman. She had been on her way to establishing herself as a midwife by then, our mum and grandmother having taught us the skill. I am not sure how she got involved with saving unwanted bairns or bairns in danger of their lives being snuffed from them right after birth, she told me it was better I didn't know. One of the midwives who was part of the group of women who had banded together to help the vulnerable women and bairns was discovered and she lost her life. All involved feared the woman had been tortured to reveal the names of others involved. The group was

283

quickly abandoned and all fled, fearful for their lives. When I was suddenly claimed insane and taken to the abbey, I feared it might have had something to do with my sister's past. It was either discovered I was the sister of the woman they searched for, or I was mistakenly believed to be Eudora."

"With the Lowlander's arrival today, I would assume you had been sent to the abbey to wait for someone to come to collect you," Elsie said.

Ann looked at Cavell, tears heavy in her eyes. "I am eternally grateful you did not reveal who I am."

"Highlanders take care of their own and see to their own justice," Cavell said.

Elsie brought Ann's attention back to her with a question. "Did your sister tell you anything about the bairns she saved?"

Ann shook her head. "She would not speak of them, fearful of the danger it could bring me and, truthfully, I did not want to know. When I heard your da speak of it, I got frightened for my sister all over again."

"Your sister is still alive?" Cavell was quick to ask.

"I do not know. She only stayed with me a short while, then left, insisting she would not put me in any more danger than she already felt she had. I have not heard from her since the day we hugged and parted ways, yet I have continued to worry about her all these years, and I have prayed every day that she is safe."

"You have no idea where she may have gone?" Elsie asked, realizing it was imperative they find the woman.

Ann shook her head. "One thing about my sister is that she is good at hiding. Sometimes when she didn't want to do her chores, she would hide and my da would get angry that he couldn't find her, and he would have no choice but to see to the chores himself. Then she would suddenly appear and pretend that she had forgotten. I am glad she has such hiding skills, for I fear what her fate would be if she was found."

Cavell and Elsie sat in silence after Ann took her leave, the only sound the pop and crackle of the flaming logs, though there was the occasional rumble of thunder heralding an approaching storm.

Elsie broke the silence after a while. "My da says we should leave the past in the past, but I fear that is not possible. The warrior you killed to save my da had asked him which one of us was she and when my da told him he didn't know, he said he would collect and kill us all."

Cavell bolted forward in the chair. "And you did not think to tell me this?"

"There was so much going on, the attack, worry about my da, but mostly fear of losing you that I forgot about it until now."

"It was not fair of me, wife, to be angry at you," Cavell said, guilt gnawing at him for snapping at her. "I am glad you finally recalled it. It tells us that the search is to find one of you with the intentions of seeing that person dead though they would not stop at killing all three of you to accomplish the mission. Yet the Lowlander's mission is to return with the young woman he was sent to find. Either way poses much danger for you and your sisters."

As his words hung in the air, a chilling silence once again descended upon the room. Elsie's heart pounded loudly in her chest, drowning out the rest of the world. She felt a knot forming in her stomach and color drained from her face. She clenched her fists, trying to steady herself, but the weight of the news was too much to bear. Her thoughts raced, trying to comprehend the reality of the situation. Her da had been right to fear for her and her sisters' safety. Their three lives were at risk. Someone wanted one of them dead and was willing to kill all three of them to successfully complete his mission. And an abduction was possible as well.

Cavell had his wife out of the chair and into his arms and returned to his chair to sit with her tucked in his lap with ease and speed.

"I did not give this enough thought. For someone to want another dead so badly he would allow others to be killed to make certain the intended person died means this person believes the child, who is now grown, would be a hindrance or danger to him," Elsie said, trying to make further sense of it. "And that means—" She stopped, fearful of speaking her thoughts.

Cavell finished for her. "The person is powerful and possibly influential. Brother Emanual told me that he gave his word to an unnamed nobleman that Edith would remain under his care until her dying day but with the arrival of the Lowlander I would guess something changed those plans. I also wonder over the accusation that Edith had stolen the breaths of bairns at birth as a sign that they knew she had stolen the bairns at birth and she would pay for it. Your da was right to worry over your sisters and your safety. But you have no worries, wife, I will keep you safe."

"I do not fear for myself. I know I am safe with you," she said and kissed his cheek.

He never thought he would be comfortable with any woman kissing his face ever again. Elsie changed all that and he was glad she did.

"It is Leora I fear for out there somewhere all alone with no one to protect her and no hint of where she may be."

"Noble will find her and once he does, she will be safe with him," Cavell said, trying to reassure her.

"Once he finds her, but until then she is vulnerable and in danger." Her brow frowned in puzzlement, and she slipped off her husband's lap to pace in front of him. "Numbers make sense to me. You add, subtract, multiply, divide and have an answer. But what has happened here multiplies without making sense. My da weds his three daughters to keep them safe. Rogue warriors haunt the area. All those at the abbey are slaughtered. A Murdock croft was attacked, the family almost killed. There was an attack on Clan Murdock by rogue warriors. A troop of Lowlanders show up searching for an old woman. The old woman is the one from the abbey, or so we assume, only to find out it is not her at all but her sister who is the one who delivered me and my sisters and rescued us from certain harm." She stopped pacing, shook her head, and continued. "How does this all connect, make sense, provide any answers at all? "

"Maybe we look at it wrong," Cavell suggested. "Maybe someone is desperate to find this child, now grown, while another someone is desperate that the now grown child is not found. Perhaps the acknowledgment of this person's existence threatens someone's inheritance. The trusted midwife would know who the rightful parents are of the bairns, providing proof. A possibility to consider and one that would make the situation that more dangerous since when a large inheritance is involved, a person would do anything not to lose it."

"Our only recourse is to find Ann's sister Eudora and see what she knows about mine and my sisters' true parents."

Chapter Twenty-four

The clouds overhead reflected Elsie's somber mood as she walked through the village. The rain had stopped a short time ago, leaving its mark on the land. Children splashed in the puddles left in its wake, laughing while dogs barked, joining them in the fun. Tree branches hung heavy while leaves dripped with the last of the rain and people gathered in talk, relieved to have a reprieve from the rain that had fallen since early morning.

Elsie was troubled and had been since her talk with her husband far too many days ago. He had told her that it might not be possible to find Eudora after all this time and that she might not even be alive. If that proved true, there would be no one left that would know the truth about her and her sisters' true parents. What then? How did they stop the threat she and her sisters faced?

She shook her head at her bothersome musings, trying to shake them away. There were many things she should be pleased with, like how most of the men wounded in the attack had recovered well, with only two needing a bit more healing time. And how the men in the clan had taken well to the teachings of the

289

Gallowglass warriors when it came to battle and weapons. It was obvious Clan Murdock was growing stronger by the day and it was all thanks to her husband's wise leadership. Her da had even begun to improve since Cavell was visiting him daily and was discussing how the clan could benefit by being part of a trade route that Slayer had begun. Her da had been thrilled with the idea and had suggested different possibilities.

She had much to be grateful for and yet she had much to worry her as well, Leora being her biggest worry, though Sky was not far behind. She was anxious for Melvin's return and news about Sky. For now, she would settle for a hot brew and the warmth of a gentle fire, the rain having left a chill in its wake.

She was surprised to find Wadely in the Great Hall, not that he never came there, he did, but only at mealtimes. He talked with any and all, having an easy tongue but then a merchant usually did.

"Mistress Elsie," Wadely greeted with a smile. "I was looking for Chieftain Cavell. I have his vest here." He pointed to the table.

Elsie ran her hand over it, admiring the skilled piece. "It's padded and the stitching is beautiful."

"The padding and tight cross-stitching will help protect him when in battle," Wadely said with pride.

"That is good to hear," Elsie said, finally smiling. "Where did you learn such skill?"

"On my travels. The leather garments I saw stitched intrigued me, so I learned and practiced, though a skilled stitcher taught me her trade."

His response had Elsie thinking, and she asked, "In your travels have you ever come upon many women living all on their own?"

"Nay, I would not likely come across a woman on her own since my travels take me to clan market days, or individual clans, and some monasteries. My travels have taught me that most women who live removed from others are not spoken about with any favor. They are either deemed a witch or believed touched with madness or so says the wagging tongues," he said with a chuckle.

"Have you heard talk of any such woman?"

"Do you look for someone in particular, Mistress Elsie?"

How could she phrase this without alerting him to the true issue?

An idea came to her. "I was told the midwife who delivered me lives alone and I was wondering if I could find her and talk with her about my mum."

"Do you know what area she might be in?" Wadely asked.

"Unfortunately, I don't."

"The Highlands are vast, Mistress Elsie. Without an idea of where she may be it would be difficult to say."

Wadely almost echoed her husband's words.

"If there is anything distinctive about the woman that might help?" Wadely offered.

"Hiding," Elsie said with a laugh. "She is good at hiding from what I was told."

Wadely stared at her as if speechless.

"You heard of such a woman?" Elsie asked anxiously.

"Oddly enough I have heard someone speak of such a woman, a healer who preferred to live alone," he said, sounding as surprised as Elsie looked though with a sadness in his eyes. "Unfortunately, I also heard of her passing about two years ago." Wadely quickly offered some encouragement when he saw the disappointment on Elsie's face. "Perhaps she is not the one you search for."

"You're right. The Highlands are a vast place. The chance of her being the woman I search for is probably not likely." Still, Elsie felt disappointed.

The door to the Great Hall opened and Elsie did not have to look to see who entered, she felt her husband's potent presence as soon as he stepped into the room. His steps were powerful, the wood creaking beneath his confident footfalls.

"Chieftain Cavell," Wadely greeted with a bob of his head. "I finished the vest you requested."

"It is beautiful craftsmanship," Elsie said as she turned to face her husband, her stomach fluttering at the sight of him, her heart beating a bit faster, and her face lighting with love for him.

"Aye, it is," he agreed, though it wasn't the vest he looked upon… it was his wife.

Elsie blushed, still trying to get used to the fact that her husband thought her beautiful.

Cavell slipped his arm around his wife and eased her against him as he spoke to Wadely. "Show me the vest."

Wadely snatched it off the table and displayed the front and back, explaining how the side straps would hold it firmly in place.

"You do exceptional leather work," Wadely. "You are welcome to make a permanent home here and provide us with your skill if you ever choose to."

"I will give it thought, sir," Wadely said and after placing the vest back on the table, took his leave.

Cavell's other arm went around his wife as he kissed her lips gently. "I love seeing how your face lights with love for me. It fills my heart with joy."

"I am glad it pleases you since I cannot help but brighten with love for you when I see you."

"That's because I am irresistible," he said with a chuckle.

"Only to me, no other woman," she ordered sternly.

"Is that an order, wife?" he said with mocked annoyance.

"Aye, an order you better obey or else?" she threatened playfully.

"What punishment do I suffer if I don't obey?" he whispered near her ear before nibbling along her neck.

She sighed softly. "You will lose favor with me."

His lips left her neck suddenly, his head shooting up to look at her. "I never want to lose favor with you."

"I was but teasing," she assured him, seeing how much her words had disturbed him and feeling guilty for upsetting him. "I will always favor you, always love you, always desire you, on that you have my word."

He kissed her hard and strong, forever sealing her words.

Cavell assisted her in taking a seat at the table near the hearth rather than the dais and they shared a brew as they talked.

"I asked Wadely if he ever came across a woman living alone and he said the same as you that the Highlands are a vast area, though he asked if there was anything specific, I knew about the woman. When I told him that she was good at hiding, he was surprised. He knew of such a woman but said she died about two years ago. If, by chance, it was Eudora, it means we will never know who mine and my sisters' true parents are."

"Not so," Cavell encouraged. "Someone searches for one of you, so someone knows the parents of at least one of you three. As difficult as it might be, you need patience in this, wife." He grinned. "Thankfully, you have me to distract you."

She returned his grin. "As you did this morning when I woke with endless questions on my tongue. Your kisses and teasing touches quickly distracted me."

"A perfect way to greet the morning."

"On that we agree, husband."

The door opened and Elsie's smile faded as warriors entered who she didn't recognize, but obviously her husband did since he smiled and nodded at them. Then she spotted Melvin and her smile returned.

"Melvin!" she shouted.

He hurried his way through the warriors, to the table, and spoke to Cavell first. "Lord Slayer sent these warriors," —he raised his voice and snickered teasingly— "a helpless bunch if you ask me."

"Far more skilled than you," one warrior called out with a laugh.

"Far better features as well." Another laughed.

"It is generous of Lord Slayer to send you all," Cavell called out.

"There are far more than just us few, Chieftain Cavell," one warrior said.

"I am most grateful to Lord Slayer, Henry," Cavell said, knowing not only the man well but the others with him. He had fought many battles alongside them.

"Lord Slayer takes care of those who pledge their fealty to him, and he knows you will be there without question if he should need you," Henry said.

Cavell stood. "With sword in hand, ready to fight."

Henry nodded knowingly. "You always were quick to join the fray. Never saw anyone move as fast as you do."

"Sit and enjoy some food and drink. We will talk once I finish speaking with Melvin." Cavell reached out to his wife and when she took his hand, he helped her to her feet, then turned to Melvin. "My solar."

Melvin barely closed the door when Elsie asked anxiously, "My sister Sky, you spoke to her?"

Melvin cast a quick glance at Cavell, then seemed to struggle to respond.

"Is my sister all right? Please, Melvin, tell me," Elsie asked, her stomach knotting with worry.

"Lord Slayer would not let me speak with her. He gave his word he would relay the message, but he refused to let me see her and believe me, Mistress Elsie, I tried, knowing how important it was to you. Though

295

he did tell me to inform you that she was well and safe and there was no need to worry about her."

"How do I know that for sure if you never got to see her?" Elsie said, having hoped for a response from her sister to know for sure she was well and safe.

"When Slayer says that your sister is well and safe believe him," Cavell said, hoping to ease his wife's worry. "Trust me on this, wife. He is a man of his word, a man of honor."

"I have little option than to do anything else, though I do trust your word, husband," Elsie said, her worry calming some.

"What did Lord Slayer have to say when you told him that Sky and her sisters were in danger, Melvin?" Cavell asked, eager to know if it was news to Slayer or that he had already found out.

"He knew, though how I don't know, but he is aware of it."

Cavell was surprised that was all he said about that and went on delivering more news.

"He was not happy to hear about Clyde. Naturally, he plans to revenge his death, though presently his thoughts are heavy on his father and brother's deaths. He believes the rogue group of mercenaries may be responsible for his brother's death, but he does not know who poisoned his father. His thirst for revenge is great and I can tell you now that he intends to make the culprits suffer horribly for it. And he will do the same to whoever killed Clyde. He was furious when I told him of Clyde's death. He is out for blood, Cavell, and I fear he will spill much blood before this all ends."

Cavell was afraid of that and worried it might mean endless battles before the truth was finally discovered.

"Did he say anything of Noble?" Cavell asked.

"Noble was tracking for Slayer, but when he received news of being wed to Leora and discovered her missing from the abbey, Slayer released him from the chore to go find his new wife."

"There has been no other word of Leora?" Elsie asked, her worry growing once again. At least she knew that Sky was protected, not so Leora. She continued to be all on her own somewhere.

"Only that Noble has grown frustrated that he cannot find her," Melvin said. "Unusual for him since I don't believe anyone has ever eluded his fine tracking skills."

Elsie did not want to think of what it might mean that a skilled tracker could not find her sister, but it was unavoidable. She feared Leora had met a horrible fate and lay buried somewhere she would never be found.

Cavell could see the fear on his wife's face for her sister and hoping to ease her burden of worry, he offered a bit of encouragement. "It seems that your sister is as brilliant as you at avoiding being found. I would not be surprised if she disguised herself as a monk just as you did."

"I can only hope," Elsie said, praying her husband was right.

Melvin kept his eyes on Cavell as if purposely avoiding a glance at Elsie. "There is something else Slayer discovered that he wanted to make certain you know, but he says it is for your ears alone."

"Does it have to do with my wife and her sisters' parents not being their true parents?" Cavell asked, the thought having come to him when Melvin spoke of Slayer releasing Noble from his duties."

Melvin's brow scrunched. "How did you know?"

"Slayer would have never released Noble from tracking his father and brother's killer unless something proved more imminent and since we discovered it as well, I assumed it was what he would want me to know as I would do the same for him. Did Slayer say how he found out?"

"From friends in the Lowlands, though he did not elaborate on the friends," Melvin said. "He did, however, say they were an extremely reliable source. Someone searches for a female, taken at birth, who belongs to a prominent, aristocratic family."

"And this prominent family just discovered this?" Cavell asked.

"Slayer does not know if it is the family who searches for the woman or even why after all these years someone searches for her," Melvin said. "The search led to unwanted bairns or bairns in danger when born that were placed with couples in the Highlands. Three females were placed with Chieftain Norris and his wife, Terena. But the origin of each female is unknown and so the hunt is on to find one particular one. Slayer is trying to find out more and says he will send word if he learns anything. In the meantime, he says to remain cautious, and Noble has been warned to do the same. He also sent a generous troop of warriors to reside here leaving it up to each one if they wish to make a permanent home here. Several volunteered to come once they heard they could have a permanent home. Slayer has secured the safety of the clan for you."

"And I am grateful, though he also benefits from it since it secures him a clan that will serve him whenever necessary."

"The ways of the Highlands," Elsie said.

"Aye, so it is," both men agreed.

"You did well, Melvin, I appreciate it." He nodded toward Elsie. "My wife suggests that you would make me a fine, trustworthy counsel, but I know battle is a way of life for you... unless you now think differently. If so, I would be pleased to have you at my side offering guidance whether I agree with it or not."

Melvin smiled. "There was a time I would not have given your offer thought, but I find I favor it here." His smile grew. "There is enough battle to sustain me, intrigue that entices, and people who welcome me as family, though most importantly, a woman I have come to love to my great surprise. So, I humbly accept your offer and will serve you with honor and respect."

"I am pleased to hear that. We will talk more tomorrow since I am sure you will want to spend time with May today."

Melvin grinned widely. "That I do, sir, that I do!"

Melvin left the solar still grinning and Cavell turned to his wife. "I must talk with and see what, if any, orders Slayer may have given Henry. Also, the warriors will work with the clan to get shelters built throughout what is left of spring and into summer so they will have homes before the winter sets in. I will also have them hunt for more food since what food we have will be depleted soon with so many more mouths to feed."

"We will extend the planting fields and more meat will need to be stored for the winter as well as root plants," Elsie said. "I will see to getting it done."

Cavell ran his hand gently down her arm. "I look forward to later tonight when we are finally alone and left undisturbed."

Elsie eased toward him, her body falling gently against his. "As do I."

Her lips reached for his when Melvin burst through the door. "Two of our warriors have arrived with injured Lowlanders."

Chapter Twenty-five

"They came out of nowhere, roaring like banshees, swinging their axes and swords, severing limbs, leaving men screaming in agony as they lay dying. I have never seen such ferocious warriors. If it were not for the men you sent to follow us, we would have been massacred," Frewen said, taking a needed breath and wiping away the blood dripping down the side of his head with his sleeve-covered arm. "I am most grateful to you for seeing to our safety."

Cavell was once again impressed with the young Lowlander, one of the Gallowglass telling him that the Lowlander fought bravely and skillfully. Unfortunately, others with him did not. He lost half of his troop, and the other half were left wounded, a couple of them seriously.

"The Highlands are no place for Lowlanders," Cavell warned.

"So I have discovered, though I must say while the Highlands are wild and unpredictable, I never imagined the beauty it possesses," Frewen said.

"Far more than any realize," Cavell said with pride in his homeland.

"Sit and let me tend to your wound," Elsie offered, joining the men and pointing at one of the tables in the Great Hall where she had just placed a fresh bucket of water and clean cloths.

Frewen appeared hesitant.

"You cannot be of any help to your surviving men if you do not have your own wound tended," Cavell advised. "Besides, my wife not only has a gentle touch, but she works quickly. She will be done with you in no time."

Frewen bobbed his head and went and sat on the bench at the table.

Cavell talked with Melvin while his wife tended to the Lowlander, his glance going around the room at the many injured warriors being tended to by several women in the clan.

"You say May is tending a seriously wounded warrior in her cottage and the other badly wounded warrior has died?" Cavell asked.

"Aye, the poor fellow was beyond help and May says the other is barely clinging to life and will not live long," Melvin confirmed and shook his head. "The attack makes no sense. The Lowlanders were no threat to the mercenaries."

"But they could have been a benefit to them," Cavell suggested.

"How so?"

"Someone could have paid them to attack the troop and make sure they never returned to the Lowlands, fearing they discovered information."

"Are you saying that we are dealing with two different people, one who wants information and another who doesn't want the information found?" Melvin asked, his brow narrowing. "We fight two foes?"

"I believe so. I have found out more in your absence that you need to know about. We will talk later in my solar," Cavell said, intending to discuss what had gone on here in his absence.

"What do you intend to do with the Lowlanders?"

Cavell glanced around the room again. "If I am right, they will never make it back to the Lowlands, at least not until we discover who, out of the three sisters, is the one wanted by this unknown person who wants her returned. They would be wise to remain here until then, but that is not my decision to make." He nodded toward Frewen, the blood gone from his face and a thick coating of honey on a small wound by his hairline, busy talking among his men. "He needs to see to his men right now. I will discuss it with him soon enough."

"A camp will need to be set up for them. The Gallowglass warriors who returned with me are setting up camp, we can add the Lowlanders camp onto theirs," Melvin said with a sheepish grin.

Cavell smiled and shook his head, thinking someone had told Melvin what had happened when the Lowlanders arrived here. "Do you want to see them all die of fright?"

Melvin laughed.

"Do what you think is best," Cavell said.

"Truly? You leave the decision to me?" Melvin asked, surprised.

"I trust you to do what is right."

"Aye, sir, I will," Melvin said, bobbing his head. "Warriors who fight a good fight should always be treated well."

"And that is why you are my counsel," Cavell said.

"I will see to it right away and look forward to talking with you later," Melvin said and hurried out of the room.

Cavell felt a gentle hand at his back that followed along his arm and to his chest as his wife walked around from behind him.

"He is proud to serve you," Elsie said, leaving her hand to rest on her husband's chest.

"And I am glad to have a trustworthy friend to help me." He brushed stray hairs that had fallen loose from her braid off her face and while he could see fatigue creeping up on her, he knew she would never admit to it. "You could use a douse of fresh air. Come walk with me a bit before I go and speak with the Gallowglass who returned with Melvin."

"A most welcome invitation," Elsie said with a smile and hooked her arm around her husband's.

The village was abuzz with busy chaos, the clansmen doing all they could to help settle the large Gallowglass troop that had arrived to help protect them. With some trepidation, older children took food and drink to the warriors and Elsie didn't blame them.

Many of them were massive men with numerous scars that marked their battle worthiness.

Elsie had to smile when she spotted Kara walking through the troop of warriors without fear and knew she was busy counting.

"That lass is fearless," Cavell said, having spotted her as well.

"And she will have a good count of warriors, who recently arrived opposed to those already here and then a compilation of them all, for us when she is done," Elsie said with pride in the lass and pointed in the distance near to where a camp with makeshift shelters was being constructed. "Is that the area where you will have more dwellings built?"

Cavell nodded. "Aye, though they will be longhouses like Slayer has for his unmarried men. I want to make sure the warriors are housed well before winter sets in. With the amount of warriors who arrived today that should prove no problem and I hope to have a few single dwellings done as well since I expect some of the warriors to find wives here."

"Our clan grows," Elsie said, beaming with joy.

"I would not be surprised if next summer a slew of bairns are born."

"I hope to contribute to that slew," she said.

He looked at her as if expecting news.

"Not yet, but it shouldn't be long now before a possibility turns positive and as I promised, you will be the first to know."

Cavell grinned and lowered his head and voice, saying, "With as much as we couple, I do not know how you could not be with child."

"You are right, and we should continue coupling so your seed has no choice but to take root."

He chuckled. "I whole heartily agree." He kissed her quickly. "While I would love to continue walking and talking with you, I have duties to tend to."

"As do I," Elsie said, already feeling her husband's absence in her heart and it growing as he walked away.

She turned around to return to the keep when she saw Ann speaking with Wadely, by the stable, though it appeared they argued more than conversed, Ann being the aggressor. Elsie hurried toward them.

"You are lying!" Ann accused, shaking her finger at Wadely.

"What goes on here?" Elsie asked, her tone firm.

Ann turned to Elsie, clearly upset. "I just saw the leather vest Wadely stitched for Chieftain Cavell and recognized those perfectly crafted cross stitches. There is only one person who could have taught him that skill… Eudora. My mum taught her, but she perfected the stitches. I have never seen another hand do such skilled work until today when I saw the vest. He learned that skill from my sister Eudora."

Elsie's heart pounded in her chest at what that news might mean.

"I always believed you a trustworthy man, Wadely," Elsie said, keeping her voice calm, though her insides churned, and her heart continued to pound. "It is why you were generously offered shelter here whenever necessary and now a permanent home if you so choose. So, I will ask you for the truth and trust that you will speak it."

"I would like to hear that myself."

"Harcus?" Elsie's brow narrowed, surprised yet suspicious to see Cavell's brother appear from behind the stable.

"Aye, and we are all going to talk but not here."

Elsie saw the dagger then, though realized he intended her to see it and Wadely to feel it since he poked the point of the blade at his back.

"The three of you are going to casually step behind the stable and do not be foolish and think to draw attention for I will see at least two of you dead before anyone can reach here and one of those will be Elsie."

Ann reached out to take Elsie's hand as if she could somehow protect her.

"Move!" Harcus commanded low and harshly.

The three did as he ordered, Elsie casting a quick glance at the village to see if anyone spotted them, but no one glanced their way, all too chaotically busy for anyone to notice.

"You all are going to walk quietly into the woods and go where I tell you," Harcus continued to command.

Elsie's heart continued to hammer in her chest, but it was from fear this time. Fear she would never see her husband again and never live to bear the bairn she suspected she carried but had not wanted to say until she was certain.

Harcus grabbed hold of her arm once in the woods, keeping the dagger planted near her side. "If either of you try anything, she's dead, though it will not be a slow death."

Elsie realized fear would do her little good in this situation. She needed to keep a clear head and bide her time as best she could. Once her husband discovered her missing, he would search for her and he would find her, of that she had no doubt. She only hoped he discovered her absence soon.

"Why do you do this, Harcus?" Elsie asked, curious for answers.

"Why does any man do anything?" he asked with a laugh.

Elsie did not have to think of a response, it came easily. "Wealth and power."

"Something my da craves but he takes too long to achieve, and his craving does not come close to the wealth and power that I crave. He thinks by having small, insignificant clans pay allegiance to Clan McCabe that we grow in strength and power. It takes wealth to grow power, and do you know what brings great wealth?"

"Information," Wadely said, helping Ann maneuver through the forest.

"I discovered just how dearly noble men and women would pay for information and how the information could be used to gain even more wealth."

Elsie understood what he meant. "You sell the information to whoever will pay the most for it, increasing your wealth substantially."

"My da never looked past your plain features but the few times I visited your da, I saw who was responsible for the daily running of your clan and the exceptional job you did. It is a shame my brother must lose such a good wife so soon after his marriage."

Fear sent a chill running through her, though she kept herself from shivering. She would not let Harcus see her fear. She would stay strong no matter how frightened she felt.

"You joined forces with rogue mercenaries?" Elsie asked.

"A motley crew, but a necessary one that I secretly formed," Harcus said.

Elsie kept him talking to learn all she could. "Then it was your crew who slaughtered the monks from Dundren Abbey?"

"A necessary evil," Harcus confessed. "They failed to keep you and your sisters there and the old woman who could provide the proof needed as to your true parents. I could not let that information go to anyone else."

"I am not Eudora. I know nothing," Ann said.

Annoyed, Harcus snapped, "So, I discovered."

Elsie was beginning to understand it all. "You and your crew were hired to find a woman and kill her, but then you learned that the woman was potentially more valuable to someone else if kept alive." She shook her head. "Which is what brought the Lowlanders here, the person you crossed found out and sent another crew to finish the task you started."

"If I had been offered more money the task would have been completed, but the price was too hefty for the person to match or go beyond," Harcus said. "After hearing the three of you talk, it seems like the merchant might know the whereabouts of Eudora." Harcus gave Elsie's arm a yank. "If I can confirm you are the woman the person searches for and wants returned, then I will see that you are delivered posthaste. If not," —he shrugged— "I can't have my brother discovering what I

309

do. So unfortunately, I will need to kill you. The two with us die regardless of what I find, though if either one of them can tell me about the true parents of you and your sisters, I might reconsider since I could earn a good amount of wealth with that information."

"You won't let us live," Wadely said. "You would worry the information got out to others before you could earn a good amount for yourself."

"You have a sharp mind, merchant. I will remember that," Harcus warned. "Now keep moving and don't think my brother will come to your rescue anytime soon. There was enough chaos today with Melvin's recent return and the attack on the Lowlanders to keep everyone occupied and then some."

"I don't understand why you had the croft attacked or why you attacked the clan. And whyever did you kill the lone Gallowglass warrior or that innocent woman, the one with hair the color of Leora's?" Elsie asked, intending to ask endless questions of him.

"My crew attacked the croft but not the clan. One of my men realized the fellow from the croft had spotted him on market day at different clans. One of those times I was there speaking with him, and I could not be sure if he spotted me or not. And I was not sure if he mentioned it to his family, so I had little choice but to eliminate them all. Unfortunately, the attempt failed, though when my brother did not come after me, I knew the fellow never spotted me, so it all worked out well in the end. I know nothing of the lone Gallowglass warrior, but the woman, you must have guessed by now, was nothing more than mistaken identity."

Elsie continued with her questions. "You kept an eye on Leora on those days?"

"I had an eye kept on all three of you. It simply proved more difficult to keep an eye on Leora since she flits around talking to everyone and men cannot seem to take their eyes off her. They stare as if mesmerized by her, not that I blame them. Your sister is a beauty."

Elsie ignored his remark and continued to probe. "This mission you accepted came after my marriage to your brother?"

"It did and I believe I will be doing him a favor getting rid of you. He hadn't wanted this marriage to begin with and now he will be free of it and still retain the title of Chieftain of Clan Murdock. And he will be free to wed a woman of his choice."

If Elsie wasn't sure how much her husband loved her, she would have believed the nonsense Harcus spouted. But she did not doubt her husband's love, not even for a moment. She saw the love he had for her in his eyes every time he looked at her, felt it in his tender touch, felt it every time they made love, felt it every time he took her in his arms, and every time he kissed her. The list could go on forever. Her husband loved her with his whole heart, and she loved him.

Another question came to mind, and she asked, "Did you have anything to do with Lord Bannaty and Warrand's deaths?"

Harcus stopped abruptly. "Are you crazy? Every sane person knows to avoid Slayer. He is utterly insane. Though I was more than surprised when I heard of the marriage agreement between Warrand and Sky." He started walking again. "Enough talk. We are almost there."

Elsie's worry grew when they came upon a camp occupied by three rouge mercenaries… some of Harcus's crew.

"You got the right one?" one of the men asked.

"Not sure yet, but the other two I've brought along should help determine that," Harcus said, and the man nodded, looking pleased. "Keep watch, though we will not be here for long. Once I learn what I want we will be on our way."

The three men there remained watchful, and Elsie wondered if the three men were all that were left of his troop, though somehow, she doubted that.

Harcus shoved Elsie toward Wadely and Ann, and she stumbled though kept herself on her feet.

"I heard you two," —Harcus pointed between Wadely and Ann— "arguing about stitching and the name Eudora was involved. The name of the woman many are searching for, so how is it that you both know the name? And so that you know… I have little patience. You will taste the blade of my dagger if you do not speak up."

Ann spoke immediately. Eudora is my sister, but I haven't seen her in almost twenty years. The stitching pattern that Wadely did was familiar to my sister's stitching work, and I was so shocked to see it that I accused him of knowing my sister."

"And do you know her, Wadely?" Harcus asked.

Elsie watched Harcus, his movements, the way he spoke. He resembled his father in certain ways. Though he was taller than his father though not near the height of his brother. She realized then that her husband had gotten his fine features from his mother and no doubt his teasing ways as well since Harcus's stern expression never wavered, the lines between his eyes deep, an indication that his brow was often drawn together in annoyance or anger.

"No, sir, I do not," Wadely said.

"The old woman's story sounds more believable," Harcus said and with a quick swing of his dagger, he slashed at Wadely tearing through his sleeve and along his arm. Blood poured out soaking his torn sleeve. "Let's try that again."

Chapter Twenty-six

A strange feeling that he needed to see his wife poked at Cavell. Instinct was a warrior's best friend, so he had learned not to ignore it and was glad he hadn't when he couldn't find her.

"Melvin!" he shouted, spotting him talking with May.

He and May hurried to Cavell.

"Have either of you seen Elsie?" he asked, worry having made him irritable.

"Last time I saw her was with you," Melvin said.

"The last I saw of her was in the keep tending to the wounded," May said.

Both were before he left his wife to talk with the Gallowglass warriors. Where could she have gone?

"I cannot find her," he said, his remark sending a rash of fear racing through him.

"She must be here somewhere," May said, "perhaps she is with her da."

Cavell shook his head. "Nay, I went to see for myself. She was not there and her da was sleeping."

"Have you asked around the village?" May asked.

"Someone saw her walking toward the keep which was where she was going when I left her."

"There was much chaos today with Melvin returning and the Lowlanders being attacked. She is probably busy helping someone," May said and spotted Mab with Kara. She waved them over. "Have you seen Mistress Elsie, Mab?"

"I saw her a while ago by the stable with Wadely and Ann. The three were talking," Mab said.

"Four," Kara said. "There were four of them. A man was behind the stable."

"Did he join the three?" Cavell asked, grateful the young lass had a penchant for counting, though he did not like hearing someone lurked behind the stables.

"I don't know. My mum called out to me and I had to rush off."

"Mab, you and Kara go and fetch a treat from the kitchen for being so helpful," Cavell said, fighting to talk calmly when he wanted to roar with anger.

Kara squealed with delight and took Mab's hand to tug at her to walk faster.

"Bloody hell," Cavell said and spit out several more oaths. "I am a fool. The attack on the Lowlander troop was a diversion to keep us busy so they could snatch what they've been after."

"One of the three sisters," Melvin said and looked ready to hurry off. "I will get a search started.

315

"Have them search for Ann and Wadely as well," Cavell ordered. "And ready the Gallowglass, they go with me."

***

Elsie tore at the hem of her underdress to wrap the strip of cloth around Wadely's arm.

"You will be naked by the time I get done with him if he doesn't stop lying," Harcus warned.

"Tell him what he wants to know," Elsie urged Wadely.

Wadely acquiesced. "I know Eudora. I have stopped by her place frequently through the years and we established a close friendship."

"Close enough that she confided in you?" Harcus asked, his patience waning.

Wadely hesitated.

Harcus brandished the dagger in his face. "I grow impatient."

Regret that he betrayed his friend's trust could be heard in Wadely's voice. "Eudora told me that she ran from trouble she had gotten into in the Lowlands. She never said what it was, and she never made mention of birthing bairns."

"Where is her home?" Harcus asked.

"Three days from here and secluded in the forest," Wadely said.

"You will take my men there," Harcus ordered. "This is where I leave the three of you. I need to visit my brother and keep him busy so that he doesn't realize his wife is missing until you are far enough away that

316

he cannot find you. And if my men find that you lie, Wadely, your death will not be quick and painless."

"So, you spare none of us?" Elsie asked.

"If you are the right woman, your fate will be decided in the Lowlands, if not?" Harcus shrugged, then grinned. "You get to stay in the Highlands… under a mound of dirt. That is if my men take the time to bury you. Otherwise, the forest animals will feast well."

Harcus left them to talk with his men.

Elsie fussed over Wadely's wound so she could whisper to him. "You spoke the truth?"

"Partially," Wadely murmured.

"What part might that be?" Ann whispered, her back to their captors.

"Eudora is dead."

Elsie understood. "You delay giving my husband time to find us."

"Aye," Wadely agreed, "and he will find us. He is Gallowglass."

***

Cavell turned numb. It was necessary when going into battle, not to feel anything, not to care whether you would meet death that day. Not caring gave you power. It allowed you to swing your weapon without thought, strike down the enemy with not an ounce of regret. He needed to remain numb hunting for his wife, for if he allowed himself to think about her and what she might be suffering, he would lose his mind and the ability to rescue her.

"What goes on here, brother?"

Cavell turned, shocked to see his brother Harcus dismounting his horse. He may have been surprised to see his brother, but he was more surprised he had not heard him approach. It confirmed what he feared. If he did not remain numb, he would fail to rescue his wife.

"What are you doing here, Harcus?" Cavell asked.

"Duties have kept me busy, but I thought it was time we talked after the incident when I last was here. But I see I have chosen a bad day for a visit. I saw Gallowglass gathering as if for battle, injured Lowlanders, and worry in people's expressions upon my arrival, so I ask again… what goes on here, brother?"

"I have no time to explain it all. I need to find my wife. She has been abducted along with two others in the clan." Anger flashed in his eyes hearing his own words, blaming himself, and fighting to keep himself numb to it all.

"I will join you," Harcus said, keeping his tone steady while silently cursing his brother for discovering far too soon that his wife was missing.

"Father would not approve.

"Father is not here," Harcus said, needing to remain close to his brother so he could save what he could of his mission to find the right sister.

Cavell had no time to argue with him… Elsie came first. He also had no time to waste thoughts on his brother or father.

Melvin rushed toward him. "We found the tracks."

"Lead the way," Cavell ordered and followed Melvin, Harcus trailing behind them.

318

They went on foot, not to disturb the tracks, men and horses trailing behind them. Cavell kept his focus on one thing and one thing only… rescuing his wife.

Clouds moved in overhead darkening the sky, signaling the arrival of an impending storm but a far worse storm brewed on the ground as Cavell followed the tracks through the woods. The atmosphere hung heavy with anticipation though not for the storm whose first faint rumbles of thunder echoed in the distance. It was the anticipation of what they would find and who would die today for daring to abduct Cavell's wife.

The rustling leaves quieted, and the distant call of birds fell silent, sensing the imminent tempest. A strong breeze turned gentle, brushing through the treetops, as if whispering a warning to the creatures below. The once serene forest now seemed anxious, its inhabitants seeking shelter and safety from not the impending deluge but from fear of what the scarred Highlander would rain down upon their home.

Cavell kept a steady pace, a double-sided axe gripped in his hand as he trudged through the woods, his footfalls heavy and determined as he followed the tracker.

***

Elsie tried not to think of what would happen if her husband did not find her. The thought of dying was bad enough but being taken to the Lowlands never to return home, never to see her husband again tore viciously at her heart. She would do whatever she needed to do to return to him, but what if she was with child? How could she dare try such a dangerous trek while round with child and what if her child was not welcomed where they took her? Would they take the child away from her? The thought was unbearable to consider. She had to do whatever she could to delay their journey to give her husband time to reach her, the two possible fates not at all to her liking.

She wondered why they were still traveling on foot, though she was relieved they did. It gave her husband time to find them. Her relief was short-lived when only moments later they came upon a troop of men with horses drinking from a rushing stream.

"We cannot get on those horses," Elsie whispered to Wadely and Ann as they huddled close once brought to a stop, one of their captors going to talk to the men already there while the other men snatched up what food was left on the fire spit.

"These are ruthless men. They will hurt us if we do not do as they say," Wadely said.

"I am exhausted," Ann said, looking at the stream and licking her dry lips. "And parched."

Elsie was just as parched and she called out, "We are thirsty."

"Drink your fill," the man who led them there ordered with a nod to the stream.

Wadely helped Ann to her feet and to the stream, and Elsie followed.

A thought came to her and after they were settled at the edge of the creek, she whispered in between drinking the water she scooped up in her cupped hand. "They need me. If I accidentally fall in here, they will have to go after me. We will gain time that way."

"They need me more, let me do it," Wadely said.

"It must be me," Elsie insisted.

The matter was settled for them when a man approached them.

"It's been decided. We only need two of you," the man said.

Elsie realized his intentions and as he raised his booted-covered foot to give Ann a shove into the stream, Elsie grabbed hold of her arm and went tumbling into the rushing water with her.

She heard another splash follow her in and worried the man went in after her, then she heard Wadely shout her name and knew he had jumped in of his own accord. This would gain them much time, though could cost all of them if not one or two of their lives.

Elsie was grateful to Leora for forcing her and Sky to learn how to swim and though the rushing water was in command, she managed to keep her head above water, not so Ann. The strength of the rushing water had ripped them apart as soon as it got hold of them. Ann now flapped her arms in a desperate attempt to keep from going under, but she was not successful. Her head dipped beneath the water again and again.

Elsie did her best to reach Ann and caught her before she went under for what Elsie feared would be the last time. The woman latched onto her, and Elsie struggled to keep them afloat. She had to get them to shore, the water was too cold to remain in too long.

Wadely bumped into them, and Ann lost her grip on Elsie and the raging water swept her up and away.

Elsie wanted to scream in frustration as she went after the woman. Ann disappeared around a bend and

Wadely was already out of sight. She feared both were lost and the cold would get her soon if she did not get out of the water.

She came around the bend and was ever so relieved and grateful to see that Wadely had gotten hold of Ann and had almost reached the bank. She tried to reach them but couldn't, the strong current rushing her away.

"Hide!" Wadely called out.

He may have cautioned her to hide, but he was also letting her know that he intended to do the same with Ann.

Elsie found herself further downstream than she hoped to go but it enabled her to get out of the stream more easily, the force of the water slowing. She lay exhausted on the bank of the stream listening for footfalls, fearful someone had chased after them, following their plight from along the bank and waiting to capture them once they got out.

Cold seeped through her, shivering down into her bones and she told herself to move, find a place to hide, but that took strength and she feared she had none left. A moment more, just a moment, and she would get up.

That was when her ear caught the sound of horses' hooves pounding the earth.

***

Cavell waited for Melvin's return. He and two other Gallowglass warriors scouted ahead to learn what awaited them. It seemed like Melvin was taking forever when he had only been gone a short time. His glance darted about, sensing something was wrong and fearing

322

what his delay could mean for his wife yet knowing from endless battles he could do more harm to her than good if he were not patient and learned what awaited him and his warriors so that he could reposition his warriors and adjust his plan if necessary.

"I have your side, brother," Harcus said, waiting beside him.

Melvin finally appeared. "Twenty men no more and something is wrong. I do not see Elsie or the other two and the men run frantically about yelling at each other."

"We go in," Cavell said and took off without waiting for Melvin, fearing what may have happened to his wife though thinking she may have escaped them. Whatever way it might be, he needed to find her.

He let out a tremendous roar that echoed through the woods as he descended on the camp, a signal for his fellow Gallowglass warriors to attack and they did, pouring in from all sides. Swords and axes clashed, the rogue mercenaries skilled warriors but by no means a match for the overpowering Gallowglass warriors. Even his brother fought bravely, taking down three men with ease. But he needed some left alive so he could find out what happened to his wife.

Cavell made sure to wound not kill those he fought when possible and the battle ended quickly though not fast enough for Cavell. He rushed the surviving warriors on their knees, some with wounds that still bled.

"I will ask this once and if I get no answer, I will cut out every tongue here," Cavell threatened with an intensity that left no doubt he would do as he said.

"Where is my wife and the other two people you abducted?"

All went to speak but one was faster than the others. "They all went into the stream."

"Only the old woman was meant to go in, but the younger woman grabbed hold of her as if to try and prevent her fall and she was dragged in with her."

"Then the man jumped in after them, "another man said.

"Only one of us can swim and not well," one other man said.

Cavell knew his wife well. She would have never let Ann drown if she could help it. And to help the woman she would need to know how to swim, and no doubt, her sister Leora had taught her. He also had told his wife often enough that he would keep her safe. She would have no doubt that he would come to her rescue and the only thing she needed to do was to bide her time for him to reach her. He would not be surprised to learn that the thought of purposely falling in the rushing stream had crossed her mind. He had a brave and foolish wife.

"Find out who commands them?" Cavell said to Melvin as he headed to his horse, anxious to go find his wife.

"We don't know who commands us," one man said, having heard Cavell. "Only certain men know."

"Who are they?" Cavell demanded.

"They are dead," one of the men said.

Chapter Twenty-seven

Elsie got to her feet with difficulty, exhaustion at surviving the raging stream taking its toll on her, not to mention the weight of her wet garments. She needed to hide, no longer hearing the sound of the approaching horse and worried someone lurked nearby. She struggled to take steps up the bank, feeling as if she could barely lift her legs.

"You are a troublesome woman."

Elsie raised her head with a bit of effort and smiled at Harcus.

"You greet me with a smile?" he asked perplexed and shaking his head.

Her smile widened. "Aye. I am happy to see you since it means my husband is near."

Harcus scowled. "Not near enough to save you."

"You lack your brother's intelligence. No doubt he already knows you are responsible for what has happened."

He laughed briefly. "You think too highly of him."

325

"And you unwisely think too little of him, a costly mistake, in more ways than one for you," she warned.

Harcus's brow creased in confusion. "You make no sense."

"Your plan is ruined. Your brother will learn everything, if he already hasn't, and he will seek retribution against you."

"I am not the fool you think I am. Only three men knew who commanded the rogue warriors and I made sure they did not survive the fight. Unfortunately, I have no choice but to see the same fate for you."

"And if I am the woman the Lowlander searches for, what then?" Elsie asked, keeping him talking to give her husband time to reach her.

"I will convince the person you were the woman they searched for but unfortunately met an untimely death," Harcus said confidently. "I will accept only half the sum of what they offered and use it to form another troop of mercenaries so I can continue to grow my wealth and power."

"Wadely and Ann—"

"Are dead," he said. "You will drown by my hand, and I will convince my brother that I tried to save you but failed and be ever so upset about it."

Elsie took a quick step back when he stepped toward her.

"By all means return to the raging stream," he encouraged. "You will never survive another dunk in the stream. You are too exhausted from the last one."

"HARCUS!"

Elsie sighed, grateful to hear her husband's powerful voice and watched him quickly dismount his horse. He was a sight to behold, a powerful warrior, confident and strong and with a look of rage in his eyes that would frighten the bravest soul. She was also grateful that he wore the leather vest Wadely had stitched for him, providing extra protection.

Harcus turned. "I did not want to have to kill you, brother. You were never to find out. Now you leave me no choice. You both must die."

"I knew before arriving here, it was you who commanded the mercenaries." His brother's stunned look was what had Cavell explaining while he took stock of the situation and weighed how best he could keep his wife safe. "Your men gladly informed me of the only men who knew your identity, and I recalled seeing you kill all three, not maim, so I could talk with them as my warriors did with those they fought. You, on the other hand, drove your sword through the three men, your intention, to kill. I did not see you after that, no one did. It was easy to surmise why."

"It matters not," Harcus said with a shrug. "You both die today."

"There is only one person here who will die today," Cavell said and drew his sword.

Harcus laughed and drew his sword. "She dies first."

Elsie rushed back away from the sword and into the raging stream.

"I didn't even need a sword to kill her." Harcus laughed again and charged his brother.

Cavell had to get to his wife fast, having seen how she barely kept herself on her feet. She would not last long in the water and he could not let her be swept too far away from him, which meant he had to kill his brother fast. He ran at him.

**

Elsie did her best to keep her head above the water, but she had little strength and her garments felt far too heavy. She feared she did not have the strength to swim to the bank and pull herself out.

Fight. Cavell will come for me.

She recalled something Leora had once told her. If you fall in angry water and grow too tired to swim, grab onto the nearest branch to help keep you afloat until you reach calm waters. She gave a quick glance around but didn't spot anything she could grab onto. She was about to go under, too exhausted to keep her head above water, when she saw a branch land in the water not far in front of her. With what little strength she had left, she swam for it and latched her arms over it, relieved for the reprieve. But with her strength waning, she would not be able to hold on long.

She thought she heard a splash and the next thing she knew someone grabbed hold of her.

"I've got you."

**

Cavell realized soon enough that his brother avoided close battle with him so that he wouldn't have enough time to save his wife.

"I learned to dodge Da's quick hand better than you and the skill has served me well," his brother taunted. "This ends only one way, brother… one of us dies and it is not going to be me."

"You're right," Cavell said. "Only one of us dies today.

Harcus gasped and his eyes shot wide, staring his brother in his face that was so close that he could feel his breath on his cheek.

"That is a dagger you felt shoved into your gut," Cavell said.

Harcus's mouth hung open, but no words fell out.

"I dodged Da's hand with far more speed than you, something he never expected, and he missed me every time, never having seen me coming just as I've done now with you." Cavell twisted the dagger deeper before yanking the blade out of him, then shoved his lifeless body to the ground.

He didn't give his brother a second glance as he mounted his horse and took off, keeping close to the bank of the stream, ready to rush off his horse and into the water to save his wife.

He grew anxious when he didn't see her and feared the worst. Then he spotted something on the bank ahead. He urged his horse on and nearly flew off it when he spotted a body on the grassy bank.

He stood staring at his wife, lying on her back, her arm stretched out, and her hand clasped in the woman, lying on her back, a short distance from her… her sister Leora.

***

"It was Leora? I wasn't dreaming?" Elsie asked wrapped in a cloak and snug in her husband's arm as they rode toward home.

"You weren't dreaming," Cavell assured her. "It was Leora who saved you. I sent her ahead with Melvin since she would not stop instructing me how to tend you."

"That's my sister," Elsie said with a soft smile. "I am so relieved she is home and safe."

"And I am relieved that you are in my arms and safe." He kissed her brow.

"As am I," she said, tightening her arm around his waist. "I knew you would come for me."

"Always, wife," he said and lowered his lips to hers.

Elsie greeted his lips eagerly, ever so grateful she was safe in her husband's arms and that the day would end well.

"I love you, Elsie," he whispered after his lips left hers.

"And I am grateful you do love me, for it was your love that kept me strong, kept me fighting to survive, kept me confident I would come home to you."

"I had no intentions of returning home without you no matter how long it might take to find you."

"I am glad it did not take long, for I prefer to sleep in our bed tonight." She grinned. "Well, maybe not sleep."

"You need to rest," he chastised, though he welcomed her playfulness. It meant she was feeling well.

"I can sleep later," she said relieved she had survived and wanting to celebrate it in the best way possible... making love with her husband.

"We shall see," he said, not having as much confidence in his words as he should.

Her response overflowed with confidence. "Aye, that we will."

They arrived home just as a rainstorm unleashed upon the land and darkness fell.

Elsie barely entered the Great Hall when Leora captured her in a tight hug.

"Thank the Lord you're safe," Leora said, tears in her eyes.

"You saved me, Leora," Elsie said, tears gathering strongly in her eyes that she soon would not be able to stop from falling.

Cavell watched the two women and had to agree with all who talked about Leora's beauty. Even though she was disheveled from her dunk in the stream, there was no hiding her fine features. He understood why men could not take their eyes off her. Her features were strikingly beautiful, the eyes unable to look away from her, needing to feast on her rare beauty. And while Cavell could appreciate such beauty, he found his eyes drawn more to his wife and his heart as well.

"Sky?" Leora asked, worry in her tone.

"Sky is not here, but she is safe," Elsie assured her.

"We need to talk. Melvin would not tell me anything. He said it wasn't his place and I had to talk with you," Leora said.

"In the morning," Cavell said. "You both need food and rest."

"You will not stop me from talking with my sister," Leora said, her look stern.

"Aye, I won't, but you will not talk with her until morning," Cavell said.

Melvin chuckled and Leora sent him a scathing look and he had the good sense to remain silent.

With so much to tell her sister and how Leora might feel when learning they weren't sisters, it was better they waited and faced the news after a good night's rest since no doubt there would be endless questions.

"My husband is right, Leora. I am too exhausted to talk tonight. Tomorrow we can talk. There is much to tell you."

Leora's shoulders slumped in disappointment. "I am tired myself and hungry, and I desperately need a hot bath."

"I will see to all of it for you, Mistress Leora," Alda said, approaching them.

"I thank the heavens for you, Alda," Leora said, putting a wide smile on the woman's face.

"Come and I will see you settled in your bedchamber while the bath is prepared," Alda said.

Leora was about to follow Alda when she stopped and looked at her sister. "Da?"

"He improves each day and knew nothing about what went on at the abbey."

Leora sighed, nodded, and sent a scowl to Cavell. "I will talk with my sister as long as I want to tomorrow." She swirled around and led Alda from the room.

"She's a handful," Melvin said when Leora was no longer in sight.

Elsie chuckled. "That she is."

"Before I take my leave, I wanted you to know that Ann is resting in her cottage and Wadely is resting in May's cottage," Melvin said. "They both are doing well."

"I am so relieved to know they are alive," Elsie said, happy to have heard it from her husband on their ride home. "I believed Harcus when he told me they were dead."

"That's because he believed it as well. Wadely planted his vest and Ann's shawl among the rocks in the stream to make anyone searching for them assume they had drowned," Melvin explained.

"Wadely was so helpful in helping to delay our journey, lying to Harcus and willing to jump in the stream so they would have to search for him, which would have delayed us even more, giving you a chance to find us, husband," Elsie said.

"I will make sure he knows how grateful I am for his efforts."

As soon as Melvin left, Cavell led his wife to their bedchamber where a bath waited for her along with food and drink.

"I will bathe after you," Cavell said and went to the table to fill two tankards with wine.

Elsie didn't argue. She was chilled and the heated water was just what she needed. Though she wished the round tub was large enough for them both. It would have been nice to relax naked in her husband's arms.

333

The heated water engulfed her, and she sighed with pleasure. Relaxing, she found the strength to broach the subject she had been avoiding.

"I heard the Gallowglass talking. They say you killed your brother."

"He left me no choice."

"I didn't think he would, and I am sorry that he did that to you. It must have been difficult."

"Not really," he said. "He sealed his fate when he abducted you. There was no way I would have ever trusted him again and he knew that. He just didn't expect he would lose to me. He never lost to me. He beat me in everything, excelled in everything, which is why he thought it would be easy to kill me. What he didn't know was that I let him beat me every time. I knew if he didn't our da would beat him for failing to be stronger than me since he was heir to the clan."

"You are an honorable man, husband."

He grinned. "If you knew what I was thinking, you would not think me honorable."

She returned his grin. "And if you knew what I was thinking, you would think me wicked."

"Hurry and wash so I may wash," he ordered. "I will not come to you with the blood of battle on me."

Though exhausted from all she had been through today, Elsie hurried to bathe, eager to make love with her husband. She kept a drying cloth wrapped around herself once out of the tub and sat at the small table, piled with food, ready to eat so her gurgling stomach would not disturb them while in the throes of lovemaking.

She watched him undress and even with the grime and blood of battle on him, he was appealing as always, and she found her need for him spiraling. She drank the wine and nibbled on the food, eager for him to finish.

Cavell watched his wife lean back in the chair, saw the fatigue on her lovely face and how she fought to keep her eyes open. He had an aching need for her, and he silently cursed the toll the day had taken on her. He could hurry and wash and share a quick poke with her, but he wanted more, his love for her insisted on more than a quick poke.

He lingered in the tub after washing, the water already chilly, until he was sure she slept. He got out, dried himself, then gently loosened the cloth around her so when he lifted her into his arms, the cloth fell away. He carried her to the bed and gently placed her on it, then pulled the blanket over her.

He did not trust himself to get in bed with her, not yet. He went to the table and sat in the chair still warm from his wife's presence and turned it toward the hearth, so he did not look upon his sleeping wife and think of her naked beneath the blanket. He refilled his tankard with a generous amount of wine and drank it, it slowly flowing down his throat and crashing into his stomach, not having eaten since early morning. He grabbed a piece of bread and munched on it.

It was better they did not couple. He killed today and his hands should not be touching her. He feared he would not be as gentle as he should be with her. Still, he ached for her.

He let his glance linger on the flames in the hearth, but his thoughts kept going to his brother. His father would need to be told, but did he tell him the truth or let him continue to believe that Harcus was the son he most admired, the son he most respected?

It was not an easy decision to make, for either way, truth or lies, he would suffer for it in his father's eyes. At one time that would have mattered to him, but Elsie's love had changed all that. He cared what she thought of him, what his clan thought of him, and what their future children would think of them. Nothing else mattered.

Her hand on his shoulder surprised him and he rubbed his cheek across it, before taking hold of it and drawing her around in front of him to rest in his lap.

"You need to sleep."

"I cannot sleep without you beside me, though presently I would prefer you inside me."

He rested his brow against hers. "You make it difficult to do what is best for you."

"You know what is best for me, for us both, especially after the day we have had. So, please, husband, do what is best for me."

His arms slipped beneath her bottom and in one swift lift he was on his feet with her tucked safely in his arms. He walked to the bed as he brushed a kiss across her lips, then lowered her down on the bed, slipping over her.

She pressed her cheek to his and whispered, "Slow and easy, husband, so I can enjoy the feel of you inside me."

He obliged her, slipping his hard shaft inside her gently and setting a slow steady rhythm. They kissed along with his easy thrusts, tasting slowly of each other, satisfying a thirst that had lingered in them since he had found her on the bank of the stream.

"I love you so much," she whispered between kisses.

"I love you more," he whispered back.

And so it went the back and forth of kisses and thrusts that built slowly, deeply, until it overwhelmed and Elsie cried out, "I cannot wait."

Cavell felt the same and they soon became lost in a spiral of pleasure, the sensation growing stronger and stronger and when he heard his wife cry out in climax, felt her body burst with it, he did the same, roaring out his pleasure.

Sleep claimed his wife as soon as he rolled off her and took her in his arms. He lay there, the blankets tucked over them, his warmth seeping into her and he thanked the heavens that his father did one thing good for him… he found him the perfect and most loving wife and he was forever grateful.

Chapter Twenty-Eight

Leora sat staring at her sister in Cavell's solar, not uttering a word after Elsie explained how she, Elsie, and Sky were not truly sisters and how it all came about. And how someone was searching for one of them and how it endangered all of them. She had yet to tell Leora that she was not the only one their da had married off.

"I don't care," Leora said abruptly, breaking her silence. "Joined together by blood or not, we are still sisters and always will be." She reached out and took hold of Elsie's hand as if committing to their bond.

Elsie smiled, pleased to hear Leora felt the same as she did and squeezed her hand to let her know she felt the same.

"And how brave of Mum and Da to take unwanted bairns into their home and raise them as their own," Leora said, then shook her head. "So, no one truly knows who our true parents are?"

"Not according to Wadely, who knew Eudora. She hadn't even confided in her sister, Edith, the older woman in the abbey with us who now resides here.

Though we call her Ann for her own protection since she was thought to be Eudora."

"Where is Sky?" Leora asked anxiously.

Elsie hesitated to tell her, but having no choice, said, "She is with Lord Slayer."

Leora's cheeks heated in anger. "What is she doing with that savage and why do you refer to him as Lord Slayer?"

"His brother Warrand was killed in an attack when he left here, and his father was poisoned shortly afterward, the title now belongs to Slayer."

"How terrible, but what does any of that have to do with Sky?'

Elsie continued to explain, anxious as to where this would lead them. "Da agreed to an arranged marriage between Sky and Warrand. Lord Slayer went and rescued Sky from the abbey to protect his sister-in-law. Da thought he was sending us to Brother Kendrick at the abbey. He did not know that he died and was replaced by Brother Emmanual and that he changed the abbey from a peaceful retreat to a place that housed the insane. Da did it to protect us, having discovered someone was looking for a female child that was brought to the Highlands after birth. He had promised Mum to keep us safe and marrying us to Gallowglass warriors was the only way he could think to keep us safe."

"Us?" Leora said, anger sparking in her green eyes.

Elsie cringed, expecting Leora's anger and understanding it, and not sure how to make her sister realize that with the current situation, it was for the best.

"Are you telling me that Da arranged a marriage for me as well and I now have a husband?" Leora asked, trying to contain her temper while attempting to absorb the shocking news.

"Aye, he did," Elsie confirmed.

"To a Gallowglass savage?" she asked, getting to her feet.

"Aye. His name is Noble—"

"I don't care what his name is, he is no husband of mine," she said with such certainty that she had Elsie believing it.

"It might be best since we are still in danger," Elsie suggested.

"Danger? Do you know who is in danger? The fool who agreed to this marriage and thinks I will honor it," Leora said with a hard rap on the table.

"Do not be hasty, Leora, give it thought. My marriage worked out well. We found love and I could not be happier."

"And I am happy for you, truly I am, Elsie, but I told Da that I and I alone would choose the man I wed, and he gave me his word. He will dissolve this marriage or there will be hell to pay."

"Da is finally improving. You don't want to upset him," Elsie said, trying to make her sister see reason.

"Upset him? What did he think he did to me? I will not stand for this, I won't," Leora said with a harder rap on the table. She let out an angry groan and hurried to the door.

"Nay, Leora, do not go and upset, Da," Elsie urged.

"He had no right," Leora yelled and swung open the door.

"He had every right," Cavell said, his body consuming the doorway.

"This does not concern you," Leora said. "Now get out of my way."

Cavell stepped forward, the overpowering size of him forcing Leora to step back, and he shut the door. "You will not go and upset your da. He is doing well, and he did what he did to keep you three safe. He married all of you to Gallowglass warriors."

"Not Sky," Leora argued.

"Maybe not, but Slayer being Sky's brother-in-law is enough to keep her safe and I believe that was enough for your da to wed her to Warrand. Presently, she is at the safest place she can be. And you would be wise to understand and accept your marriage to Noble, for it is the safest place for you."

"I am safe here in my home," Leora insisted.

"Not if someone comes and proves you are the woman they search for and insists you return to the Lowlands with them. The Highlands will not go to war with Lowlanders over one stubborn woman who could have prevented an altercation between the two fractions by agreeing to a marriage."

"At least remain wed until this can be resolved," Elsie suggested, feeling a twinge of guilt recalling how her husband said that Noble would take the marriage seriously and remain in it no matter what. "Please, Leora, just give it thought."

A rap at the door interrupted them and Melvin called out, "Your da draws near."

He reached out and gave his wife's arm a gentle squeeze. "I need to speak with my da alone. Go with

Leora and visit with your da. He knows she is home and is eager to see her."

Elsie stepped close to him. "You will be all right?"

"Aye, I will, and I will see you as soon as I am done with him."

Leora did not protest, she followed Elsie out the door and when they reached the staircase, Leora asked, "You do truly love him, don't you?"

"With all my heart and more," Elsie said, her heart aching for what her husband had to do.

They had talked about whether he should tell his da the truth about Harcus. Her opinion was the same as Melvin's. Secrets were difficult to keep. They eventually made themselves known. Her husband would tell his da the truth.

Leora stopped at the closed door of her da's bedchamber. "How do I not let him see my anger at what he has done?'

"Think of how much he loves you and what it must have taken for him to break a promise to you. It was not something he did lightly," Elsie said and rapped on the door before opening it.

"Leora!" her da said and went to get up from the chair he sat in with some difficulty.

"Stay, Da," Leora said and rushed to him, to hug him as she helped him sit.

Elsie saw the worry in her sister's eyes for their da and she knew Leora would say nothing to upset him.

"I am so sorry, Leora. I broke my word to you, something I never thought I would do. I had to keep you safe. Your mum and I promised each other that no matter what happened we would both do whatever was necessary to keep you three safe. Please, forgive me. I am told Noble is worthy of his name and will make you a good husband."

"I forgive you, Da, worry not," Leora assured him.

Elsie, however, did worry since Leora said nothing about agreeing to the marriage.

***

Cavell's father stood staring at him, his mouth agape until his silence turned to rage. "You lie! Harcus would never do what you say. He was a better man than you. You were always jealous of him. You killed him on purpose. You lie to cover your treachery."

"Nay, Da, I don't," Cavell said calmly, having told his father all of it, including how he killed Harcus. "He abducted my wife as I told you and I have two witnesses to prove it and prove he intended to kill her. I had no choice, and I did not hesitate."

His father raised a fisted hand at him. "I will see you pay for this."

"You may want to think about that, Da. I am your only son, the only one who can provide an heir to Clan McCabe, the only one to see your legacy continue. Someday a son of mine, a true McCabe, could rule Clan McCabe and continue its legacy."

His father dropped down on a chair, accepting the truth weighing heavily on him and his legs unable to support him any longer. "Why? Why would Harcus do such a thing?"

Cavell continued to tell him the truth, no matter how difficult it might be for him to hear. "You were going too slow in building wealth and power. He was impatient for both and found a way to gain wealth faster and power along with it. You two are alike, both wanting the same, but he wanted it faster than you and he did not care how he got it."

"We were not alike. Harcus did something I would never have done. He dishonored the McCabe name," his father said, looking as if he had just fought a difficult battle and lost.

"He only did what you taught him, Da."

His da looked perplexed. "What was that?"

"Take what you can, no matter the cost or who you hurt."

***

It took several weeks for Wadely to gain his strength back, having turned ill with a cough and nearly dying, so Elsie was glad to see him finally getting about, slowly but improving just like her da, who was up and about himself.

"It is good to see you doing well, Wadely," Elsie said.

"Aye, I can thank May and Ann for that. They took good care of me, and Ann kept me entertained with stories of her youth with her sister. Having come so close to death, I gave thought to something and made a decision. I need to talk with you, Mistress Elsie, and I think your husband and Ann should hear it as well."

It did not take long to gather everyone in Cavell's solar, Elsie curious as to what Wadely had to say and

Ann just as curious and a bit uncomfortable as if she should not be included among them.

"Are you sure you want me here, Wadely," Ann whispered to him.

"Aye, I am sure," he said with a gentle smile.

Have your say, Wadely," Cavell said, standing beside his wife where she sat, his hand resting on her shoulder.

"Eudora asked me to keep a secret."

"More secrets," Cavell said, shaking his head annoyed, secrets having caused far too many problems already.

"A secret I believe that will prove helpful."

"Then tells us," Cavell commanded.

He tilted his head back and looked up. "Forgive me, Eudora, but it is the wise thing to do." He looked at Elsie. "Eudora is your mum. She had you when the trouble was nothing but rumors. She feared more might come of it and what would happen to you if she was discovered. She decided to find a good home for you. It broke her heart to give you away, but she did it to keep you safe. It took years for her to trust and confide in me and ask a favor. She told me where you were and that she had named you Elsie and had asked that your name be kept, but she did not know if the couple had done so. She wanted me to stop here and find out what I could and tell me how you were doing." Tears clouded his eyes.

"She was thrilled when she found out the couple had kept your name and that you were doing well. I continued to stop here and report back to her through the years. She wanted to see you so badly, but she

345

feared bringing you harm. And she was right in doing so. She heard stirrings of someone searching for a bairn given away around the time she had helped women give their bairns away out of fear of what might be done to them."

"Did she confide in you who Leora and Sky's parents are and what of my da?" Elsie asked.

"Your da was a man she knew briefly and never saw again. She remembered the two bairns she placed here with Norris and Terena. She knew who the parents were but would not tell me, fearing what harm it might bring me."

"You must look like your da, for I do not see my sister in you," Ann said, tears rolling down her cheeks.

"I told Eudora the same, that I did not see her in her daughter, but when I told her about your soft blue eyes, she smiled and told me that you had your da's eyes. The lovely color of his eyes had been what had drawn her to him. You also got his skill of numbers, so I discovered when I told her about it."

"This goes no further than this room," Cavell ordered, fearing what might happen to his wife if it was discovered she was Eudora's daughter.

"You have my word," Wadely said.

"And mine as well," Ann said. "I will not see my niece harmed." She smiled. "I am so pleased that I will spend the rest of my days with true family."

"You will tell me about my mum?" Elsie asked, eager to know all she could about the woman who gave her life and unselfishly sent her away to protect her.

"I will tell you everything about her," Ann said, her tears continuing to fall.

The door flew open, and Leora stood staring at them. "What goes on here and why was I not included?"

"When that door is closed, you will knock," Cavell ordered.

"I doubt that, now tell me what goes on here," Leora demanded.

Elsie laid her hand on her husband's where it rested on her shoulder, feeling him tense, her gentle touch eased him and she eased as well, glad she had averted a fight between her sister and husband, which they had been having quite a few of lately. Then her husband spoke.

"I cannot wait for you to meet your husband."

"He will learn soon enough he cannot dictate to me," Leora said. "Besides, I have yet to decide if I will honor the marriage agreement. Now why is Ann crying and my sister looks like she is about to?"

"Come in and close the door and I will tell you, but you must swear to speak of it to no one," Elsie warned.

"Not even to Sky? We never keep anything from each other," Leora reminded.

"Nay. We shall share it with Sky," Elsie said.

Satisfied, Leora closed the door and sat and Wadely once again revealed the secret.

***

Cavell grabbed his wife's hand and hurried her through the keep and up to their bedchamber. It felt like it had been ages since he got his wife alone during the day. Leora and Ann spent endless time with her, and Elsie spent extra time with her da now that he was

347

getting around well. And he was busy himself with all that needed to be done before winter set upon them.

But he had an urge to be alone with his wife, not so much to make love, though he wouldn't mind, just to be alone with her if only for a little while.

Elsie hugged her husband tight, then gave him a kiss. "I am so glad you stole me away for a while. I have wanted to get you alone."

"We think alike, wife," he said and nibbled at her neck.

She scrunched her shoulders, his nibble sending gooseflesh racing over her. "There is that, but first I must tell you something."

He groaned. "I beg you, not another secret."

"A secret between you and me for at least a little while," she said and took hold of his hand to place on her stomach.

He looked at her speechless, then hurried to say, "You are sure?"

"Aye," she said. "I am sure our child nestles inside me."

Cavell scooped her up in his arms and planted a firm kiss on her lips. "I am thrilled, wife, and I agree. It is our secret for a little while."

She nibbled at his neck. "Now before anyone notices that we disappeared, let's make hasty love in celebration of the news."

"A perfect way to celebrate," he said and before he made it to the bed a rap sounded at the door.

They both groaned in disappointment.

"You better get to the Great Hall," Melvin called out.

Melvin was gone when they opened the door, and they made their way to the Great Hall worried what trouble there may be.

"Do what you will with him. I have no desire to meet him," Leora said and rushed out of the room.

Melvin grinned. "Noble, her husband, has arrived."

***

Read about Noble & Leora in
The Fierce Highlander

Blood & Honor Highland Trilogy

The Scarred Highlander
The Fierce Highlander
Highlander the Conqueror

Cavell, The Scarred Highlander, was first introduced in Highland Hearts A Cree & Dawn Novella.

You can find more of Donna's books on her website: donnaflecther.com

Note from Donna

Get in touch!

I love hearing from readers so drop me a note and give me your thoughts on the book, say hello, introduce yourself, let me know what you enjoy reading, and any questions you have are welcome.

You can reach me at donna@donnafletcher.com

Newsletter

Consider subscribing to my newsletter. It goes out twice a month, more if there is some unexpected news to share. I keep readers updated on forthcoming books, future books, and alert them to giveaways, offer a free book now and again, share recipes, and leave you with a cute joke to put a smile on your face. So don't miss the fun… subscribe!

Reviews

Some people enjoy leaving reviews, others don't. If you like leaving a review it is immensely appreciated. If you don't like leaving a review, consider spreading the word to your reader friends about the books you've read.

Thanks for reading my book!
Donna

351

Donna Fletcher